the Albatross

the Albatross

Nina Wan

MACMILLAN
Pan Macmillan Australia

Pan Macmillan acknowledges the Traditional Custodians of country throughout Australia and their connections to lands, waters and communities. We pay our respect to Elders past and present and extend that respect to all Aboriginal and Torres Strait Islander peoples today. We honour more than sixty thousand years of storytelling, art and culture.

First published 2023 in Macmillan by Pan Macmillan Australia Pty Ltd
1 Market Street, Sydney, New South Wales, Australia, 2000

NATIONAL LIBRARY OF AUSTRALIA
A catalogue record for this book is available from the National Library of Australia

Typeset in 11.9/17 pt Adobe Garamond Pro by Post Pre-press Group

Printed by IVE

For William

Golf is played by striking your ball with a club . . .

You should normally play the course as you find it
and play your ball as it lies.

Player's Edition of the Rules of Golf

1

I forget why I went to Whistles that day. I do things all the time without knowing the reason. *When* is easier – the unadorned fact, no more, no less. That is where I should start, at almost noon on a day in May, in the year I am thirty-six years old.

I'm driving through the gates, past the sign that says *Welcome to Whistles Public Golf Course* and, a moment later, ploughing the car into a bush I do not see until it's too late. The mangled vegetation – of a kind I do not recognise – is in a dense state of bloom. The flowers are a papery purple, as pale as frost and quite beautiful.

What a pity, I think to myself. Nevertheless the car is parked.

The only person around is a teenager with a cheeseburger in one hand and a garden rake in the other. A blue cap is on his head backwards, the plastic snap cutting a transom into his forehead. He must be no more than seventeen years old, but has the air of someone who is responsible for the place. Why else the rake?

He looks at me as I get out of the car, and might've waved if his hands weren't so occupied. 'Hi there,' he says, brightly.

'Don't worry about that,' meaning the bush. 'It's not the first time that's happened and it always grows back.'

He seems unbothered by the fact that he is standing in a puddle left by the rain; he may, in fact, have been standing there for some time. A gust of wind whips across the car park and kicks the water up at his trousers. Unperturbed, he holds up his burger and proceeds to prove to his mouth just how much food it can accommodate at once. The orange cheese and the tomato sauce, previously conspiring to escape from the bun, now try to do the same from his lips. The whole thing looks simultaneously appetising and stomach-churning.

Chewing, he asks: 'You know this is a golf course, don't you?'

'Yeah,' I reply. 'Your big sign out there says as much.'

'Oh, just checking.'

Still he seems curious, confused. I guess it must be what I'm wearing – a gauzy blouse and a pair of jeans, and slingback heels that seem the very definition of irony in this weather.

All through the morning it rained, the kind of rain that erased pigeon stains from the heads of public statues and threw chaos over the metropolitan train system. It rained so hard that traffic lights were replaced by policemen in ponchos, and graveyards of broken umbrellas sprang from the roadside. People on the radio were calling it a 'freak weather event', warning of more storms, bigger storms, on the way.

Less than a day ago there was sun and blue sky, a lingering summerness that coaxed feet out of socks and bugs into song. Now the promise of a new season pervades the air. The faint smell of funghi rises from the earth, the way nature intends for a day in late autumn.

'Everything's under water out there,' the teenager informs me, his eyes moving in the direction of the old canal. We cannot see it from here, only the faint rise of vegetation that hints at the curvature of its banks. A bird, a mere shadow of outspread wings, flutters briefly out of the thicket and disappears into the tall grey mist.

'You won't get very far today, unless you're happy to swim. The little bridge over on the fourth hole is inundated.'

Despite the break in the rain the sky above us is no brighter. It feels as though we are standing in the great shadow of an invisible tree, the daylight barely filtering through its canopy. The teenager looks at me, at the way I'm trying to hide my hands in the pockets of my jeans, the way I'm hunched against the wind. I must seem strange to him, like a new species arrived from a foreign habitat.

'Are you alright?' he asks.

'Perfectly fine. Why?'

At my frown, he diverts his gaze and turns it to the sky, where a new storm is visible to the west and heading slowly across the bay towards us. Matter-of-factly, he says, 'We'll be standing in water for days.'

With the rake, he begins to stir the water he is presently standing in. The water turns quickly into a tumble of leaves and mud and colourful bits of plastic rubbish. He puts the burger between his teeth so both hands are free to do the work. The more he churns, the more the water gurgles. Small bubbles rise to the surface and form larger ones; soon an eddy emerges and, through the spinning current, a glimpse of the metal grille in the ground beneath it. He rakes away at the grille until there is a comfortable clearance around it. Then he watches, in wonder, as a not insignificant amount of water hurries into the abyss.

'This place really loves to flood,' he says, his mouth once again available for speech. It occurs to me that he sounds a lot older than he looks. 'Even a few drops of rain can turn into a downpour. Water has a way of coming at us from every direction. All this is meant to be swamp, you know. In a way, it's just the land going back to its nature.'

The wind has picked up pace, running circles around us. I wish I'd put on a jacket, or at least worn better shoes than these silly slingbacks with their tiny unsteady heels. They were the nearest pair within reach as I hurried out of the house. Now my feet are growing numb from the cold and the leather straps have cut raw imprints into my ankles.

After a pause, the teenager asks, 'So, what actually brings you here?' It seems to have been gnawing at him. 'To be honest, we don't see a lot of people like you around here. They're usually, I guess, a bit older, and male.'

He watches, amused, as I do up the top button of my blouse and try to shake the weather out of my body.

The truth is I hadn't planned on coming to Whistles. All morning, after leaving the house, I'd been driving around aimlessly, going left or right in accordance with the car ahead of me, following it for as long as I could until it pulled off the road and a new vehicle took over as my lead. I didn't know where I was going or where I wanted to go and, for all that driving, I didn't seem to make much distance either; I was only going around in a large loop, I came to realise.

All the while it rained as I drove past schools where children were kept inside, past sports ovals overrun by ducks. I came across the same supermarket three times and, by the third time, resigned myself to stopping in order to pick up some groceries. Then I was back in the car, feeling spent and determined to go home at last. But I took the wrong turn, perhaps several wrong turns. A hostile chorus of horns rang out around me as I stopped in the middle of the road to make a U-turn.

The rain was easing by then. As I looked around, I saw, to my surprise, the rusty roadside sign, its half-hearted welcome in faded red paint.

I hadn't thought about Whistles for years, and all that time it had stayed exactly the same, everything from the jungle of trees at the boundary to the weeds growing in the car park. The clubhouse, with its Stetson-shaped roof, still seemed to have the same abandoned bird's nests clinging to the eaves. I looked at the ugly chain-linked gates that sagged to the side like bad teeth, and the empty takeaway cups dancing half-circles on the ground. Never too late, I thought as I hit the accelerator. The average age of the golf-playing public was what? Sixty-five? In golf terms, I was positively early.

'The fact is . . .' How do I explain all this to the teenager? Words are evaporating quicker than I can say them. 'The fact is. Well . . . I don't have any clubs.'

He smiles, makes an affirmative noise. It seems to be just the answer he wanted. Excitedly, he says, 'Don't worry, we have some here for purchase. But let me just say this: it's really great that you're here. Do you want to know why?'

He doesn't catch my scepticism, doesn't wait for me to shake my head.

'You might not know this – so don't freak out when I say it – but you're sort of, part of, the future.'

'The future of what?'

'Of golf!'

'Really.'

'Yeah, absolutely! Every new person who decides to give this a go counts. That's what the game depends on to survive.'

He starts to talk in a kind of gibberish, something about supply and demand and the declining trends in golf membership. He's so worked up by what he is saying that it seems unkind to stop him. Bouncing off his heels with a special energy, he launches into a prolonged speech which loosely translates into this:

No one plays golf anymore – certainly not here in the inner city, where trendy people prefer to stay home with their indoor plants. This is not ideal.

We live in the age of the YouTube golfer, who makes the game out to be all about subscribers and free merchandise. Again, this is not ideal.

The sport is devolving into a bunch of hacks playing baseball. For example, 'long drive' – just a drive, no hole, no strategy – is now a legitimate competition watched by more people than the US Open. For further example, frisbee golf – yes, frisbee – has become an accredited sport played by thousands of amateurs who somehow think they can demand equal respect for their sportsmanship.

To make matters worse, golf must now be inextricably

linked to a man like Trump, who displays none of the qualities the game demands: grace, humility, honesty. You can't turn on the TV these days without seeing the man take a swing as if dispatching a wrecking ball down the fairway.

So, in summary, the situation facing golf right now, in the year 2019 (he says the year as if it's a harbinger for worse things to come), is decidedly a dire one. In fact, there is such a decline in the sport that golf courses everywhere are now seen as mere real estate portfolios to be sold off and carved up for profit. That, beyond doubt, is the least ideal thing of all.

'Excuse me for asking' – I wait until the last word has exited him before saying – 'but how old are you?'

Instead of replying, he only bites his lip, smiles vaguely. Perhaps he has been asked that question too often. Perhaps he is suddenly embarrassed by his own impassioned monologue.

He plants his rake in the ground, prongs up like a trident, signalling that it is time for him to go. Somehow, despite all the talking, he has managed to finish his food and clear away the rubbish from a second gutter. The debris left by the water has been raked into small neat mounds.

'Okay,' he says, turning towards the clubhouse. 'I'll find you some clubs inside, when you're ready.'

I watch him take the shortcut across the practice green, unsure if I should follow. It seems just as easy to get back in the car and drive off into the traffic.

By now the rain is starting to come down again, but only in disorganised patters like crumbs from a biscuit. The wind does little pirouettes as it dances between the trees. And there, unexpectedly in the melaleucas, the figure of a woman in a brown parka and a scarf over her hair, walking with her collie. The dog is very old, or at least seems to be as it limps along on three legs, the fourth never daring to test the ground. Painfully they advance together, the dog always an obedient two steps behind – a monarch and her subject, slow enough for a painter to capture in oil.

A minute must go by, equal to a stagnant hour. They continue to advance until, abruptly, the dog stops. It seems to be processing something that cannot be humanly understood, an inaudible command carried in the wind. And suddenly it lunges forward, sheer joy propelling it towards a bean-shaped bunker in which the sand has turned a dark grey in the wet. The dog dives into it, rolls wildly. It rubs against the sand this way and that, four legs in the air, so mad that I think it must have fleas.

Funny what such a thing can make you remember: Kodak moments that you never suspected yourself of keeping. A little Alsatian, all fur and black eyes, brought home in my father's arms; my mother objecting, while my twelve-year-old self, airborne with delight, promises to be good for the rest of my life in exchange. The tiny animal taps the carpet with one paw, tests the texture. Finding it agreeable, it jumps down in one fluid movement that only a cat can imitate. Home. I lay myself down, cheek flat to the carpet. From here, you view the world as if through a microscope. Little black legs trot around me, clockwise and back, upside down and right again. I laugh: we have built our own galaxy, a girl and her dog floating through childhoods being lived simultaneously.

A pair of magpies swoop; the rain follows. I cross my arms for warmth, and start down the path towards the clubhouse.

'Michael!' I can hear the woman calling from the trees, her voice dispersing like dust being thrown at the wind. '*Michael-angelo!* Come. Here. Now!'

For a second time the collie freezes, its ears stiff against the wind as it weighs up the options. Even for a dog, there must be the occasional agony of choice. Which is better? The exfoliation of sand on his back, the freedom of resting his three good legs in the air, no more doing the work of four? Or the companionship of a mistress who takes walks on a golf course, untroubled by the danger of being hit by a hard white ball?

Whatever spirit that whispered to the dog is gone. He rises, wags his tail and, lowering his head, as if recognising his error, stumbles towards his keeper.

I find the teenager in the poorly lit pro shop adjoining the clubhouse. He looks up from the counter as I enter, and pops a red something into his mouth.

'Okay, good,' he says, sticky between the teeth. 'Let's see what we've got.'

'Anything will be fine,' I say to him. 'I won't notice the difference.'

He walks out from behind the counter and from his pocket produces a packet of Skittles. Picking out two more red ones, he says, 'We used to have a whole range of good stuff here. But not anymore.'

He nudges his hand towards the empty wall as if to indicate that it had once been filled with merchandise.

The place has certainly seen better days. All the shelves

are empty now. A pile of rubbish waits on the floor for the vacuum. The aluminium table by the window looks like it hasn't been wiped down since January, which is no matter since the vending machine next to it has run out of food.

There is a glass-panelled door that leads from the shop into the darkened clubhouse, where walnut plaques bearing gold letters hang on the walls and stacks of meeting chairs are turning grey with dust. It doesn't appear to be in use anymore.

'I was thinking we could look over there,' the teenager suggests, pointing me to a bunch of old golf bags next to the vending machine, each with an assortment of sticks poking out at various lengths. 'Do you mind second-hand? If you're just starting out, they'll do you fine. They are five dollars.'

'Five dollars a club?' I ask, not quite believing the public-course value for money.

He turns his cap around so it now casts a glum shadow over his face, all the way down to his lolly-stained lips.

'No, five dollars a bag.'

Up close, the clubs look more like their worth, but what little options I have are dwindling still.

'These are men's clubs,' the teenager apologises as he wades through the bags, handling them roughly by the neck in a process of elimination. 'Sorry, these ones are for someone taller . . . Sorry, this one's broken . . . No, these are left-handed.'

He is shouting above all the shifting and rattling.

'We found all these in the shed when we were cleaning the place out, probably left behind over the years by our members, for one reason or another. There used to be two hundred members here at Whistles. But, as I said, not many people bother with it anymore.'

A plume of dust envelops us like some archaeological curse. The grips on the clubs, ragged and peeling, could have been lifted from an Egyptian mummy. I cough on purpose, hoping the guy will stop all this rummaging.

'Wow,' I hear him say for no reason that I can see. Like all discarded things, the clubs have a look of embarrassment about them, which rubs off on those in their presence. I find myself moving nearer to the door.

'Wow,' he says again. This time he has a reason: a single bag planted in front of me with a thud. He grins. 'Pretty cool, isn't it? I didn't know we had this!'

This is a bag as thick as an elephant's leg and so tall it almost levels with my chest. It looks like something out of a Vegas show. Elvis white, with splashes of blue, red and gold.

'Is this . . . leather?' I can't think of anything else to say.

There is no waning in the teenager's enthusiasm. His cheeks are a hot red, his eyes jacked open by invisible toothpicks.

'Look at this.' He points to the embroidery on the side pocket. A fat gold chalice overlaid with big loopy letters. *Presidents Cup 1998*.

'Royal Melbourne,' he chimes. 'The only time the Internationals ever beat the United States.'

None of his words are registering and he can tell.

'Ever heard of Peter Thomson? Ernie Els? . . . *Nicklaus*?'

I shake my head and he shakes his.

'Anyway, the bag is heirloom. Just take my word for it.'

But he has no such praise for the clubs. I reach out and pick up one with a long shaft and a knobbly head. It feels heavy and greasy in my hand; the grip is sweating a little.

'Is this a driver?' I ask.

He clears his throat. 'That's more of a fairway wood.'

A fairway wood. It sounds like something you read to your children at bedtime. Though I've never heard the term, its existence now seems perfectly logical. It is a fairway wood, a wood to be played on the fairway.

'The equipment used to be very confusing,' says the teenager. 'You would've needed a dictionary to know what you're playing with: niblick, mashie, brassie, all sorts of weird names for the clubs. It's easier now, everything is really intuitive. The irons are numbered. The woods are numbered. Just remember a wood goes further than an iron, and a lower number goes further than a higher number. That's really it. You're Goldilocks.'

'This all rings a bell,' I say. 'I think I've had that explained to me before.'

'Oh yeah?'

'Yeah.'

An old image of Peter comes to me, and of the sun, the grass, the shiny arm of his club tracing the time as it swung at the ball. He was always talking about the aerodynamics of the equipment, and about how the way the grass was cut could impact the pace of the ball on a particular day at a particular hour. As I recall, he was not a natural golfer – a mid-handicapper who drove long and putted short – which only seemed to add to the appeal for him. It was the reason why he agonised over the distribution of force in his arms, how the back path of his swing dictated the forward path of the ball. He had the habit of leaving golf clubs around his house as if they were reminders of all the things he needed to know.

That summer we were together, when we were so much younger than now, Peter had brought me here, to Whistles. It was very hot that day, I remember. There was a drought, or at least the beginning of one. The grass was dry and the trees were full of cicadas. There was hardly any water in the canal. Peter was playing with some clubs he had built by fitting together various heads and shafts that he'd collected from garage sales.

As I walked with him, he told me how much he liked this place. He said that for every hole here, there was one way to play ambitiously and another way to play conservatively, which meant that everyone could enjoy them, no matter who they were and what their skill level. He had found that attractive, that sense of equality.

I guess I must've been sixteen then. I think, if I tried hard enough, I would be able to remember more, about what happened to us and how it happened, and why it came to be that we fell away from each other. But is there a point in recalling something that took place twenty years ago? My father has always told me the past has an expiration date. I think he is right.

Now I have a fairway wood. And, hiding in plain sight, the driver. It is vintage-car red and has three screws on the head like tiny cameras. The slender shaft reveals itself as I pull it out of the bag. It carries a lifetime of accidents, not an inch of it unscarred. But no matter the small details. I have two clubs and I'm feeling more confident.

Next there is the putter, easily recognised. The head is dirty and heavily scratched. Someone has been dragging it across gravel all its life. The word *Ping* on the steel is worn to a faint, shallow impression, but the club feels sturdy, solid as a weapon in my hand.

There is one last club in the bag. No game is complete without an iron. This one is a six, or a nine – who can tell? Either way, it is good enough for me.

An inexplicable satisfaction fills me as I drag my acquisition to the counter, even more so as the teenager offers me a bag of old balls and tees. It doesn't even bother me when he catches sight of my hands, the blood oozing from between my fingers.

'That looks pretty painful,' he says, trying not to wince.

'Yes, it's not particularly pleasant.'

'What happened?'

I tuck them away under my arms. And, sensing my reluctance, he looks away, rubbing at the beard he does not have.

Outside the rain is falling in a mist, tugged in every direction by a wind that has lost its way. I look down at my clubs, at the empty space in the bag where more clubs should be.

'It's fine. Thank you. Everything is fine.'

2

The ground underfoot is now a soupy slush. Little rocks vie for room inside my shoes as I drag my clubs onto the grassy mound at the beginning of the first hole. From here, the fairway stretches out straight for a good distance before it dog-leg kicks to the left. The view of the flag is obscured by a huge tree that hangs over the route, brown syrup spilling, grape-like, from its blackened trunk.

The woman with the dog is walking across the grounds in the distance. A row of cypresses stands guard over them as they mount a green on the other side of the canal, and brush their way past the flag. The woman finds a stick on the ground, picks it up and swings it about in the air, at the rain. The dog barks at the performance. She throws the stick at him, and he catches it in his mouth, carries it as they walk again. Their figures are just smudges of pencil through the rain that is once more growing dense and determined. Her jacket billows like the train of a wedding dress being carried into church.

They say the first woman to have played golf was Mary of Scots; that she was so mad about it that even the brutal murder of her husband did not stop her from going out onto the links. Is this how she might have looked in the winter of 1567, as she trudged across the course in the Scottish rain, trailed by a loyal servant who carried her clubs? She should have been doing any number of other things. Grieving. Rejoicing. Plotting. Why golf?

I stick a pink tee into the wet earth and place a ball, the only pink one I could find, on top of it. The set-up looks unexpectedly fetching, like something displayed in a dessert cabinet.

With the driver in hand, I move into position, or what I estimate to be roughly the position. I'm sure there is a right way and a wrong way of doing this. I can recall the way Peter used to practise his swing in the backyard of his house, legs apart, winding up at the waist. The club in his hand would swoop down and up, over and over, drawing an inverted arc over a ball that was not there. He made it seem intuitive, simple.

I swing my driver and look out to see where the ball has flown. But it is nowhere, gone. I step back, turn a full circle, searching. Then I realise it is right in front of my feet, where it has always been, unmoved. The club has not connected with the ball at all, but the tee is now lodged in the grass about five metres ahead.

The fact that such a thing can happen impresses rather than discourages. It's pure wonder to me that the clubhead should have been able to clear the tight space between ball and ground so effortlessly, so exactly, as to send off the tee without ever kissing the ball.

The clouds have suddenly turned a deep violet. Thunder faintly rumbles. Again, I tee the ball up. Eyes on it, I tell myself. This seems to apply universally to all ball sports; it must equally apply to golf. I swing as hard as I can.

The club connects this time, sends the ball off with the sound of a muted bell. The ball arches through the rain and, helped by the wind, seems to extend its flight a moment beyond what gravity would allow. How strange that a bit of rubber pressed with resin could produce such a motion. It lands on the fairway without bouncing, looking resigned for a moment, done. But to my surprise it wills itself forward, rolling, skidding, helped by some allowance on the ground I can't perceive. It is travelling, not in a straight line but in a gentle curve to the left, over the sodden grass. The sky flashes. The ball goes on, swishing up a tail of water. And it might have gone further still, if not for the land which is now sloping up unforgivingly as it reaches the bend. But where it comes to rest seems remarkable all the same. It's the first time in my life I have hit a golf ball. It is almost halfway to the green.

The rain is so heavy, so blinding that the ball seems to drown instantly once it comes to a stop. Soon there is no trace of it, only the flicker of elation in me, like an afterthought of a dream that lingers in the morning. If this is golf – this madness of pitting the motion of a small object against rough terrain and bad weather, this dogged insistence on distance and precision in the face of incomputable variables, the rain, the wind, every nuance of the land – then it is surely worth repeating.

I take another ball from the bag and set it down. I'm almost ready to take a swing when I hear a voice calling to me from behind.

'Hey! Stop! Put the club down!'

I turn to find the teenager running out of the pro shop, hunched against the wind, his shirt speckled with raindrops. His arm is up, pointing at the rumbling sky.

'Lesson number one: never play golf in a thunderstorm.'

Turns out he is not a teenager at all. His name is Josh and he has played golf for seventeen years, since he was five. He has just finished his maths degree at uni, but no one is surprised to find him working on a golf course.

This he tells me after pulling me back from the first tee, or what he assures me was a statistically significant chance of being struck by lightning.

Under the porch, I feel no drier nor warmer than before.

'Wait here,' he says and, after a while, returns with a towel. 'Here, dry yourself, if it's at all possible.'

The rain is drumming on the tin roof above us. Even though he is only a step away, I can hardly hear him. I take the towel, and run it over my face, my hair. It has the smell of something kept too long in a cupboard. I wrap it around me, grateful all the same.

'You should consider yourself lucky,' Josh says, shouts. For a moment, I think he is still talking about the lightning. 'The course is closing. If you had come any later, you might've missed it completely.'

'When will it close?'

He glances at me sideways. 'By the end of July this'll all be a construction site.'

'Pity.'

He's not quite convinced of my sincerity. His fingers come together to make a square frame, and he moves it around like a movie director trying to locate just the right shot. When he finds it, he says, 'There. See that?'

'Sorry, see what?'

'This view. Look through here.'

And through his hands I find the ninth green – the final green – and the fairway coming up towards it, towards us. A line of willows on either side pose like the offspring of the taller cypresses further away. The fairway is very long and straight, built as a boulevard fit for a golfer's homecoming. It's the longest hole, the only par 5 at Whistles.

'Now look behind you, inside the clubhouse,' says Josh. 'The wall to the left.'

I think he must be playing games, but turning around, I catch sight of something made all the more surprising by the decrepitude of the building which contains it: a painting the size of a small blackboard, framed in flowering gold. I squint through the window, trying hard to see through the grime into the darkened room, to take in the details of the painting. It bears the same vista as the one framed by Josh's hands, except the storm is gone and in its place a day that has barely left its dawn. The light, low on the horizon, pools as if it were too sleepy to rise.

Josh says, 'That was Whistles in 1934.'

The brushstrokes are quite impressionistic, yet very vivid. You can sense every blade of grass, every dappled leaf on the trees as they posed for the painter all that time ago.

There is something unusual about the perspective of the

painting, at odds with how you imagine such a picture should look. Most landscapes seem to demand that you look far into the distance; they hint at a place, yonder, to which you should yearn to travel. A hill, or the sea, or the spire of a church. But this one begins where most finish. Your eyes start at the destination – the green in the foreground adorned by nothing but a white flag licking at the wind. You get the distinct feeling that you have already arrived, that there is nothing left to do but wait for someone to come up the fairway to join you.

'Not much has changed since then; since even before then,' says Josh. 'The view is pretty much the same as the day it was made.'

Suddenly he seems a little sad; his head drops like it's heavier on one side.

'Actually we've been here since 1880. We're just about the oldest there is, in this part of the world.'

His choice of pronoun seems odd. It reminds me of those married couples who go around telling people 'we're pregnant'.

'The lease is up and there are no more options to renew. Truth is we've been struggling to keep this place going for years. It's been running on a shoestring budget. Bare essential maintenance. No one plays golf anymore. Who's got the time and the patience?'

Though the question requires no answer, he lets it hang in the air for a while, as if testing its validity.

'This used to be a full-length course, eighteen holes. About thirty years ago, the council sold off half the land and put a road through it.' He says the word 'road' as if it were a profanity. 'After that we had nine holes. And soon we'll have none.'

He doesn't have to go on. The big council notice, tacked to a nearby post, says the rest. Six hundred new dwellings spread across ten apartment buildings. Flowering avenues and exercise facilities. Solar-heated pools on rooftops. Cafés with liquor licences. A lake in the middle with swans that eat hot chips right out of your hand.

I look out over the land. On a clear day you must be able to see the glinting silhouette of the city in the distance, beaming like an advert for the proximity. The potential for these urban hectares is endless. Anybody can see that.

The green on the ninth is now a small atoll, surrounded by a mirror of water. The rain is pooling at our feet. The ground is waterlogged everywhere. I take a step back, but the water follows me, and I must resign myself to standing in it after all.

'Let me ask you something,' I say to Josh. 'Has anyone ever finished the ninth hole in just two strokes?'

He looks at me curiously, considers. 'Two strokes into the hole on a par 5? We call that an albatross. I'm not sure if anyone ever has, but I'd say it's unlikely. Why do you ask?'

I don't know how to explain it to him; it would require too much time, too much effort to recall. It is easier to simply say, 'I sometimes wonder about it, that's all. I've been told it's a very difficult thing to do.'

'You need to find a word better than *difficult*.' He chuckles. 'Let me just say that you would've had a greater chance of being struck by that lightning.'

He seems to sense that I want him to go on, that I don't fully comprehend.

'It's just about the rarest thing in golf – the odds are pretty spectacularly against you, six million to one, or something close to that. We're talking about more than half a kilometre of fairway. But it's not just the insane distance that makes it hard. There's something oddly complicated about it, I guess – the fact that you have to hit not one but two great shots, consecutively, to make it happen.'

He pauses, and joins his hands, takes two big swings at the air as if demonstrating how it should be done. He reminds me of Peter, of the way he swung the club that year, his eyes fixed on the green as the ball travelled through the air.

'Here's the funny thing. Believe it or not, I've met lots of people who dread getting a hole-in-one. They're superstitious about it. They think that it drains their luck, that they'll never be able to win the lottery afterwards. But an albatross, like the one you're talking about, here on the ninth hole – that would be a totally different story. People pray for that. You can even call it the holy grail for golfers.'

'Now I'm confused,' I say. 'You're telling me that people might actually find more fulfilment in achieving something in two strokes than one?'

'Sure they do, plenty of them.'

'Doesn't that go against the whole idea of golf?'

'I don't know. It depends on how you look at it, from your perspective.'

He takes a moment to think, before adding, 'The way I look at it, a hole-in-one, anywhere on a golf course, is really just a random event, a fluke. It's not your own doing. But an albatross on a par 5, on the longest of holes . . . Ask anyone who has seen one, and they'll tell you that it's a thing of beauty.

One. Two. It must be very deliberate, very thoughtful, one superb shot followed by another. You can say it's got to take a degree of belief. You've got to really want it, and aim for it, and try for it. That's what I think.'

Maybe he's right. The mere idea of it, to deliver a ball over 500 metres from tee to flag in no more and no less than two strokes, seems to require something beyond luck. You must hit a long drive, and follow it with a deftly accurate shot from the fairway into the hole. In the alternative, you'd have to drive the ball straight onto the green, over what must be an improbable distance, and sink the ball with one putt. Neither approach appears to be particularly feasible, and yet each, in its own way, seems faintly possible given the right person, the right amount of resolve.

The wind has shifted. The rain is falling at a different angle, away from us now. Still, the lightning flashes, the thunder always chasing, trying to keep up. In a minute, I will have to make a run for the car. It's been hours since I left the house. Will Adrian be wondering where I am?

'So, you'll be back again?' Josh asks as I hand him the towel. 'There is still time before the door closes.'

It is hard to look at him for long without feeling unease. He has the kind of eyes you see a lot in baby animal calendars; he seems to be wanting a promise of some sort. But would it really matter if one more person chose to play here in the time that remains, on this land that is abstractly dying?

'I hope you don't take this the wrong way,' I say to him. 'But of all the things people do to pass their time, I think golf must be the strangest.'

'Yeah, I know. Golf makes absolutely no sense to anyone.'

Then he blushes, produces a laugh which on account of the thunder I can only see but not hear. It isn't clear to me at all if he meant what he said.

3

A trail of mud and rain follows me into the house. Halfway up the corridor I have to kick off my shoes to keep myself from tripping. Cans and packets and apples are tumbling out of my bags and by the time I'm in the kitchen I have willingly let go of the rest. The sound of it all hitting the floor is a relief, even if the yoghurt is now a constellation of blotches at my feet.

The room is dark. I turn on the light and now it is the colour of weak tea.

Adrian is in front of the fireplace, a glass of water in his hand. There is no fire, so why does he stand there? We have never used the fireplace in this house, despite the logs we keep on the front verandah as if to prove to the world we are wood-burning people.

He drinks his water, scrutinises me. 'What happened to you?'

'I went out for groceries, as you can see.'

'But your clothes,' he points out.

I realise as I look down that I may as well be wearing nothing. My blouse is clinging to my skin; you can see right through to my bra and belly button. Was it like this the whole time I was at Whistles? I pull at the fabric, try to dislodge it from my body. It's no use. The whole thing is stuck to me like I've just walked into a giant spider web.

'I was held up in the rain. Sorry.' I don't know why I am apologising. 'The traffic was terrible. They blocked out half the lanes on the highway. We had to go around the potholes.'

'Primrose,' says Adrian. 'You look like you fell *into* the pothole.'

I try to laugh. 'Don't be ridiculous.'

'You left in such a hurry,' he says. 'We were in the middle of a conversation and you just got up and bolted.'

'That's not what happened, Adrian.'

'No? We were right here. I was saying something about an email I got from Terence. The next moment you were out the door. What's the matter with you?'

'Nothing is the matter. We needed groceries. It was raining and I got wet. That's all there is to say.'

Still he looks at me doubtfully. In the time that I've been gone he has made no effort to dress himself properly. He is wearing an old jumper with a rip across one shoulder. The front of his sweatpants is all scrunched up on account of the draw-strings, which have to be tightened beyond what the fashion would normally permit. Even though he is almost back to his old weight, his clothes still have a way of reminding me just how much of him is missing.

'What about you?' I ask. 'I thought you had class today.'

He shrugs. 'Someone from the faculty is filling in for me.'

'Again?'

'Yes, again.'

'Won't your students mind? You've skipped a lot of class time, haven't you?'

'It doesn't matter much.'

'How? How can it not matter that you aren't showing up for work?'

He moves towards the couch, glass still in hand.

'People don't take philosophy courses at uni in order to get an education, Primrose. They've already done all the Google-assisted learning by the time they turn up to class. They are only there to be argumentative and self-righteous.' Then he adds, casually, 'Anyway, they've got Simone if they really feel like asking questions.'

'Simone? She's the one filling for you?'

'Yes, I said that already.'

'That's nice of her, I guess. Always helping you out.'

We could go on like this forever – me probing him about his work and him about my day – and neither of us ever quite getting to a point of satisfaction. It's a relief when Adrian finally sits down on the couch, his back to me, and turns on the TV.

The afternoon news bulletin is full of fallen trees and car accidents in the storm. Even when it digresses from the weather, it lingers on tragedy: out west, a funeral for a well-known climber who plunged to his death while scaling the quartzite rockface at Mount Arapiles. He had ascended without much trouble, but the grigri decided to speed things up a little on the way down.

On the coffee table Adrian's phone is doing that familiar, low-key buzzing. He won't answer it. He simply sips at his water and makes a shape with his mouth as if it were liquor – maybe it is. The urgency of the caller grows with each vibration until voice mail finally sends it into silence.

A poorly tied knot was the cause of the climber's fall, the news reporter is saying. Sadly, such human errors occur much too often. Friends of the climber say his fiancé is devastated, but there is comfort in knowing he died doing what he loved most.

'Why do they always say that?' says Adrian. 'Surely it's the opposite of comfort to die when you are at your happiest.'

His phone is buzzing again, but still he chooses to ignore it.

'Adrian, please, just answer it.'

He keeps his eyes on the TV, swishes the last bit of liquid in his glass.

'In a minute,' he says.

In the laundry, I try to change out of my wet clothes, the blouse first to come off, its buttons taking forever. The latch on the window, broken for months, is squeaking in the breeze like sound effects from a horror movie. I remind myself to get it fixed, or to remind Adrian to get it fixed.

The jeans are no easier to tackle than the blouse; they're so stiff from the mud and the rain that they refuse to budge past my ankles. Granted, this isn't the best place to change. I can't bend an elbow or stand on one leg without bumping into the cardboard boxes that have taken over the room like a poorly played game of Tetris. What has happened to this place? There is hardly any room to move.

More boxes seem to have arrived in the time I was out. The stacks have grown higher. As I pull the jeans free, one box tumbles and knocks me against the wall. Cursing, I kick it out of the way. I don't have to open it to know what's inside.

Life Meal. Balanced nutrition for life.

For almost a year now, Adrian has lived on this stuff. The recipe is simple: you add water and you stir, and no matter the flavour, it promises to enter and exit in the same sludge-like consistency. He grew used to it during all the months he was in the hospital, when the nurses gave it to him to curb the weight loss brought on by the treatments. Somehow the habit stuck, or perhaps he made no efforts to let it go. Now boxes of Life Meal fill the house, as if we are slowly building a brick wall around ourselves.

I get dressed, feeling somewhat warmer in a dry jumper and shorts. And after rearranging the boxes, I can finally reach the sink, where the bucket is already waiting to be filled and carried away. The work needs to be done; it cannot be delayed. I pull on a pair of rubber gloves through gritted teeth. My hands sting, but leaving those muddy footprints in the corridor would be out of the question.

It's another hour before I have to pick Bebe up from school, a luxurious hour of slaving over the floor.

As the water from the tap splashes against the bucket, I add the usual bleach and detergent and, for good measure, a generous pour of oregano oil. The oil disappears into the foamy water and fills the room with its sharp, bitter scent. If the internet is to be believed, the oregano alone will be enough to blast away all the evils in this house: the yeast, the mould, the *staphylococcus aureus* and *salmonella*, and even drug-resistant *E.coli*. It will make the house smell like an ashtray, but that is beside the point.

I load the bucket with more oregano, more bleach, more detergent, and take the steaming concoction into the corridor where, in the short time since I left them, my puddled footprints have begun to look set in wax. I will start with them, then the yoghurt.

By now I have a routine for cleaning this house, of working with a brush, then a cloth, as thoroughly as I can. I used to clean with a long-handled mop; that took less effort but produced results that were merely token. I could never properly address the corners, the tiny dimples in the grout, the molecular variations on the surfaces of wood or porcelain. It is infinitely better this way, more effective to be on my hands and knees, like some beggar picking up the change.

My hands will hurt; I'm sure of the splitting pain that will come with each flex of the fingers, the new, weeping blisters that will somehow find room on my already crowded hands. The gloves can no longer protect the hands from the wear. But it all seems a small sacrifice for the relief that will wash over me once everything has been scrubbed clean and raw, to within an inch of its existence.

I get down to work; it feels less like work, more a dirty, shameful pleasure. One footprint at a time. One floorboard after another.

The cloth will have to be rinsed at regular intervals. Not a speck of dirt should be allowed to remain on the fabric when it is reapplied to the floor. Once the water in the bucket reaches a light grey, it must be changed, and more bleach, more detergent, more oregano oil added.

Adrian has kept the TV on in the kitchen. Someone is saying something about more rain to come and, in the alpine areas, even the first snow of the year. Outside, the rain lives up to this promise, unrelenting. And inside, the sour water from the bucket quickly begins to pool around my knees.

If Elaine were to see this, she'd surely try to talk me up from the floor with her studied, temperate words. She'd tell me, as she always does, that the amount of time I spend cleaning the house is preventing me from leading a normal life, that everything I'm doing is a superficial manifestation of something deeper that grips me. But I am not due to see her for days. For now: one footprint at a time, one floorboard after another.

Elaine is someone I see every fortnight. She has an office in the city, in a building full of dentists. The building has a tiny lift that takes nearly a minute to arrive at the eighth floor. Riding in it always makes me think of the poor claustrophobics who must take the stairs to get to their sessions.

During our allocated time, Elaine and I talk a lot about my attachment to the water in the bucket, about the state of my hands, about Adrian. Around and around she goes, the same questions, the same advice. While I talk, she makes interjections to show she is listening and takes fastidious notes in pencil on a Spirax notepad. She is like the trusty animal that mills the flour, never a hint of impatience as she walks her circles around my thoughts, grinding them to dust.

Adrian appears in the doorway, or perhaps he has been standing there all this time. He seems a little more cheerful, his mood lifted by something on his phone.

'That email from Terence,' he says. 'I never finished telling you about it earlier.'

'I don't need to know everything between you and your brother,' I tell him. I'm still bent over the floor, hair falling loose over my face. 'You've told me he's coming down from London, in July. That's all I need to know.'

'Well,' says Adrian, coming nearer. There's yoghurt on his shoes, smacking the floor like unwanted kisses. 'I know you wouldn't mind, so I've asked him to stay with us while he's in town.'

'And what does he say to that?'

'He's agreed.'

Adrian is looking for some indication of excitement. He adds, 'It would be nice to spend some time with him, don't you think? We haven't seen him at all since I got out of the hospital, and that's over a year ago.'

There is an area on the floor where the polish has worn thin. I scrub it hard and watch the timber blacken into a wet, irreversible wound.

'I can't seem to get this floor to look the way it should,' I say, more or less to myself.

I am not blind to the fact that the house has never thanked me for my efforts. It has chosen to wear my hard work as scars, as damage. The more I clean, the more things seem to take on the appearance of being dirty. When people visit the house, they do not directly comment on how clean it looks. Rather, they say things like, *Oh, you've really given the place a scrub, haven't you?*

In Elaine's view, my compulsions were defensible in the beginning. They started for practical reasons, to protect Adrian when he was sick all those months ago. At the time the chemo had obliterated his body's capacity to defend itself. The most common germs would have sent him into a downward spiral of fevers and infections. He had no immunity against the world, thus my devotion to cleanliness was logical and necessary – one might even say essential. But now, in the context of his return to health, she thinks my behaviour is rather carried away.

I must understand, she tells me, that everything around us can cause pain or illness or other unpleasantness. Everything has the potential to harm us, even kill us. But excessive vigilance is not a sound strategy against dying. It is a sure path to living miserably.

Elaine has no doubt, through our conversations, that I should continue to take the Sertraline. She gives me a new script every now and then. I don't have the heart to tell her I've never filled any of them.

'Hey, Primrose,' says Adrian, 'are you listening?'

'Yes, you are saying that you've asked Terence to stay here, with us, in this house.'

'I know Bebe would love to have him here. She always looks forward to a visit from her Uncle T. The two of them have a lot in common, don't you think?'

'She's nothing like him,' I say, to the floor.

Adrian does not hear me. 'Primrose, will you stop for a minute so I can talk to you properly?'

I try to get up, only to realise my legs have gone to sleep. In the end I am half bent, half standing, saying, 'Adrian, can we please discuss this later?'

'Why is it so complicated that it needs to be discussed later?'

He gives me an arm so that I can straighten myself. I try as hard as I can to get my rubber gloves out of his way. My hands feel clumsy; my neck is stupid with pain as I look up at him.

'Terence has his own apartment in the city,' I point out. 'Don't you think he'll be more comfortable there? If he's in town for work, it would make sense for him to stay there.'

'I think he'd rather spend time with us. It's only for a few days, so I can't see the problem. In any case, I've already invited him and he has said yes.'

'I'm sure he's only saying yes because he feels obliged. He's not the kind of person who seeks out closeness with his family. Maybe you can't see that about him, but I can see it as an outsider.'

'Primrose, you're not an outsider. And why would you even say that about him? I don't understand.'

Adrian is looking straight into my eyes as if searching for a direct route to my thoughts. I try to look anywhere but at him.

'After all that Terence has done for us, I think we owe him at least the invitation,' he says. 'Why're you so wary of him? Does he intimidate you in some way?'

'I am not intimidated,' I reply. But I think I am merely resigning, feeling my legs again.

Every marriage contains at its heart something that is unnegotiable; for us, it must be Terence.

Terence, fifteen years older than Adrian, is more than older brother. He is, to Adrian, friend and confidant and father figure all rolled into one. In fact this persona extends well beyond brotherhood into all realms of Terence's being, which only serves to strengthen Adrian's view of him. In many circles, Terence is considered a big deal because he happens to have a very successful career. He manages a lot of other people's money and has a lot of money of his own. Most people think of Terence as someone they'd like to have on their side. Not much is heard from those who want to run a mile.

I drop my gloves and walk into the study where, through the window, I can see the rain drawing arrows as it falls on the cars and the pavement. The big house across the street seems to be quivering in the downpour, fishlike, as if ready to slip away into the ocean.

I don't know whether to sit down or to stand. I stand. Adrian walks in, puts his hands on his hips.

'I just don't see the problem in inviting Terence. This is his house after all, remember? It's only because he's generous, because he's my brother, that we are living here. And we haven't given him anything in return.'

'Yes, this is his house,' I reply. It is hard to argue with that. 'You're right. It's his house.'

'He has done a lot for us, don't you think?'

'Agreed,' I say, as plainly as I can. 'He will stay here with us, if you want it that way.'

'Good. I'm really glad.'

Satisfied, his body softens. He leans in, encircles me with his arms. He gives me a peck on the mouth that turns into a kiss. There was a time, when he was frail and defenceless, that we would've never dared to kiss in this unguarded manner. Now a sense of unauthorised thrill forever attaches itself to these moments.

'I'm glad that you're glad,' I say.

I let him sink his hand beneath the waistband of my shorts, and down further to where he wishes it to go.

Each day he seems better to me than the day before. Not long ago the treatments had whittled him down to the bare essentials of a man. Nights spent next to him felt always interminably cold, subterranean. And most mornings, I didn't get out of bed until I felt him stirring beside me. I just pulled the blanket over my head and waited and hoped and prayed for some humanly sign that he was still alive.

Louisa, who lives across the street, thought I was mad when I told her. *But who knows?* I said to her. *Anything could happen during the night.* There were stories of people expiring in their sleep all the time, even young people who ate well and trained for triathlons. Who were we to tell children not to be afraid of the night? Nights scared me straight.

I reach up and touch Adrian on the forehead, feel the roots of his hair against my fingertips. He almost has that put-together look again, the appearance of someone who was once broken but is now mended.

'You look good,' I tell him, with conviction.

He smiles, but in a way that does not fully believe. His eyes wander over my face. He says, 'Tell me, where did you really go today?'

His arms are still around me; we seem to be caught in a

dance that has no way to finish. Put us in nicer clothes and this could pass for a wedding portrait.

It feels so exposed to be standing here, in full view of the street. It seems as though the whole world can see us holding each other in this manner, that someone, anyone, might be standing out in the rain, gazing in. Even Peter – a fleeting, basic shape of Peter, glancing as he passes. I know it sounds crazy but it always seems possible, entirely and lucidly possible, that he is out there looking in at me, passing judgment on the way life is arranged within these walls.

'So,' says Adrian. Is he still waiting for an answer?

He watches as I place my hand over his chest.

'I told you the truth, Adrian. Don't we always tell each other the truth?'

Either he is unsure what I mean or he does not want to answer. He lets out a breath, loosens the embrace. A bashful look crosses his face, and all I can see as I remove myself from him is the rain falling over Whistles, an entire prairie turning into marsh.

4

At school, Peter and I were two years apart; he was ahead. I have a memory of the library, filled with Form Sixes on the day an assignment was due. I remember Peter and his friends taking over the big round table in the middle of the room, a graphics calculator being passed among them like contraband.

Most of the boys were wearing their school shorts very low, defying both gravity and the school rules. That was, I remember, the fashion. It was the nineties after all, very late. In fact, it was less than three months till the year 2000, which everyone was calling the new millennium even though, technically, they were a year too early.

Peter's voice is what I remember next.

'Should you be reading this?' he asked, in the way that all Form Sixes talked to the lower levels. 'How old are you, twelve?'

I didn't see him get up from the table; I wasn't sure whether he had walked over to me intentionally or was merely passing by. Could he have me confused with someone else? That seemed like the most plausible explanation for why he was talking to me.

'I'm *sixteen*,' I said to him from the floor, beside a pile of books.

He got down, and picked a copy of *Rabbit, Run* from the top of the pile, thinking that he did not need to ask.

'You like reading, don't you? I always see you in here, like this.'

I didn't say anything.

People often had that impression of me. In reality I spent a lot of time just looking at the books, trying to figure out how to read them and why they were worth reading. When I opened a book, the first thing I saw was patterns made out of words, words made out of letters. They were just as complicated as my mother's knitting patterns or an architect's plans for a building. It took me forever to read a book from cover to cover, which was why I was always surrounded by them.

'This one is a waste of time,' Peter declared. 'Take my word for it, don't read it.'

'Why? What do you have against Updike?'

'Nothing. But the whole Rabbit character is pretty lame. He spends all his time cheating on his wife and messing up his kid.'

Peter began to rummage through the books on the shelf behind me. It made me uncomfortable how close he was. I wondered if it would be impolite to move away.

'This one, read this instead.'

He grinned as he pulled the book off the shelf, placed it in my lap. There was gum in his mouth and the faint smell of Lynx on his collar. His hair was a black mass of gel, the front of it standing up like the edge of an uncut lawn.

'It's an Updike too, but way better,' he said.

The book was a collection of essays about golf. On the cover was a picture of a man with his club up in the air, like he had just taken a slightly awkward swing. It was the last book in the world I wanted to read. I was not into sports and I didn't even understand the scoring system in golf.

I opened the book suspiciously, looked at the first page. The words made no sense at all, even when I read them over several times, once backwards. It made me nervous, the way Peter was staring at me, waiting for a verdict. I hated it when people did that, when they put a clock over me while I tried to make sense of things. I'd never been much into foreign language movies for the same reason. Not enough time to get through the subtitles.

'You're on the golf team,' I said, though I didn't mean to say it out loud. It was just a thought that came into my head, one that might explain why he was going around recommending golf books to people he didn't know.

He smiled. 'Yeah, me and Davo Robson. We were in the regional finals last week.'

'Did you win?'

'No.' He rubbed the back of his head. 'We overplayed the course a bit.'

I must have looked confused, having no idea what he meant.

'You've got to know the map pretty well if you want to win,' he added. 'We thought we could just wing it. We didn't study hard enough. We didn't know the lay of the land.'

He made it sound like a skirmish, with boys holding toy rifles, hiding in ditches. I tried to look at the book again, and the words on the page stared back at me, reading themselves out loud.

They steal upon the sleeping mind while winter steals upon the landscape, sealing the inviting cups beneath sheets of ice, cloaking the contours of the fairway in snow.

I imagined Updike in thick coat and heavy boots, a club in his hand, his footprints on the ground.

'Thanks for the suggestion,' I said to Peter. 'I'm not really sure if it's my kind of book.'

'You haven't even read past the first page.'

'The words are beautiful but . . .'

I thought about my dad then, about what he'd say about a book like this. He once told me that golf was just another excuse for people to form clubs and cliques that some could belong to and others couldn't. He said that about a lot of things. As a general rule, he was very offended by anything that was capable of dividing people into categories. The first English words he ever made sure I understood were 'blue collar'. Then he told me never to use them.

I glanced at Peter and put the book back in his hand. 'Thanks anyway.'

He left the book on the carpet and shrugged, overly nonchalant. His friends at the table were looking at him, laughing.

'Alright,' he said, getting up, turning to go. 'See you around, Primrose.'

The last thing I saw as he walked away, as he said my name, was a protractor poking out of his blazer pocket, its edges stained with blue ink. This, for some reason, was what I always remembered afterwards. Even years later, I would see that protractor whenever I thought of him at that age, as if it were proof that everything did happen.

A few months after the day in the library, it was summer, almost Christmas. I was on a shift at the café on Newton Street where some of the local kids worked during the school holidays for a bit of pocket money and what their parents liked to call 'character building'. As for me, I was there for an altogether different reason – because my parents actually ran the place, and the arrangement between us was that I didn't so much get paid as I was repaying my debts to them.

A lot of people at school knew about me because of the café, and I couldn't remember a time when I didn't feel embarrassed about it. About how we served and smiled and cleaned up after our customers, how we had to endlessly remark on the weather and say thank you when a tip went into the jar. There was no way to hide in a place that opened itself to the street with a flashing 'Welcome' sign at the door. There was no way except to hope that, with an occasional lie, I could be excused from my shift so that the remainder of the day could be spent upstairs with Bob, where no one could see us lying side by side on the floor, counting away the time with the taps of his tail.

Bob, my Alsatian other: his name a tribute, as my dad would put it, to the greatest prime minister in all of Australia's history. When we first got Bob he was eight weeks old, no more than a baby to me. Now I was sixteen and he was four, almost thirty in a man's years, marching steadfastly towards his prime. He was the older and wiser of us.

My bedroom upstairs was the easiest place to be on earth. Being in it with Bob was like floating through outer space. There was no colour, no language, no sound that begged to be understood. Only me, left with my own thoughts, my dreams of what I'd do once I finally left high school behind.

I still had two more years of school. For me, archaeology came closest to what people might call a dream. I thought constantly about going to see the Nile and the Valley of the Kings and the temple built by Hatshepsut. My dad was always telling me it was one of the most dangerous places in the world to visit. He knew I didn't believe a word of it, but it was better than telling me straight that he didn't put archaeology in the same basket as law or commerce or medicine.

If archaeology was out of the question, I wanted to do something that allowed me to write. Writing was a breeze compared to reading; my teachers always said I wrote very well. But write *what*, I was not sure. Something for a magazine, perhaps. A column in a newspaper. My dad was more open to this idea. But get a useful degree first, he said. Then write.

'Primrose,' said Erin, in the café. 'Are you doing anything special for Christmas?'

We were untying our aprons after wiping down all the tables. Erin had let her hair out of her braids and now it looked all crimped and voluminous, as if she'd been through a wind tunnel. She had lovely black hair tinged with a shade of auburn that must have come from spending a lot of time in the sun, playing tennis, maybe, or sailing.

'December's usually pretty boring for me,' I said to her. 'It's just one hot day after another. Nothing exciting ever happens.'

'Really? That's a pity.'

It always felt odd talking to Erin. We were in the same year at school but we had different friends, and those friends in no way intersected.

'Christmas is not really a thing for us,' I said. 'We never even have a tree. I don't know any of the carols off by heart.'

I could tell Erin was feeling sorry for me. She squished her mouth together so her lips were no longer visible. 'Christmas is kind of overrated.'

She didn't mean that. All day she'd worn an elf's hat while serving the customers and nobody had even asked her to.

'What are you doing, then?' I felt obliged to ask. 'For Christmas.'

'My mum's taking us skiing,' she said, of course.

'Good for you.'

'We're going to Japan.'

'That's nice.'

'I love to ski.'

'I've never skied.'

Erin laughed. 'You know that's not true, Primrose. Remember when we went to Lake Mountain for Form 3 Exodus?'

'Oh yeah, cross-country. That's not real skiing, is it?'

She laughed again and I could see all her back teeth. They were like white fluffs of popcorn.

Earlier she had pulled a perfume strip out of a magazine someone had left on a table and rubbed it between her wrists like she was making a fire. Now she smelled like Mrs Karagianis, our chemistry teacher.

'Anyway, Japan has the most awesome snow, if you ever want to check it out. Especially around Hakuba, which is where we always go. The food is really good too.'

'You're lucky. My parents never take me anywhere.'

This was not entirely true. At age eight, they did take me on the mother of all trips: Shanghai to Melbourne via Singapore, no return flights necessary. I still remembered my father's grand announcement as our plane touched down: we were now on the largest island in the world, exclamation point. It was probably the only time I ever saw him get excited.

In hindsight, what he said seemed a touch irrelevant when there were so many other things he could have said. He could've said, for instance, that the first year here would be like being a deaf mute, running around guessing at what people meant and in what way they meant it and if they were even talking to you. He could've said the second year would be only marginally better; that it'd be like finally realising you could talk but that you spoke with a stutter. He could have also taken the time to mention that by the third year you would feel almost normal again – since, like the rest of the children, you could now eat a meat pie piping hot from the tuckshop without having the fillings or sauce drip all over your jumper – except for the fact that sometimes you'd remember the two years prior, and the way kids looked at you, then looked at each other, and once you remembered that, it would be clear that they could never be properly forgotten.

Yet on the day our plane taxied into Terminal 3, he didn't see fit to tell me any of that. Needless to say, I now had an aversion to taking family trips anywhere.

Erin was the reason we came to Australia. Not Erin herself, of course, but the essence of Erin: what my dad liked to call 'the long-term good'. To him, Erin's family was testament to what our family could become in five generations. Her great-great-grandparents had been gold-rush people from Canton. They went from digging gold to trading furniture in one generation, then from trading furniture to banking and investments in another. By the time Erin's dad, Robert, was growing up, the Loys, in mild seriousness, could call themselves a dynasty. They could be whoever they wanted.

Looking at Erin was like looking at proof of what life could be after a hundred years in this country. It was like peering into the future and knowing in your heart that you were in the right place despite all the feelings of not quite belonging. That was what my dad liked to tell me. He made it sound lovely and meaningful, but what he really meant was that I was a non-Erin. I was just a stepping stone on the way to a future generation of Erins.

So, by contrast, here was Erin, five generations ahead of me, despite us always sharing the same shift. She was part of the popular crowd at school. She had her birthday parties on her mum's boat every year. Her dad had a boat too, by the way, which some people said was more correctly called a yacht. But Erin happened to live with her mum, so her mum's boat it was.

Donna, Erin's mum, was from some old Malaysian Chinese family. She sat on charity boards and made documentary films about things like AIDS and anorexia. Knowing this about her mum seemed to instantly explain everything about Erin. Why she ran marathons every Easter to raise money for the homeless. Why she liked the taste of raw vegetables and did open water swimming in the middle of winter for no reason whatsoever. And why, if you walked past her house in the evenings when the lights were on, you could see a harp through the big bay window. A harp, for God's sake.

Then, of course, there was Peter. You couldn't speak of Erin without mentioning the older brother with whom she ran marathons and swam in the open water. The brother who sometimes came to pick her up at the end of her shift, who was right now waiting outside on the street in a shiny convertible he must have gotten as a graduation present, all set for uni at the end of the summer.

I could picture him in the big lecture theatre, paying more attention to the time than his notes because his future was not in any of the assigned law books but in the family bank that carried his name. As usual he'd be surrounded by his friends – not the old ones from school, whom he didn't bother to see anymore, but newer, better ones. Friends who had their share houses within walking distance of the campus and the good Italian restaurants. Friends who went to the pub every Thursday and hosted house parties on weekends.

Outside, Peter beeped his horn. Erin jumped.

'Oops, I forgot he was coming today. Bye.'

She grabbed her bag and was out the door in a flash.

I watched her get into the back seat of the car. There was another girl, in the front passenger seat, curly haired and familiar, someone from school. She was taking Peter's arm, the one he didn't need for driving, and wrapping it around her neck like a scarf. I thought her name must be Wren or Mavis, something bird-related. She was in the drama crowd and performed in all the school plays.

Wren must have been saying something funny because Peter was looking at her, laughing. And through her, his eyes seemed to catch me, inside the empty café, standing alone with my arms crossed to hide the fact I didn't know quite what to do. Or maybe, because it was only a fleeting glance, all he saw was the reflection of himself in the shop window that separated us, and the name of the place – *The Comet* – spelt out in strokes of yellow over the glass.

A week later Peter was back: closer this time, inside the doorway. He looked so different out of uniform. Most people did, I supposed. Like they'd suddenly grown legs and arms they'd never had before. The purpose of a uniform was not to clothe you but to hide you. In T-shirt and shorts he was broader and browner and older all at once.

'Erin's not working today,' I said to him, not knowing where to put the dirty plates I was holding.

Peter looked down at the ground, then at me. 'I know. I just wanted something to eat. Can I sit down?'

The only place free was in the sun between two shadows. The air conditioner was barely coping and the table was burning hot. The sugar bowl sparkled like a psychedelic cactus and, as he sat, it cast a starry sort of pattern on his arm.

'So, should I just order from you? Or is that a bit weird?'

'It's weird, I guess.'

'But technically you do work here.'

'Yeah, technically you're right. What would you like, then?'

He pinched his chin, shifted himself uncomfortably. 'Did you ever get through your pile of books from the library?'

'No, I don't really like reading.'

'Honestly?'

'Honestly. When I look at a page, all I see is the words, the individual words. I can't get my mind to work out the sentences and what exactly they're supposed to mean. My dad thinks it's because I wasn't taught English right.'

'Or maybe you just don't care about the pointless things other people find the need to say.'

We both laughed at that. It sounded nice, the way he put it. It was better than being called slow or dyslexic, which a couple of kids had done in class when I'd had trouble reading out a passage from *Heart of Darkness*.

'I did try to read the golf book you showed me,' I said.

He seemed surprised. 'What did you think about it?'

'I liked the part where he took his wife to play minigolf, but the rest of it kind of went over my head.'

'Oh. It's really just his observations about how difficult golf is as a sport, but difficult in a funny way, because people are always convinced that they can play, even when they can't. It's like it makes people delusional or something.'

Nervously he rubbed at the side of his neck, where one month of summer had left the skin red and freckled.

'Anyway, it's not important. I was being a bit of a smartarse in the library that day. I'm sorry about that.'

The apology was unexpected and confusing, and now there

was an awkward silence between us that neither of us knew how to fill.

Sometimes it seemed to me that a part of my brain was broken, the part that came up with things to say so I could have a normal conversation with people for a decent length of time. It felt like my head was refusing to communicate with my mouth, like they were two different entities that did not get along. I often watched people engage in conversations across tables or over fences or even from opposite sides of the street, and wondered how the sentences just rolled off their tongues without getting stuck in their heads. I wished I could just go through life writing letters to people instead of having to talk to them. A pen and paper would take the pressure off, knowing you could cross things out and start again.

After a while, Peter got up and said, 'I better go. I mean, you probably hate it when people from school drop in. I'm actually not that hungry anyway.'

His chair grunted as it was pushed back under the table. I could feel the eyes of the other people in the café. He seemed nervous, uncertain, which was a side of him I'd never seen at school. It occurred to me then that I didn't know much about him at all. Maybe there was no reason why I should – how well did anyone know anyone else at school? Every one of us was known by some consensus that seemed to form out of thin air and attach to us for all of adolescence, whether we liked it or not.

Peter put his hands in his pockets, tried to look casual. 'By the way, I'm having a party at my house for New Year's Eve. Just some of my friends. Come if you want.'

'I thought you were going overseas.'

He tried to process this. 'Oh, that. Did Erin tell you? No, that's just my mum's idea of herding us into liking each other. She's going to take Erin. I'm just not sure if I want to spend my last summer before uni doing the same old stuff. I prefer to have the house all to myself, go play golf or something. I really don't like the snow that much.'

'I won't really know anyone there, at the party.'

He looked amused, as if he would never consider that a reason to reject an invitation. 'Who cares? That's why parties were invented.'

I was not convinced, having never gone to a party to meet new people. I'd only been to ones where my friends and I stood around and tried not to talk to anyone else.

'Anyway, it's up to you,' he said. 'I'm at the end of Birch Grove, the house with the green stuff growing all over it.'

That was unnecessary; everyone knew where the Loys lived.

'Okay,' I replied. 'Maybe.'

Then he smiled at me. It was just an impression of a smile, imprecise, full of questions. There was no way of knowing if it meant nothing or everything, which only added to the thrill when we had time, so much time it seemed, ahead of us.

5

The sound of footsteps ring through the house as if a fairy creature is darting between the trees in a wood. It's late. The entire house is in darkness except the kitchen, where I'm crouched over the floor with a toothbrush, working over the grout. I have assumed – wrongly, it seems – that I would be alone.

Another round of footsteps, bringing me to a halt. I crawl behind the kitchen island and poke my head out. There is an inkling of a shadow down the corridor. Instinctively I duck. What is this? Hide-and-seek?

'Bebe?' I call out.

There is no reply, only a creak of the floor.

'Bebe,' I say again. And by the third time, I decide to get up, feeling stupid that I only have my sleeve to dry off my wet knees.

Another string of footsteps, ascending.

I go into the corridor and follow the sound up the stairs. The light is on in Bebe's bedroom and a mountain of blankets is piled on top of her. I walk over to the bed, uncover her face. Her eyes are closed but her lashes are quivering, her breath short and hurried.

'I know you are awake.'

I sit down on the edge of the bed and wait for her to stop the act. But she keeps quiet, lets me wait.

'What were you doing downstairs? Do you know what time it is?'

Bebe's face grows crimson and she seems to be holding on to the air in her lungs.

'You were meant to be asleep, hours ago.'

Does she want to cry? If she does, she is doing a good job at keeping the tears at bay. I pick up her arm, gently shake it. It feels limp and heavy with sleep. It's not at all unconvincing and, in fact, downright impressive for a six-year-old.

'You're in big trouble, young lady, unless you stop this game right now and talk to me.'

She was meant to be in bed; she had no right to spy on me. There is something hard growing in my throat. How many other nights has she crept down the stairs to watch me at work? For every second she lies there, it becomes more and more infuriating.

'Talk to me, Bebe.' But minutes later, her eyes are still firmly shut. This is a talent I've never known her to possess.

Unsure of what to do next, I remain seated on the bed beside her, against her frozen little body under the blanket. And for a long while, that is all I can think of doing, wanting to neither stay nor leave. So much time passes that the child no longer has to pretend. Her breath finally loosens, her body relaxes to the side, and genuine sleep claims her.

I get up close to her face; I can smell the warmth in her hair, the toothpaste in her mouth. By now the anger in me has curdled into nothing but shame. I kiss her on the cheek, feeling defeated.

'You win.'

Back down the stairs, the house is silent once again. A swell of exhaustion laps over me, but all I can think about is that little toothbrush, drowning in the bucket of soapy water, waiting. I have to cling to the wall in order to stop myself from going back into that wet kitchen.

For days now, I have been lost to the filling and emptying of buckets, the endless repetition of sponging and wiping and scrubbing and drying. Days of being trailed by the vacuum, probing into every corner of every room, ridding the place of all living organisms.

News of Terence's visit has sent me into a panic as if, suddenly, every inch of the house is about to become contaminated. He won't be arriving for two months – two whole months, according to his email. But he is already here, firmly settled in this house, present in every room. Didn't he make sure of that by announcing his plans so far ahead of time?

I shut my eyes so that I do not have to see the way to the kitchen, to that bucket. And placing my head against the wall, I let my ear grow cold.

The wall, as it turns out, has no sensible words to offer, no matter how much time I give it. It merely emits a rustling, static sound, like a radio with poor reception. It's clear that I have to call Elaine.

But Elaine doesn't pick up. What time is it?

It has never occurred to me that Elaine might be anywhere but in her office. She has never even seemed remotely human to me, a proper person with a family and a driver's licence, a life outside of her work.

I must settle for leaving a message. She still uses one of those machines that seem to require cassette tapes. For the rest of the night, I lie in bed picturing that red light on her machine flashing in the dark, and wishing with every fibre of my body that it is still flashing by morning. I keep imagining the regular beat of it, the way it goes from red to pink as it travels across Elaine's office.

When I do eventually fall into a brief sleep, I dream of that light too, only now it is flashing from a vehicle, something that resembles a wheat harvester. I have the sense of being somewhere that is distant and lawless. The harvester approaches. At first I think it is going to offer me a ride, but in fact it only wants to swallow me up, into its drum, so that I can be threshed about inside like a helpless little rag, no voice to scream.

Yet all that threshing doesn't bother me as much as the fact that I am not wheat at all. I am barley in a field of wheat and, now that I am mixed up with all this wheat, how in the world is anybody ever going to recognise me? How will they find out who or where I am? How will they know what kind of menace did this to me?

I am frantic with unknowing in this dream, which plays like an old, silent film, jammed between moments when I can almost feel myself waking. I can see my little dead barley legs dancing with the spin of the drum and, though they are dead, they go on dancing with no will of their own until someone calls out: *Mama!*

Then I am spat out onto a freshly shorn field, facedown in the wheat stubble.

Nothing has changed. I am still barley in a field of wheat, not knowing how far I must be blown by the wind to be back where I belong.

To my relief, Elaine calls in the morning.

'What has triggered this latest panic?' she asks, sensibly.

Now that I have her on the phone, I don't know what to say, except: 'Everything.'

'Everything, meaning Adrian?'

'Yes, Adrian. And everything.'

She says, evenly, 'Do you feel that, by continuing to clean the house in this manner, you are rewarded with more than the ridding of germs? Has the act of labouring, of tormenting your body, become a purpose in and of itself?'

She talks that way sometimes, like she's reciting Proust.

'I've seen this happen to people, this enactment of guilt and shame through a physical deed of hurt and punishment. You blame yourself. You are still, after all this time, plagued by the cat, are you not? Therefore you determine to torture yourself, over and over.'

The cat. The mention of it sends a shudder through me. This, I'm sure, is Elaine's way of raising the temperature, of getting a reaction out of me. She knows how much I hate being reminded of the cat for, in a way, the cat was how everything began.

The morning before Adrian received his diagnosis, I had

run over the cat in the driveway. It was a black kitten – ours – rescued from an animal shelter only days earlier. Its body had felt like no more than a pin cushion under the wheel of the car. I had to scoop it up and bury it in a shoebox. How perverse it felt to have killed something for which I was meant to be the saviour.

That night the phone calls began. First a young woman from the lab, her voice sounding junior and nervous. Something in Adrian's blood test wasn't right, she told him without explaining. If he felt unwell he ought to go to the hospital right away.

Within a few minutes a man called from the same lab, using funny words like 'blasts' and 'neutropenia'.

'But don't panic, Mr Gillings.' He kept referring to Adrian by surname. 'Stay calm and wait.'

'Jesus, wait for what?'

'For the doctor, Mr Gillings.'

And, as promised, the doctor. Like the final act in a dystopian play, the script so badly written you had to hear everything twice to get the drift.

Don't panic, the doctor said too. As bad as it was, it wasn't as bad as it sounded. There was a chance of a cure. The chance was forty–sixty.

I didn't know what to make of that. Was it possible to live with a 60 per cent chance of dying? And in the reverse, could he really die when there was a 40 per cent chance of living? It was anyone's guess what would happen to Adrian from there.

We sat on the bed and waited for the taxi that would come to collect him for the hospital. When it arrived, it sounded as big as a truck coming up the driveway.

The driveway. That was the exact moment I mentally connected the dead black cat with my half-dead husband, and once I had made that connection it seemed that all the bad things that would happen to him, no matter how small or large, were going to be tied to me forever whether I liked it or not.

But Elaine is unperturbed by my silence on the phone, my refusal to take her bait. She seems quite content to study the sound of my breathing.

What I need is a new regimen of some kind, she suggests eventually. A way of channelling the troubles I'm having into a more healthy occupation that not only distracts the anxious mind but overrides it with new purpose.

I can hear papers rustling as she looks over her notes.

Didn't I have a job some years ago? she asks. A job that I enjoyed, and was rather good at? Isn't it possible that I might go back to working again?

She makes a sound with her pen, like she has underlined something.

Journalism. Is it feasible to go back to that?

I tell her that I can't, that I haven't contemplated working for years. I'm happy to be home.

But she perseveres: all those things I was writing about – the wrongs of the corporate world, the greed and subterfuge, moral obfuscations and social inequities – it had an agenda. Sometimes life needs an agenda. What was the name of the publication? Here, *Criterion.* She has it written down. It all seems rather promising to her, from all angles. She has the distinct feeling that I'd extracted some sense of meaning from the work. Isn't it a pity to give that up permanently?

And so it goes on, her milling, until I start to regret ever leaving her a message. Finally, I tell her in no uncertain terms that I would never write another word. I am tired of that kind of work, of having an opinion and of having people harangue me about it. I only wish to empty my mind, that it might be so empty that I'd no longer have so much as a fleeting dream at night.

Then, she says rather firmly, at least go out more, in a physical sense. Get dressed and join the world. Engage in something that requires removing myself from the house. I should be outside as much as I can. Find a place to occupy my mind in a way that diverts me from my usual routine, not reinforces it. At least do that. Are there such places I can go?

I can think of only one, I tell her.

One, she says, is enough.

6

The golf clubs have been waiting patiently in the pool house since my visit to Whistles, among boxes of toys that Bebe has long forgotten. It's the perfect place for them to hide. Nobody else has been near the pool for weeks. The oak tree has begun to shed over the water, and the leaves are starting to look like islands.

Everything smells of damp wool inside. A cold but sunny morning has produced trails of condensation that have run down the window and collected in puddles on the sill. The clubs are just the way I left them, filthy from the storm that day. With an old cloth I give them a wipe, which gets rid of the muck but does nothing to help that irreparable look about them, the way the sunlight catches on the edges of all their damage.

In the bag pocket, which I did not think to inspect last time, I discover a time capsule of sorts – an array of tees and pencil stubs, some Minties wrappers, a golf glove and a silver key without its lock. There is an old *par avion* envelope too, with barber-shop edges and stamps of the Queen, addressed to a Margaret Reed of Elwood. Inside, the handwriting in the letter looks laboured, somewhat shaky.

Dear M,

When you are better, Musselburgh in East Lothian is the place you must visit. I played at the Old Course yesterday, in the Scottish wet, as unforgiving as anything I've seen in the tropics. I thought of you as my ball got trapped in a bunker of epic proportions. A pity you were not there to guide me, or at least laugh at me.

Afterwards I found myself at the town museum (across the street from a bakery in which the most heart-stopping shortbread was sold). And I discovered this little fact I am sure you will enjoy – the first ever women's golf tournament was played here in January, 1811. There aren't many details of the day other than what was minuted in the club records, but we know the ladies who competed were the Fisherwomen of Fisherrow, the prizes being a fishing basket and handkerchiefs.

Apparently the fishwives were just as keen on golf as you, M. They played on their days off, in between the hard work of carrying their creels of fish into town for sale. Their husbands were at sea a lot. I suppose golf was a way of passing the time.

I left Musselburgh this morning, currently en route to the island of North Ronaldsay where, they say, there is some interesting golf to be played. There's terrible wind. The little plane is making me nervous, though the pilot assures me he has flown this route since 1976 and never run into any trouble of the fatal kind. Some comfort.

I will write again soon. For now I leave you with my score card from the Old Course.

Love always,
C

The score card, also in the envelope, is a wrinkled thing that might have been soaked with rain and dried in a hurry. It's dated Wednesday, 28 April 1999. Despite the bad weather, C did rather well – more pars than bogeys, even a birdie towards the end. It seems a more than respectable outcome for any golfer on an ordinary weekday.

But what a strange token to leave someone, a pencilled record of a golf game played far away on the other side of the world, as if to say, *I thought of you as I played and how I played was because of you*. And there it's been, in the pocket of the bag, kept by Margaret all these years so that she might have something to look at whenever she thought of C.

It feels wrong of me to stand here and read these long forgotten words between two people I've never met. Even the clubs seem to be staring at me as if I've pried too deep into the past. I put everything back in the envelope, the letter, the card, and look around for a place to put it.

The only place that seems fitting is a box of old books in the corner, books that I read years ago but couldn't bear to throw out. Plath and Hemingway and Updike, and a copy of *Ulysses* that I never managed to get through. I tuck Margaret and her C between the dusty, browned pages. It isn't quite Musselburgh, but Dublin may be close enough.

'Wow.' Suddenly, a voice from behind. 'It's like the Museum of Domestic Bliss in here.'

How long has she been standing there?

The voice belongs to Louisa, who lives across the street in the big house the neighbours jokingly call *Moby*, both because of its size and the way the glass façade curves in and out like an elementary drawing of a whale. She has a habit of letting herself in through our side gate without warning, a habit which I probably should have discouraged from the start but is now too late to reverse.

As usual she is dressed in her exercise clothes, tight black leggings and a windcheater left unzipped to reveal a neon sports bra and the sculpted contours of her breasts.

She steps into the pool house, looking around with a judgmental twitch of the nose. With plier-like fingers she retrieves Bebe's broken stethoscope from a pile of toys.

'Hey Primrose, are you saving these for when she goes to medical school?'

The stethoscope wriggles like a worm, a dusty green worm. Repulsed, she puts it back and steps away, almost rolling her ankle over an old rubber duck. *Squeak*, the toy goes under her foot. She looks down at it, eyes widening as if it were a rodent.

Children's toys are not Louisa's natural milieu. She does not have children herself. She's the kind of person who would prefer decorative taxidermy to real, living things. Her house is the very embodiment of cool, un-childproofed sleekness, from the seamless floor-to-ceiling windows to the razor-edged marble vanities in the bathrooms, not to mention the dangly light installation beside the staircase courtesy of a Dutch design studio with an unpronounceable name.

'Hey, what are you doing in here anyway?' she asks as she

watches me pick up my bag of clubs and lug them towards the door. 'Babe, are you playing golf or something?'

'You could say that, yeah.'

She raises one eyebrow. Tiny particles of dust are gyrating all around her. 'Is this a new thing or is it another instalment of *Things We Didn't Know about the Secret Life of Primrose*?'

'It's new. Just something I'm thinking of doing.'

'And *why*?'

'Because I thought it might be good for me. It's a reason to get out of the house more. What?'

She holds up her hands as if in surrender. 'What nothing.'

Louisa is giving me a look as if she finds me adorable. It's a look I often get from her, which makes her seem much older than me, even though we are about the same age. She has always had a casual way around me, which reinforces the fact that we are friends, despite the strangeness of how this transpired.

The strangeness lies in the fact that Louisa is married to Peter. For almost a year now, they have lived across the street. The day they moved in, I convinced myself it couldn't possibly be him. After all, he looked different. His hair was shorter; he was dressed more fashionably, in a pink shirt with rolled-up sleeves, loafers with no socks. He got out of the car and ushered the moving van into the driveway. Louisa was beside him, almost touching his ear with her lips as she spoke to him. He smiled at her. And as he looked around, he saw me on the verandah and hesitated. I hadn't seen him since high school. It had been so long that I couldn't be sure who he was. I simply walked back into the house and shut the door.

Louisa wasted no time making herself known in the new neighbourhood. In the early days, she would knock on our door (having not yet given herself access through the side gate) and invite Adrian and I over for dinner. There was no polite way of saying no to an invitation of such physical proximity, so, obligingly, we went.

She'd make us squid ink risotto or stuffed spatchcock, the kind of food that came straight out of cookbooks, then serve us dessert out on the terrace, which overlooked the beach. The evenings were always intoxicatingly pretty from their terrace. Their house was on the beach side of Fairwater Avenue. Behind it was the yacht club and a flank of dunes where people went with their dogs to watch the sunset.

Adrian and Peter got along well, more so because Adrian always made an effort to be jovial so no one would think he was feeling unwell. They discussed politics a lot, and perhaps found each other's views reaffirming. But I never said very much. The whole thing troubled me, having to pretend I was getting to know Peter from scratch. It seemed illogical, almost frightening, to see him in front of me after all those years, like someone risen from the grave.

Now, in the pool house, Louisa eyes my ill-assembled equipment. She says, 'That's very cute of you, to take up golf. But these clubs are a joke, right?'

'Why would you say that?' I push past her and out of the door with my clubs. She follows me.

'Primrose, no offence, but they look like they're from the Country Women's Association.'

'That's because they're second-hand from Whistles.'

Louisa puts three fingers on her lips so I cannot tell whether it is a smirk or a gasp she's trying to hide. There is nothing in that sentence she would find appealing. Louisa would sooner decorate her house in department store furniture than set foot on a public course like Whistles. She would find the idea of paying fifteen dollars for nine holes and a Four'n Twenty abhorrent.

Actually, Louisa is the only woman I know who belongs to a golf club – the private country club down on the peninsula with the lighthouse and the strict dress code. The place has one of those romantic-sounding names that make me think of shipwrecks. But Louisa doesn't really play golf there so much as mingle with the golfers. It's more of a networking opportunity for Peter's work, she would say. And a chance to get smashed on some really good alcohol.

She sits down by the pool, rolls up her leggings and lowers her painted feet into the blue water. The water is only blue in patches, the rest of it covered by oak leaves. Some days the leaves are as beautiful as Matisse's gouache and paper cut-outs; other days, such as today, they seem grotesquely deformed, like ears with too many lobes.

She moves her feet in circles and the blueness of the water grows all around her. She says, 'Primrose, you do know that Whistles runs a breeding program for heroin addicts, don't you?'

'That's ridiculous, Louisa.'

'I'm serious.'

'How would you know that? You who never deign to go to a place like that.'

'Well, next time you shank that ball and go looking for it in the bushes, just watch out for the used needles, that's all I'm saying.'

'You're being quite presumptuous.'

'I don't mean it in a bad way. If you think about it, it's kind of hot, all the drugs and sex that must happen there after dark.' She laughs. 'Maybe I should ask Peter to take me there for date night.'

The fact that we live on the same street, Louisa must feel, gives her a certain freedom to say whatever she likes. Slowly, I've grown used to having her around twice or three times a week after her Pilates class, and listening, with obliging patience, as she dispatches every single thought that crosses her mind.

Everything that she says relates back to sex somehow. She loves to talk about it. According to her, she and Peter have a very open relationship. The kind of sex she tells me about tends to involve third parties. She describes these encounters in a fairly liberal way and refers a lot to the anatomical aspect of things – not just the size of body parts, but the way they fit together and react to certain touches and encouragements. She seems to have slept with a lot of much younger and much older men in these settings, men who give her a great deal of attention.

She says that Peter doesn't mind it, that he is also free to do whatever he wants. In fact the presence of other women seems to create for her an essential tonic of jealousy and rivalry, without which she sees little point in any engagement between man and woman.

At times she would tell me about Peter's women as if she

had observed them up close, as if she had been right there in the room with them. How they kissed him on the mouth. The perfumes they wore. The ways in which they wanted him inside them. The fact that other women desire him is the basis on which she desires him herself; she is never embarrassed to say so.

Louisa has no idea Peter and I knew each other back at school. Neither of us has found it necessary to say anything because it seems to no longer matter. In the end we are just people who happen to live on the same street, breathing the same suburban air, waking to the same light that drifts in from the bay.

Sometimes I wonder if things would be awkward if Louisa knew, or if she would be more careful in what she tells me. But the more time I've spent with her, the more I've grown convinced that she would simply go on talking.

She seems to have an infinite supply of talk when it comes to Peter. Yet just how much of it can be believed is still up for question. At various parties of hers, it has been clear that Peter attracts a certain coquettishness from women. They love to talk to him, to touch him on the arm when something is funny. But he seems to neither acknowledge these attentions nor reciprocate them. Never have I heard anything out of him that would refute or verify any of Louisa's stories.

Nowadays Peter and I engage only in the obligatory chit-chat, when we must. In moments when we find ourselves standing next to each other, Peter will sometimes ask if my parents are well or if I still see people from school, and I will ask after his mother and sister, that is all. When we talk, it's as if we are passing a time bomb between us. Neither of us want to prolong the conversation for fear of it ticking over.

As far as I can gather, he has been travelling a lot for work. He is now the one who runs the family bank, the chosen one in the line of succession. The last time I spoke to him was in March, when Louisa threw a party for a reason I cannot remember. Everyone stood around on the terrace, drinking Moët and commenting on each other's outfits. By the end of the day a few rounds of inebriated tennis took place, played barefoot and with no concern for safety.

Peter didn't join in. Instead he spent most of his time talking with businesspeople he knew, and sometimes with Adrian. As we were leaving, I felt his hand on my shoulder, but it was only to guide me aside so that he could help me with the door.

'Primrose,' he said.

Then I thanked him, and we touched cheeks like we were children just learning our manners.

Louisa retrieves her legs from the pool, curls them up to one side. She seems to sense that her talk about Whistles has upset me in some way.

'Oh, babe, are you worried about what I said? About the heroin stuff? Don't be silly. Tell me to fuck off and do what you want!'

She puckers her lips, blows a raspberry. 'You should see the way some of the women at Lost Cove swing their clubs. Like chopping wood for winter. You'd surely do better, I reckon.'

Hearing her say that makes me feel somehow foolish and

inadequate. Sometimes being around Louisa is like that, like being back at school and forced to spend time with people much cooler than yourself. I wish she wouldn't come around so much.

There is a racket overhead and we both look up in time to see a pair of spotted doves fly into the oak's canopy. One of them starts cooing to the other, a three-noted melody that rises and falls.

'So tell me,' Louisa asks. 'How long have you been playing at Whistles?'

'Only once. It was raining so hard the pro had to call me back to the clubhouse. Then he showed me this painting of Whistles that was almost a hundred years old.'

'Hmm. I'm not really into old paintings,' she says, looking at her nails. 'Peter's always talking to me about those classics like I should be interested. But for the life of me I can't get into that stuff. Everything is so yellowed, so . . . antiquey.'

'This one was different,' I try to explain. 'It was very fresh, even after all this time. At first, all you see is an empty fairway lit by the morning, then gradually you realise what you are looking at is not the emptiness at all – it's the expectation that any minute, someone might appear in the distance and walk towards you, to join you. It was – I don't know – quite haunting.'

'That's beautiful,' Louisa mumbles, yawning through her teeth. She is clearly bored by this talk, having never made any secret of her own taste in art.

Louisa's house is an homage to whimsical, modern abstractions, all of which expensively curated. It is often hard for visitors to know the difference between a piece of furniture you can use and a sculpture you must not touch. Her pool is not so much for swimming as to display colourful floating Froot Loops that produce a bell-like sound every time they collide. And the tulip lights in her sitting room – which are perhaps the most talked-about of all her installations – will drop down from the ceiling at the click of a button to perform a kind of floral bungy dance. You sit there at your own peril.

The sun, by now, has shifted ever so slightly as to be falling squarely across our faces. Louisa puts one hand over her eyebrows like a visor, moves herself back into the shadow.

'So, to something actually exciting,' she says, straight-backed and suddenly reinvigorated. Perhaps this is the real reason for her visit today. 'I'm planning to have friends over for a weekend at the house in Flinders – for Peter's birthday next month. You've got to come. Adrian too, of course. I'll even let you bring the blessed child.'

'Oh, Louisa.' I've often heard about the Loys' house in Flinders, and I can think of nothing more unnerving than having to spend a weekend there with them. 'That's kind of you to invite us. Really.'

'What's the problem? You don't want to come?'

'It's not that.'

'It's only a short drive out of the city, Primrose, and I'm literally giving you weeks of notice.'

'We haven't been away for ages. We don't remember how to.'

'I can tell; you're starting to look like you belong in that pool house. You should all get out more. Didn't you say that yourself?'

'I guess. But listen, can I think about it?'

'I don't understand!' She prods me on the arm as if to check I'm alive. 'What is there to think about? Everyone is coming. Don't be boring, Primrose.'

I turn away and try not to grimace as she fires off a list of things she's organising for the black-tie dinner – the centrepieces, the caterer, the cake and, of course, the dress she will wear (something with tulle and silk and, oddly, spray paint).

'You'll like the house,' she adds. 'It's got old art galore.'

Somehow she makes this sound ever so subtly like a put-down.

'You're coming. It's settled.'

So this is what it has come to – being held captive in a house out in Flinders with Adrian and Peter and Louisa and all of her friends. I can just imagine the dining room, full of candlelight and flowers, of well-dressed people descending into a rich, drunken stupor as the evening wears on. It always happens like this at Louisa's parties. And everywhere I turn there'll be Peter's face, prudently looking away.

On goes Louisa, about the special cases of champagne for which strings have been pulled, and some people called Bridget and Eve and Greg and Lawrence who will also be there. She thinks I should remember them from another party of hers, though I cannot for the life of me recall any of these names.

'Peter was hesitant at first, about the party,' she continues. 'God knows why. He used to love get-togethers but I'm not sure what's happened lately. *Why can't we go to Flinders by ourselves?* he said. Sweet of him, isn't it? But I couldn't stand another weekend in the middle of nowhere, just the two of us.

The house gives me the creeps – you'll see when you get there. Anyway, I managed to change his mind, if you know what I mean. He always says yes in the end.'

She giggles into her hand, at the thought of Peter's mind being changed.

It's starting to feel so late, an entire morning usurped by Louisa. I'm tired of talking to her, of listening to her talk. Even her reflection in the pool seems irritatingly out of focus. All I want to do is go back into the house and turn on the tap in the laundry and put myself to work. My head is bursting, my hands aching at the idea.

But then a momentary thought rushes me away like a tide pulling me seaward: the thought of wide open fairways, and of reeds growing tall beside the old canal.

'Fine, we'll come to Flinders, whatever you want,' I say to Louisa, hurrying over the words. And before I know it I am up on my feet, taking charge of the day that remains. 'Now I am going to Whistles.'

7

Without the rain Whistles takes on a different quality. The sunlight exaggerates the colours of everything. The green is more green, and the blue of the sky, the brown bark of the trees, are truer shades of themselves. It's rather like looking at an old coloured photograph, from when coloured photographs were a thing to be marvelled at.

To my surprise the place is filled with people. Dozens of men are standing around in groups, smoking cigarettes and shoving at each other as they wait to tee off. There is a half-time atmosphere in the air. They are all wearing the same jersey with the same logo of connecting dots, which probably means they all arrived on the same company bus for the same team-bonding exercise.

One of the men is doing squats with a club anchored across his shoulders in what can only be described as an imaginary act of weightlifting. His mouth goes *eee-aww* with every up and down; his head steams from the exertion. I have to shout to get past him without taking a undercut to the chin. 'Excuse me. Excuse me, please.'

'Oh,' he replies, a brief glance of disinterest before returning to his task. His friend comes up, holds a can of beer to his mouth. 'Levo, look at me, *look at me*. Remember to hydrate, alright?'

By the time I reach the pro shop I'm praying that the rain will return and drive these people away. More so when Josh informs me that in order to get on the course I must be paired up with someone else, since he can barely make room for me in the schedule.

'We're fully booked today. Sorry.'

He isn't sorry at all. Every hurried movement as he works the cash register betrays his delight at the assemblage of golfers at the first tee.

'Blue moon,' he says, one hand dipping into a packet of chips. As usual he is wearing his cap back to front, a pen behind his ear as if to show how busy he is. 'I've never seen this kind of crowd before!'

For reasons unknown, the men outside have erupted into a cheer. The weightlifter raises his arm, seemingly victorious. He tosses his club; his friend tosses the beer.

'Don't worry, I'm not that cruel.' Josh realises my hesitation, laughs. 'I wasn't planning to throw you to them! No, you're playing with Harriet. I will squeeze you guys in before all the company people. She's great. You'll thank me.'

He points to a woman outside who is standing on the edge of the practice green, eating an apple with what appears to be a spoon. She's tall and slightly hunched over. Her hands are very white, almost as white as the wisps of hair under her beanie.

'Remember to keep your body still,' Josh says. To demonstrate, he bends his knees and folds his arms like a cross over his chest.

'The stiller you are, the more your club will do what you want. Pretend someone's driven a stake right down through the middle of you and into the ground.'

'Thanks. That's very vivid advice.'

With some effort I hoist my golf bag onto the hired buggy, and strap it in at the top and bottom, like a patient heading for the asylum. There is a sign reminding everyone to carry a sand bucket for repairing divots. So I fetch the sand from the sandpit and hang the bucket beneath the buggy, on the special hook provided.

The buggy is rusty all over, and the wheels snort like a donkey as I pull everything along the footpath towards Harriet.

'Hello,' I say to her. 'I'm very sorry but it seems you're stuck with me today.'

She turns her face, fixes her eyes on me. 'Oh, yes. I know precisely what Baby Josh is trying to do.'

With the spoon in her hand, she digs a chunk out of her apple and puts it into her mouth. She has eyes like diamonds set in old jewellery, sparkly against the rest of her aged face. She must be close to eighty.

'He thinks I'll move faster if there is peer group pressure.'

Even though I would've preferred to be alone, I'm relieved not to be the only woman around here. 'I'm Primrose Li,' I tell her, holding out my hand. 'It's lovely to meet you.'

From her pocket, she produces a snaplock bag to store away the spoon and the half-eaten apple. 'Harriet Boyd. People sometimes call me Hattie, but I'd rather they didn't.'

She puts her hand in mine, barely registering a squeeze. It's probably because of how coarse my hand is; it must feel as though I've handed her a pumice stone.

'A warning,' she announces, gazing out at the course. 'I do take all this very seriously.'

When it's our turn, Harriet sets her ball on the tee and takes a few steps back to consider the line of approach. She tilts her head this way and that, thinking it over. Then she walks back to the spot to reposition her tee in the ground. This process of adjustment repeats itself several times and all in slow motion. I don't know what the etiquette is on the amount of time you can spend preparing for a shot, but this has surely breached it.

The company people behind us have begun to mumble, but it doesn't seem to bother Harriet. She does a practice swing, followed by a few more, each with minor adjustments as if she is trying out her muscles for the first time. She is all straight knees and elbows, nothing like how I imagine golf should be played.

With the preparation finally over, she steps into position and lets her swing come down awkwardly, hesitating around ankle height before hitting the ball. It doesn't seem like a particularly polished way of doing it, but it turns out to be surprisingly effective. The ball is struck crisply by the club face. The club follows through and loops around behind her ears. She lifts her head to follow the trajectory of the ball.

The ball drops right in the middle of the fairway, over the bend, at least 150 metres from us.

'Well done, Harriet.'

She walks down from the tee, gives nothing away. 'Your turn.'

In my mind I pictured myself golfing in solitude. I pictured a perambulation through fresh air and greenness; in a way I pictured emptiness, an uninterrupted aloneness punctuated only by the sporadic flight of birds or a plane overhead. I didn't think total strangers could be forced to spend two hours together on a golf course and, worse still, be followed by a procession of more strangers, tailing you the entire way.

Now the urban reality of golfing has dawned on me. I push the tee into the ground and place a ball on top of it. It's rather like being in front of an audience, but scarier. No one has any interest in me except how fast I can clear out of their way.

I rush through a practice swing, more as a matter of procedure. What am I meant to be practising? With a quick pep talk to myself – *you can do this* – I step up to the ball.

I can still remember the feeling of that day in the storm, of connecting with the ball and watching it arc forward into the gloom. So here I go again.

Everything around me seems to fall into silence. I swing at the ball, but this time it shoots off sharply to the right and travels less than 20 metres before bouncing pathetically into the underbelly of a bush. Failure. I can hear cackling from behind.

'Okay, let's go.' I put the club back in the bag, ready to run away.

Harriet does not understand the hurry. 'Oh no, no, no.' She comes over, grabs me by the arm. 'Let's try that one again.'

'Don't worry, Harriet, I'll just drop a new ball further up and hit from there. People are waiting.'

'They are waiting because they are behind us,' she says evenly. 'I'm quite certain that's how a queue works.'

From her pocket she produces another ball. 'I think you are teeing it up too high. You're striking the ball with the stick instead of the club face. Try one a bit lower.'

She leads me back to the same spot, watches me set up the ball once again.

'Now this time, as the club is coming down, tuck your right elbow in a little.'

She demonstrates. Again the crowd is all silence, and the silence is all I can think about as I step up and rush through my swing.

'Okay, a little better,' says Harriet, generously. The ball has shot out low this time, and hit the ground quick. It manages to roll on a bit further and stops halfway between us and Harriet's ball. 'You'll need to work on that. Now we can go.'

It takes me eleven strokes to complete the first hole, thirteen if you properly account for the penalty incurred by the first ball that was lost to the bushes. It is near impossible to launch the ball out of the rough with my iron. Although I manage to avoid the bunkers on my way to the green, it costs me another five putts before the ball rolls grudgingly into the hole.

Nine over par on a par 4. There is no name for such a score, unless *nonuple bogey* has a place in the vernacular.

Harriet is more deft. She hits mostly small shots, but very straight and accurate, and ends up with a one over par, a bogey. It isn't clear how she feels about this as she reaches down to retrieve her ball from the cup. She merely says 'alright' as if she has completed a mundane task that she performs daily, such as taking in the laundry.

'I'll let you know a trick,' she tells me as we head on to the second tee. 'Never ever look back on a golf course.'

Which, of course, leads me to immediately turn my head to find the next group pressing down the fairway towards us.

'To be honest, Harriet, all I want to do right now is to pack up and go home.'

'With all those people behind us? You'll be in the firing line if you backtrack now.'

At the second tee we briefly lose sight of the other group. This hole is much shorter, a par 3 that seems barely the length of a council swimming pool. There is no fairway to speak of here, only a meadow of long grass turned golden in the sunlight. Tiny insects float above the softly swaying blades, drawing loops in the air. It would not be unpleasant to lie down in the middle of all that.

We hit off, Harriet first since she won the previous hole by a significant margin. The task seems as straightforward as it can be – one shot onto the green and two putts to get the ball into the hole, that would be the idea. She watches closely as the ball lands at two o'clock on the green, only a few strides away from the hole. With two strokes to spare, she has set herself up comfortably for a par. She might even get a birdie if she manages to sink the ball with her next stroke.

'Nice shot, Harriet.'

'Hmm,' she says this time.

Even though it seems like a completely achievable distance to reach the green, and Harriet has just proven it, my ball only makes it as far as its dark green edge. It pauses there for a second, looking very precarious. Will it stay or will it drift? It drifts, and in the wrong direction, further and further away from the green. It's like watching someone blow at a house of cards you've spent all your effort to assemble.

'This is a game of centimetres,' Harriet says, pragmatically. 'You wouldn't know it from all this space around you.'

Harriet has one of those buggies that come with a remote control. She lets it go out ahead of her into the long grass. The thing bobs up and down over the uneven ground, like a robot one sends into a minefield. It does well for a while, then hits a ditch. One side of it sinks and it starts to transmit a machine-like whirr.

'Silly thing,' Harriet mutters, heading to its rescue. 'My grandchildren think I'm too old to push, so they buy me a battery-operated baboon I have to reset every five minutes.'

When people mention their grandchildren, it's as if their whole lives open up in front of you. She was a stranger a moment ago; now I can imagine just who she is. I can see her at the family table, surrounded by her children and the children of her children. I can see them fussing over her, helping her with the plates while she tells them to sit down. My guess is that she is a widow now but that she once enjoyed a good marriage in which her husband seldom stood in the way of what she wanted. They might have played golf together, and it might've been because of him that she played in the first place.

It seems easier to golf with someone you know, at least someone you know by approximation. It becomes less uncomfortable, more personal. If it ever comes up, I will tell her I have a daughter, six-years-old.

The third hole is a longer par 3, and women are allowed to tee off some distance in front of the men. The fairway is lined by shrubs so thick that it seems completely enclosed, reminding me of a hedge maze. There is a huge fried-egg bunker halfway up the fairway, a very intentional trap which I manage to avoid when I hit the ball straight into the shrubs on the left, leading to another dismal campaign.

At the fourth, you have to hit an opening shot across the canal, which doesn't look so hard given you can probably jump across it with a decent run-up. But I lose three balls in that water, reducing my supply to just one. It makes me wonder how many other balls are down there at the bottom, buried beneath all the rubbish the water brings from upstream.

For the first time Harriet loses her patience with me and politely suggests that I have another go on the other side of the canal. She has not experienced much trouble clearing the crossing herself.

'Sorry,' I say to her, feeling quite ashamed. 'No one in my family has ever played golf. It doesn't exactly run in my blood.'

'Golf is not footy,' Harriet replies. 'It's not genetic, it doesn't get passed down from fathers to sons. It's open to anyone, a bit of a lottery.'

Somehow this doesn't make me feel much better. By the fifth hole, I'm doing so badly I've stopped keeping track of my score. To make matters worse, the group behind us is catching up again. This time Harriet waves them through.

'Go, go,' she shouts impatiently as they get in front of us. Clearly she is not as thrilled as Josh was about the traffic today. 'Hurry up before I change my mind.'

We watch the men thump their balls down the fairway along various deviations, none of which seem particularly desirable. They hold up their beers to us in thanks before walking on.

'I hope they don't make Whistles a habit,' Harriet says, with a proprietary air. Then she steps up to her ball and gets ready to hit.

'Won't you hit them?'

'Hah, only in my dreams.'

The men do not seem to have advanced very far down the fairway.

'Really, Harriet. I think they're too close. Isn't there a rule about this sort of thing?'

'Not at Whistles, there isn't.'

The course seems so mired in optical illusions that the relativity between one thing and another is constantly distorted. It's making me second-guess my sense of distance, of angles and directions, so much so that I think Harriet must be right, that she really wouldn't hit them.

She whacks the ball. It gives off a special, robust sort of sound.

She drops her club, shouts to the men between her cupped hands. 'Fore!' It sounds less like a warning, more a cry of excitement. 'Fore!'

The men raise their heads, each looking up at the sky from a different angle and waiting. It's hard to keep track of the ball once it is on the way down, but eventually we see one of the men duck. Then we hear a diminutive thud as the ball drops. He does a little backward hop and it looks as though the ball has bounced off the tip of his shoe. He straightens himself quickly, throws his arm up in shock at this ambush. He looks about for reinforcement from his friends, but they have already moved up ahead, eager to play on.

Harriet is taking genuine delight in all of this.

'Oops, apologies,' she shouts.

Sternly, the man shakes his head at her, ashamed on her behalf.

'That was a great shot,' she says to me. 'Straight to the point.'

'That wasn't great, that was *crazy*,' I say, thinking of all those stories of people getting killed by flying golf balls.

'Crazy mathematically, to be sure.' Harriet beams. 'The chances of me hitting that man were next to zero.'

At the sixth hole, we tee off on top of a small hill overlooking the neighbourhood beyond the perimeters of the course. Upstream, the canal is suddenly wider, with a grid of commission housing built along its fortified embankment. It looks less like a waterway, more a concrete skate park. Years of graffiti cascade down from the sides, spilling like chemical waste into the water as it flows into Whistles.

Yet the canal that enters Whistles is nothing like the one

that leaves it. Downstream, as if by magic, a riparian Eden emerges. Somewhere along its journey through Whistles – though it isn't clear to me where – the water is filtered down to a slumbering brook. It leaves the course shyly, agreeably, and runs without disturbance through a cluster of Edwardian cottages on its way to the sea.

It's terribly windy up here on the hill, enough for me to zip my jacket all the way up to the nose. We are as high as the top of the cypresses, or at least that's the illusion. From here, I can map out the rest of the round – how the seventh hole runs low and parallel to the canal, the eighth crosses back to the other side of the water, and the ninth stretches unswervingly towards home, the clubhouse.

I spend the rest of the course wondering if Harriet will try again to hit the people in front of us. And while she never ceases to give off that impression, she resists, behaves. The man ahead has grown anxious, constantly looking back to ensure a safe distance is maintained between us. His golf suffers as a result, and perhaps that is enough for Harriet.

As for her own game, she gets a par on the sixth and the seventh, and comes very close again on the eighth. The course meanders like a dream, set up just for Harriet, and I am no more than a bystander, a companion along for the walk.

Like her swing, there is something unconventional about the way she putts – it's as if she is trying to ring a bell without making a sound. There is no follow-through and the putter is retracted without delay. It's not really the way golf should be played, she explains. Not the way *she* has always played. Just how things have taken new shape as her body got older.

She spends a lot of time taking care of things that are tangential to the playing of golf. Meticulously she repairs the grass on the fairways with the sand from her bucket. She even goes to great lengths to patch up divots other people have left behind. She's also, as I discover, very good at finding lost balls: not her own, since she always seems able to keep them squarely to the fairways, but other people's. With an iron in hand, she pushes her way right into a bush without a shred of concern about getting scratched, and re-emerges, triumphant, with her loot.

The sight of Harriet foraging among the vegetation makes me think of what Louisa said. I'm almost surprised each time Harriet returns without her hands bloodied by needles. It seems plausible enough that this place might become an urban drug den at night, somewhere for addicts to shoot up in the dark low-lying shrubs. I can picture them, bleary-eyed and semiconscious, splayed on the ground like starfish in a moonlit sea. There is a strange charm to this, a pacifism that seems to fit just so at Whistles.

Then we are on the ninth tee. Of all the holes, this is the only one I can still recall from the day I was here twenty years ago. Peter stood right here that day, twirling the driver in his hand as he always did, pondering the distance that must be made, the likelihood of scoring anything under par. From here, we had the same view of the clubhouse at the end of the run. We would have taken the same steps that I would need to take now, up the same fairway, under the same trees. Nothing has changed.

'Look at it,' says Harriet from the tee, her hand flying out over the fairway. 'Dead straight. No corners to cut.'

The albatross. Now I realise just how difficult it must be for such a thing to materialise. I suppose, if the fairway was curved, one might be able to take a shortcut as the crow flies, by hitting the ball straight over the bend. But here there are neither tricks nor traps, only the distance, the 500-odd metres that lie uninterrupted ahead of us.

Harriet produces a superb drive that flies almost halfway down the fairway. With two more strokes, handled deftly with an iron, she lands the ball in the middle of the green. It takes me four shots to get onto the green myself, mainly thanks to the use of my fairway wood. (I decided some way back that my iron might be cursed.)

The way I have played so far on this hole feels like a minor miracle, the most hopeful I've felt all day. Suddenly things appear possible again, or at least more positive. I'm only one shot behind Harriet and, when I think about it, one shot away from my first par.

On the green, Harriet studies her ball from all angles, gets down low to check for breaks. The ground is sloping gently from the far side in, and also from left to right. She'll be putting uphill. She does a practice shot, decides it is too firm, tries again with a softened approach. Again and again she rehearses before stepping up to the ball and tapping it just so. The line is perfect, but the ball looks as though it will run out of puff. It slows to a crawl as it nears the hole; it stops short. No birdie for Harriet. She must take another shot to finish the hole, but still, she is walking away with a par.

'Amazing, Harriet!'

For the first time, she seems pleased, even without the

birdie that seemed momentarily achievable. 'Now your turn.'

Unlike her, I must putt downhill. With too much enthusiasm, the ball rushes forward, completely misses the hole and continues to run away until it is caught by the hairier grass at the edge of the green. The same thing occurs on the next shot, only in the reverse direction, uphill. This back and forth costs me another two strokes, ending in a triple bogey, eight strokes in total.

Harriet comes forward, watches me retrieve the ball. I shake her hand when she offers it, relieved, despite everything, to have made it to the end.

Another group of players is pressing up the fairway now, taking mock swings in our direction. She pulls me off the green, moves us out of their way. It is one thing to hit someone, another to be hit.

'You played well today, considering,' Harriet says later as we are packing up in the car park.

'Considering what?'

'Your clubs. They're horrible.'

She takes a muff out of her golf bag, places it over her driver as if she were putting a beanie on a child's head. The muff is a knitted thing with a Fair Isle pattern and a red pompom on top. Then more muffs emerge, of the same design and pattern, each one a snug fit for the club for which it is intended. Has she made these herself? Or were they also gifts from her grandchildren? Together the clubs now look like a group of siblings groomed for a Christmas photo.

'I think you're right, Harriet,' I say, looking down at my own scrappy bunch of clubs. 'They are horrible.'

'So tell me, will you be playing again? Or has this place put you off golf forever?'

I try to picture myself duffing my way through another round, shooting a multitude of bogeys and donating more balls to the bushes and waterway. Strangely, the thought no longer daunts me. I merely look forward to another display of my own ineptitude. Is it possible to feel schadenfreude towards oneself?

'Yes, Harriet. Same time tomorrow.'

8

That summer I was sixteen, Peter said to me, 'I think you're really cool, Primrose. I'm not sure if you know that.'

Cool was just about the best thing anyone could be called at that age, a summation of all the nice things that teenagers could not find the right words for. Which was why it jarred. Nobody had ever said anything like that to me before.

We were upstairs in Peter's room, sitting on the floor with our backs against his bed. It was late afternoon and the light cut in at a sharp angle. The window was framed by the tentacles of the ivy outside. It was uncomfortably hot, though a breeze had finally arrived. The door fanned back and forth, indecisively, like something in zero gravity.

Being in Peter's room gave me the feeling of being completely caught up in the modern world. He played movies on a portable DVD player and downloaded music on the latest MP3 player. He had the newest PlayStation and Sega consoles, and a fancy Apple iBook you could fold up and carry around like a briefcase. The only things that looked old in Peter's room were his golf clubs, once his father's, hanging from a timber rack on his wall.

Peter had a new Nokia phone, on which there was a game called Snake. The point of the game was to direct the meandering snake to its food so that it could grow as long as possible without running into its own tail. It had a two-player mode and you could chew up hours on that thing.

What Peter said to me came at the end of yet another game of Snake, which he won. The statement was not easy to unravel, both because of its timing and the ambiguous way in which he said it. He probably meant it in the basic way – *I think you're cool, and I want you to know I think so.* But on a more sophisticated level, could he be implying an understanding that I didn't share his opinion? Could he be doing two things at once, both producing a version of me I did not agree with, and telling me to accept it as true?

'Is there something cool about being the girl from the café?' I asked him.

'That's just a label you've given yourself, Primrose.'

'It's a pretty factual label.'

'But it doesn't mean anything. I don't think it says much about you other than what your family does for a living. My great-great-grandfather used to live in a hut made out of bark with five other people. He scraped dirt out of the ground for most of his life, hoping to find gold. Should that say something about me?'

'No, that's long in the past. People have short memories. It's enough for them that your parents are well to do.'

Peter shrugged, played with the hem of his shorts. It seemed strange to me that he couldn't accept this idea, that what your parents did for a living said a lot about who you were, in fact the bulk of who you were. He didn't seem to realise that this was the reason for everything being just so in his life. If you drilled down to it, his parents were the reason for his popularity at school, why he was chosen for sports teams, why the girls liked him and why people were willing to excuse him from Asian stereotypes. He had interesting parents who were talked about admiringly, not least of all because they had more money than most people could imagine. It was fashionable for people to pretend that this sort of stuff was not important, but it was more important than being witty or smart or even kind. I knew how kids looked at me when my dad dropped me off at school in his '81 Holden Gemini. I knew the duct tape over the side mirror said more than all my As ever could.

'If you ask me,' said Peter, 'you're too hung up about other people's opinions. In social science, Father Maine used to say that some people have too much peripheral vision. That's you.'

I didn't know what to say. We fell into a silence for a while, then he bumped me on the shoulder. 'Listen, I don't know how we got onto this. I was only trying to tell you how much I like you. Honest.'

He looked me in the eye, searching for a clue as to what I was thinking. 'I feel weird around you, Primrose. You've always made me feel that way. All those times I came to the café to pick up Erin, you never said a word to me, not even just to be polite. I mean, this might sound odd and a bit arrogant but girls tend to like talking to me, a lot.'

'That doesn't sound arrogant at all.'

Again he bumped me on the shoulder. 'I'm serious. They've always made the first move – not bragging or anything.

With you, even now, I'm not completely sure if you're interested in me.'

From outside came the sound of bicycles, and of kids playing backyard cricket. I placed my head on his shoulder, and he seemed to relax. He said, 'Just so you know, you don't ever have to tell me what you like about me. I'm aware of how great I am.'

'No time anyway. I've got to go soon.'

'Don't. Where are you going?'

'Piano lesson.'

'It's school holidays.'

'My parents don't think holidays should stand in the way of achieving excellence.'

'No wonder you're so talented.' He folded my hand into his. 'I liked that piece you played, at the mid-year concert.'

It was very sweet the way he said it, and I stopped myself from telling him how much I hated playing in front of people, how the teachers would always ask me to and I never knew how to properly say no. One of the reasons I couldn't wait for high school to end was so I didn't have to perform in front of five hundred kids who thought classical music was as redundant as VHS.

My dad made me do the same thing, but on a smaller scale. Once a week he set up an electric keyboard in the middle of the café so I could play Karen Carpenter songs to the customers. It didn't matter to him that no one remembered the Carpenters anymore. It was just about the presence of the music, he said. A way of building a conversation with the community, whatever that meant.

Peter was humming a tune that vaguely resembled Ravel's *Jeux d'Eau*. 'Is that how it went? When I heard it, I thought it was the most awesome thing anyone could do with their hands.'

He seemed slightly uneasy, embarrassed. Perhaps he felt he had been too eager with compliments.

'I always wanted to play an instrument,' he explained. 'My dad taught me the guitar when I was little. But I haven't played for years, not since he left.'

'What about the harp in the living room? Who plays that?'

'That's just my mum's idea of having tasteful decor. Also she once studied in Ireland for a year, which apparently left an impression on her. So she probably thinks the harp's symbolic.'

Then he turned to me. 'Hey, why don't you skip the piano. We can do something.'

Usually when he said this, he meant he wanted us to watch an old movie he had found. For someone who was into the latest technology, he was also quite retrospective. His favourite film era was the seventies: *Chinatown, The Godfather: Part II.* Lately, he had been obsessed with the Russian director Andrei Tarkovsky, who made a film called *Solaris*, about a distant planet that replicated human realities and in turn drove the humans insane. Peter said it was a Russian take on Stanley Kubrick's *2001: A Space Odyssey*, which seemed appropriate as that film didn't make any sense to me either.

'Do I have to sit through another Russian movie?' I asked, squirming a little.

Peter sighed. He found it mildly frustrating that I didn't share his interest. 'No, we can do something else if you want.'

'I'll get into trouble if I miss my lesson.'

Then, for a moment, he seemed lost for words, for once unsure whether he ought to take charge. He got up, paced around a little, then he sat down again. He wanted to say something, but seemed convinced that he should wait. So he did, as a cloud passed over the sun, as the kids outside argued over a wicket.

'I'll get into trouble,' I said to him for a second time.

It was barely a whisper, but he understood from it all that was not said. He came near, ran his hand over the strap of my dress and twisted it around his finger. The light around us was a rich amber, a pool of yolk.

'Then get into trouble, for once in your life.'

At Peter's New Year's Eve party, a few weeks earlier, he had come up to me as I stood alone in his kitchen and said into my ear, 'I bet you thought about piking.'

'Yes, still thinking about it,' I had replied.

He laughed. 'Stay for an hour at least.'

I was wearing a dress with poplin sleeves. The elastics dug into my arm uncomfortably and I was probably fiddling with it too much.

'You look nice,' Peter said. 'I mean, not that you don't normally look nice.'

There were a lot of people coming in and out of the kitchen. We couldn't really talk to each other without someone cutting in and saying 'Excuse me but who drank all the Sub Zeros?' or 'Hey, someone's been in that bathroom for ages.'

The main party was happening outside in the garden, where Peter's friends had set up the CD player and turned Jennifer Lopez on full volume. It was getting dark and the fairy lights draped over the apple trees were glowing. There were a few people swimming, doing somersaults. Others sat around the edge of the pool, trying half-heartedly to stay dry from the splashes.

There was another party on the other side of the street, with even louder music and slightly older people. A fair bit of shouting was going on, and there were people going back and forth, trying to get the best of both parties.

'Come with me.' Peter gestured, and placed his hand in the small of my back. 'I'll introduce you to some people.'

We went across the living room into a room that looked like a library. Three of his friends were sitting on the floor, chatting to each other. I remembered their faces from school, but I didn't know what their names were. They had a bowl of chips between them and crumbs all over the carpet. Empty beer bottles stood in a pyramid formation, looking wet and precarious.

'It was rigged!' one of them was saying, shouting. He was quite chubby and had freckles that walked across his nose like paw prints. 'They stole the republic from the people!'

'I just think you should relax,' said a second guy, who had matted hair like the beginnings of dreadlocks. He was rolling a cigarette. 'The people have spoken, man. Live with it.'

'I dispute that. Most people who voted no actually *wanted* Australia to be a republic. They just didn't want to give parliament the power to select a head of state. They wanted to be able to do that themselves, to have a democratically elected president. The whole referendum just got clouded by tangential issues.'

'How does it affect you anyway?' asked the third guy, who was wearing a T-shirt that was either dirty or tie-dyed. 'Why do you care so much?'

'Why do I care?' The guy with the freckles was practically frothing at the mouth. 'Have you considered the alternative if people like me didn't care? Have you?'

'What?'

'A country full of people like you, dimwit. Now is that scary or is that scary?'

Peter jumped in. 'Guys, this is Primrose. Say hi.'

They glanced at me and said hi in unison. Then they went very quiet for a while as if trying to work out how long they needed to wait before they could carry on as before.

Finally the freckles guy said, 'Primrose, did you vote in the referendum?'

'God, Jonathan!' said the guy with the dreadlocks. 'Are you thick? She's only in Form Four.'

It surprised me that he knew this about me. It made me think that maybe Peter had talked to them about me in some way.

Peter said to me, 'Jonathan here spent the whole year volunteering for the republican campaign. So he's a bit depressed about the outcome.'

All through the last semester at school, the Form Sixes went around like they had one extra reason to feel superior to everyone else. They put up banners about the referendum all over the classrooms and the quadrangle, mainly for the Yes side, as if to show off to the rest of the school that they were turning eighteen just in time to have a vote in this historic decision. Some of them even marched into assembly one day with huge face masks of the Queen and Prince Philip, red paint splashed across their faces to resemble blood. The headmaster was not impressed and a number of them ended up in detention. Jonathan must have been one of them.

'How would you have voted if you were allowed to?' Jonathan pressed. He clearly didn't want the conversation to stray. 'Yes for the republic? Or no for the Queen?'

It was odd, to be asked a political question like that. I didn't feel qualified to give an opinion; I played with the sleeves of my dress as I thought about it. In some ways, I was drawn to the idea of the monarchy – I liked castles and hunting dogs, and when Princess Diana died, I had felt very sad for her. But did that amount to a proper opinion? In the end, I found myself saying, 'My dad voted yes. He thinks the monarchy should've been abolished two hundred years ago. He says the French got it right.'

Actually my dad said a lot more than that, but it didn't feel like the right place to be going into Mabo and Rudyard Kipling and the Opium Wars. Jonathan seemed pleased enough with my abbreviated reply.

'See that?' he said, contented. 'I rest my case.'

A wave of people flooded down the hallway towards us then, yelling about some fight that had broken out on the street, between the two parties. Someone grabbed Peter's arm – it was the girl with the bird name, Wren. 'We need you, Peter,' she pleaded, damsel-like. 'Come and tell those knuckleheads to go back to their side of the street.'

And without delay, the human tide receded down the hallway towards the front door, carrying Peter away with it. He looked back at me as if to say he would be back in just a minute. I considered whether I should leave.

Jonathan was saying something about how he'd never vote for the Liberals, who had set the Yes campaign up to fail. The guy with dreadlocks said that was too bad for Jonathan because people were already saying Howard could be in for at least another term. And the third guy, with the T-shirt, said to Jonathan, 'You'd better move out of this electorate, then, because it's as blue as the flag, and when did a single Labor voter ever count in a place like this?'

Then they looked at me from the corners of their eyes. There was an awkward sort of pause and I got the feeling they'd be more comfortable without a girl in the room. Actually I was starting to find their discussion mildly interesting, even if I wasn't especially keen to participate. I'd often heard my dad lament that no Labor candidate had ever won an election in this seat. He talked about it like it was a source of shame, because he'd always admired Hawke for showing compassion to outsiders and Keating for standing up for Indigenous rights. All of which had always given me the feeling that we'd be imminently moving to a part of town that was more Labor-centric, where people were more diverse and, shall we say, less affluent. We never did, though, because the Comet was where we made our living, and having a living to be made was marginally more important than politics.

Now Jonathan looked at me and said, half-asking, 'So you're in Erin's year level, are you?'

'Yeah,' I said. 'But I'm in Byrne and she's in Mitre.'

'That's nice,' he said, for no real reason.

To make an effort, I asked if they were all going to uni in the new year. They nodded, and Jonathan said, 'I'm going to do law at Melbourne, maybe arts as well, so I can major in politics.'

His friends gave him a look, as if to say, *of course you will.*

'Peter's the lucky one,' Jonathan continued. 'I guess his dad pulled some strings, made the appropriate donations.' I must have looked blank, as he went on: 'He's going to Columbia. New York. You didn't know that?'

I'd never heard of anybody going to America for uni. People from my school went to either Melbourne or Monash, or they took a year off to go to Machu Picchu.

I shook my head and said, 'We're not really friends.'

I went to the kitchen after that, to get a drink of water. There was a group of girls with their heads in the fridge, arguing about whether the strawberries had gone bad. One of them was wearing low-cut jeans and I could see a picture of a spade tattooed just above her right buttock. When they emerged from the fridge, they popped the strawberries into their plastic wine flutes and giggled as they ran off up the stairs.

I really wanted to go home then, but the thought of walking home in the dark, in the middle of a street brawl, was not particularly enticing. So I went up the stairs too, hoping to find a quiet spot and avoid making chitchat.

There was a timeline of photos on the wall beside the stairs, of Peter and Erin at different ages: swimming at a beach, riding their bikes, wearing beanies and backpacks hiking up a mountain. Their mum must have taken the photos, since she didn't appear in any herself.

It was much quieter upstairs. The girls with the strawberries had locked themselves in one of the rooms, still giggling. There were a handful of other people around, sitting on the windowsills, drinking. I paced up and down the corridor for a while and, when I was sufficiently bored, sat down to watch two drunk guys hang over the handrail, their arms stretched out like the wings of planes.

Downstairs the phone rang; the answering machine picked up, and a woman started talking. It was hard to hear above all the party noise, but something was mentioned about hotels and ramen and a happy new year. I wasn't wearing a watch, but I thought it was probably not long before midnight.

From outside came a loud plunging noise as someone cannonballed into the pool. I could hear the heavy splashes of water and some people protesting about getting wet. A couple of boys were cheering in fake baritone voices.

Then the girls with the strawberries came charging out of the room, shrieking like those people in old Beatles footage. It was probably to do with the song that had just come on, 'Last Kiss' by Pearl Jam. It was strange to see them so worked up over such a depressing song. I had to stand up to make room as they raced past and gyrated down the stairs into the brightly lit garden.

It was then that I heard Peter say, 'I thought you'd left.'

He was at the bottom of the stairs, looking up through

the dark-wood spindles. Then he began to walk up to me. He didn't have any shoes on.

'I think your friends are crazy,' I said to him.

'Yeah, it probably wasn't a great idea to introduce you to Jonathan.'

He stood next to me, leaned against the wall. He didn't realise I was referring to the hysterical strawberry girls. 'They're all nice guys, but they don't know how to turn it down a notch. Jonathan doesn't like losing any arguments. He's really invested in his beliefs. It was a bit much. Sorry.'

'That's not what I meant,' I said. 'Don't worry about it. Actually, I liked them.'

Peter got close to me so that our clothes were touching. He said, 'I should've mentioned this earlier but I'm really glad you came tonight.'

'It's been fun. I love . . . Pearl Jam.'

He thought that was funny. He leaned in and kissed me briefly on the lips.

'Are you going out with Wren?' I asked him.

'Who?'

'The girl with the curly hair, from your year. She was in the car with you the other day.'

'Um, you mean Dove?'

'Yes, okay. Dove.'

'She's nice, but we're just friends.' Then Peter lowered his voice, even though no one else was listening, and whispered, 'I don't want to get into it, but I'm pretty sure her dad is running the biggest insider trading ring in Australian history.'

'I don't know what that is.'

'It's stuff that'll put you in jail.'

'So you don't like her because you think her dad's a crook?'

'No, I just don't like her in that way. I know who I like.'

He put his arms around me and, pulling me closer, kissed me again as if he were trying to draw my breath away. I let him have it, my breath, and everything left behind was a tingling effervescence. He smelled like summer, like night-time.

Downstairs, someone had begun to count down the last minute of the year. Sixty . . . fifty . . . When the number got down to thirty, more people joined in. The house seemed suddenly very still. The music was gone, and there were only voices now, ringing all around us.

Peter didn't wait for the counting to be over to kiss me a third time, and it didn't seem at all excessive. It was just a moment on a night when 1999 turned into 2000.

Whatever doom people foresaw for the new millennium remained elusive in the new year. Computer bugs left the world alone, and life went on as usual. The days lasted forever; the nights were short and sleepless. The heat came, not in waves, but in one lingering spell unpunctuated by rain. Which meant nothing except long afternoons by the pool at Peter's house, under the shade of the apple trees.

From there, I watched on as Peter swam back and forth, from end to end, his arms glistening with every stroke as the water yielded to the disturbance of his body. The more he swam the more he seemed to demand a battle from the water; he almost seemed bored with the lack of resistance. It must have been, to him, the very contradiction of the ocean into which he plunged, inexplicably, every winter.

Sometimes he dived to the bottom of the pool and returned with a golf ball in his hand, which he would bring to the lawn and, with a club he always seemed to have at hand, try to chip over the pool to the other end. He didn't always succeed, and at times he succeeded by too long a margin. Each time this happened, he returned the ball to the same position to try again.

Everything seemed to be an opportunity to better his golf handicap. He was taking lessons from a pro who had once coached his dad. He kept a notebook in which he wrote reminders for his arms, and drew diagrams of various holes on various courses where he wished to do better in the future. Sometimes he even made clubs for himself, mad little experiments in which disparate club heads and shafts were cobbled together in the hope of producing otherworldly results.

Why golf? I asked him eventually. Why not basketball or volleyball or table tennis? Why not hockey, which equally required a bent stick and a ball?

He thought about it, as if I was the first person to ever ask such a question. And then he said, 'Because no two courses in the world are the same. There's no template in golf, it's up to you to work it out.'

Some days, when Donna was home, she invited me to stay for dinner.

She was the kind of cook who liked to throw things in the oven, a concept I was not used to since my own mother used our oven to store her sewing machine. Donna had not one but two Gaggenau ovens in her kitchen, both of which seemed to be constantly in use. She made roast lamb with roast baby carrots, and stuffed roast chicken with roast cauliflower. The food came straight to the table in big roasting trays, rustically adorned with sprigs of rosemary she cut from the garden.

The way the Loys gathered around the table was peculiar. The meal always began with everyone seated: always Donna and Erin on one side, Peter and I on the other. There was an orderly distribution of food; each person had a go with the carving knife, a turn with the salad bowl. But by the time everyone had waited patiently for all the plates to be filled, the formalities were considered over. Bon appétit, Donna would typically say at this point, and, with our plates, we'd go our separate ways – she to the study to work, Erin upstairs to her room, and Peter and I to the couch in front of the TV.

'You probably think we're strange,' Peter said one night, as he walked me home. It was not dark yet. All along Newton Street people were still milling about, coming in and out of restaurants. 'My mum thinks she's Jamie Oliver. It's never occurred to her that the cooking is only half the show.'

He was speaking in a dismissive manner, as he usually did when Donna was the subject. She seemed to be no more than a nagging presence to him, a fixture in the home that he must walk around. It was obvious that the parent he had greater admiration for was his dad, even though Robert had moved out of the family home when Peter was six.

As far as I knew, Robert was now living in New York and, having long ago lost interest in the family's banking business, working as an art dealer. Apparently he was well known in his circle for buying and selling old paintings. Titian and Caravaggio, that sort of thing. He was important enough to be mentioned in newspapers. Peter even kept a clipping about an exhibition Robert had staged, of European works that had never before left their home continent. The article described Robert Loy as Brobdingnagian. I had to look that up in the dictionary.

We were only a block away from the Comet. I said, 'Peter, I really like Donna. I think you have a perfect family, in fact.'

He looked at me as if I were mad. 'I don't understand what you mean.'

'Well, I mean, your parents are separated.'

'How does that make things better?'

'Because it simplifies things for you. Neither of them have to be married to someone they dislike. They don't need you to be responsible for their happiness.'

Still he was not sure.

'My parents sometimes tell me they're only staying together for my sake,' I pointed out. 'By comparison, you're far better off. Aren't you?'

He didn't reply, but he had a frown on his face, as if he wanted to say something important. We had reached the Comet by then. And I had the distinct feeling that, if we hadn't, he would have told me about his plan to go to America.

*

Now, on the afternoon in Peter's room, he closed the door. He went over to the window and drew the curtains. It was windy and the ivy outside was trying to get in, so he shut the window, and drew the curtains again. When he came back to the bed, he sat down carefully, as if not wanting it to bear his weight. The room was very quiet and the only sounds we could hear were those we made ourselves.

I lay down, and there was just enough room for him beside me. He pulled his T-shirt over his head.

'Take off your dress,' he said, wiping away the hair from my face. I let him help me, and also my underwear. Now I was only skin. He placed his palm on my throat and ran it slowly down to my breast in one stroke, as if measuring me. My body against his.

It seemed to me then that all those times in our childhoods when we were taught to be polite and civilised must boil down to this one moment – so that, when the time came, we knew how to be naked properly in front of another human being and to take in the nakedness that was reciprocated.

Peter lowered himself into me, warm and full in a way that no amount of high school reproductive ed could have prepared me for. It hurt, but rather like a prelude to something indefinably better. He kissed me all the time. And when he was done, he told me to keep still.

'Is it finished?' I asked him.

Then his hand was between my legs, and I felt a breath leaving me as I unfolded. This was the part I had never been taught. No one had ever told me about the wave that would lap over my body when it was touched in that wet and ready spot, about losing my mind for a brief moment as if I had fallen asleep and dreamt.

'Okay,' I said to the ceiling, where shadows swayed like the tasselled tails of kites. 'That is completely new.'

9

All through May, Harriet brings me clubs to add to my collection. A sand wedge, a pitching wedge, a new putter and, later, two more irons. In June, she brings me one last club, something called a hybrid, and announces that my set is as good as complete.

The hybrid is a big sort of club, like my fairway wood, but lighter, prettier. The grip is embossed with love hearts, the shaft the colour of red wine. Its head is the shape of a tadpole, reminding me of childhood days spent beside a duckweed-covered pond, my mother holding the tail of my dress so I would not fall in.

With this club, the ball launches off the ground less grudgingly and travels a few extra metres without my having to change a thing about my swing. It feels like cheating in a way, this improvement that has everything to do with the technology and nothing to do with me. But I can't quite bring myself to feel guilty about it, since it does little to improve my score.

Distance is one thing, tackling the green is another. I come to realise that putting is the most terrible part of my game, which, considering the rest of my game, is saying something. Any slim chance of making par or even a bogey is quickly stolen on the green. One putt too long, the next too short, and before I know it I have manoeuvred the ball beyond redemption.

Harriet gives me plenty of instructions on how to read the break, to line my eyes over the top of the ball, to bend my knees just a little and stick out my behind. But none of it seems to translate into results.

'Harriet, this is hopeless,' I say to her one day, at the end of yet another dismal round. 'I think a person's either born to putt or they're not.'

'False,' she replies, rubbing her nose against the cold. 'No one is born to putt. If you don't believe me, just look at Scott Hoch at the '89 Masters.'

Harriet is always throwing around references to things that happened in golf tournaments, all of which I have to look up later on YouTube just to understand what she's talking about.

She is one of those people who think that if everyone took golf as seriously as her, they'd be in with a chance to play well. That is the reason she constantly urges me to practise. Golf is not really a social thing for Harriet.

Around her, I feel like a student who has not done the homework, a rebel that I never was in my school days. No matter how many times I declare I don't care about the way I play, her reply is always the same. She tells me that I'm not practising enough, that when she was young, when her father would bring her here every Sunday to hone her skills, she practised so hard that her hands bled.

It does not escape her that my hands have been bleeding for other reasons, that sometimes I cannot be convinced to grip the club as firmly and committedly as she would like. But I have come to accept that in the matter of my hands, Harriet will not be the saviour.

During my sessions with Elaine, she tells me that I am making improvements. Small ones, granted. But steps in the right direction.

Elaine is pleased that I am devoting less time to the cleaning of the house, more time out of doors engaged in other activities. Carefully she examines the pair of slow-healing hands I hold out, and in return makes noises to indicate her half-hearted approval.

It's not that she isn't glad about the signs of progress, just that something new has now entered her consideration. She takes my left hand, turns it over. Almost imperceptibly, her gaze pauses over the fresh calluses left by golf clubs on the pad of my palm.

It is often the case, she believes, that when one door begins to close, another opens. And that dream of mine – of the wheat field and the harvester, of my lost barley body being churned and spat out – is the fresh source of her concern.

It's my own fault. I should never have told her that since I first dreamt of it, I have dreamt it again and again, so much so that some nights I cannot sleep for fear of its return. But now that she knows, she cannot help but mill around it as she does everything else. Generally this takes the form of probing questions about Whistles. From her beige upholstered wing chair, she asks me what I like about being there and how it is different from being at home. Does it help to clear my mind of my concerns? And, if so, what other thoughts have taken their place inside my head?

Like a good student I answer agreeably all her questions, and confirm to her that being at Whistles is doing wonders in clearing my mind of all the troubles with Adrian, with the pieces left behind by his illness. I tell Elaine the things I think she would like to hear. She listens and nods, but occasionally lets a glimmer of doubt cross her face. She does not seem fully satisfied with my answers. It is her job to enquire, to never be easily convinced. She is not paid to trust me completely.

Does it actually trouble me to be at Whistles? she theorises, absurdly. Is there something about the place that speaks to a different set of concerns I have not told her about? She rather gets the feeling that new anxieties have been raised. She can sense the cracks in my voice that I do not sense myself. Is it possible that the place has some buried significance that are not in her notes?

I don't remember, I tell her.

Don't remember? she says, noting it down. That seems to suggest there is something to *be* remembered.

It is curious, she adds after a pause, that of all the places I could go to distract myself, I have chosen only to go to Whistles. All through May and now into June, I have gone there whenever I can find the time. Sometimes we are driven to do things by our subconscious, but that does not mean we do such things without reason. We do them as a way of calling our consciousness into being.

I never have anything to say after such a lecture from her. I simply sigh into the silence between us and turn my eyes to the clock on the wall.

Most days at Whistles, Harriet is early and I am barely punctual. I come to expect the sight of her waiting beside her buggy, of leaves churning about her feet, an apple and a spoon in her hands.

We do not simply set off on the course; that would never do for Harriet. Instead, I am made to putt for half an hour on the practice green, or send a round of balls down the nearest fairway if the coast is clear. Again and again, she instructs me on the right way of swinging a club, which seems to come down to pretending the only arm I'm using is the left one.

She devises a drill for me, of swinging the club with my left arm while keeping my right arm tucked away behind my back. 'The left arm is the key,' she says repeatedly, neither explaining the logic nor recognising the futility of the exercise. She may as well be asking me to write with my left hand or pick up a fork with my toes.

Usually I am at a point of exasperation by the time we eventually descend upon the course, everything ahead of us feeling, by comparison, like easy butter spread over warm toast. Anything is better than being drilled by Harriet, no matter how many quadruple bogeys lie waiting on the greens.

Invariably we find Whistles almost empty, with just a handful of golfers grazing about, sheep-like. This, I've come to realise, is the norm for Whistles. I have not seen another beer-drinking crowd here since the day I first met Harriet. Like a gang of migrating buffaloes, they have watered themselves and departed for better pasture.

One morning, with a fresh westerly blowing, the course is even more deserted than usual. Yet we find ourselves delayed at each hole by the man in front of us. He is a hunch of a figure dressed in forest green, trudging sombrely ahead while carrying two clubs in his hand. You get the impression that if he were carrying anything more, he'd simply fall to the ground with exhaustion.

On account of his unhurried pace, he barely needs to stop each time he reaches the ball. He just takes a great big whack at it and continues on his way like someone playing polo in slow motion.

'He's sharp today,' says Harriet, without a hint of sarcasm. We watch him move up the fairway on the sixth, willing the ball towards the green in laboured but mostly accurate strokes.

'Do you know him?' I ask.

'His name is Matthew. He's playing awfully well today.'

We walk down from the mound where we have just teed off, and follow Matthew at a distance. The freshly mown fairway fills the air with the smell of vegetable juice.

As I look across the canal I can see only three other men, also progressing along on their own, collars up against the wind. This has become a familiar sight to me, even if I can never be sure whether they are the same people. Not one of them is particularly distinguishable. They wear the same earth-toned clothes, the same invisible weight on their backs.

Louisa was wrong about this place. It is no haunt for junkies, merely a refuge for those fleeing other people's company. Something I have noticed is that most people here seem to have no desire to engage in human interaction. They quicken their pace if you are too near, or withdraw to the bushes until you have passed. Perhaps golf to them is a kind of religion, with prayers to be whispered in solitude.

As Matthew climbs onto the green, Harriet remarks, 'He will take two more putts to finish, which will make it a ten for him.'

On a par 4, taking ten strokes to get the ball into the hole seems to me a horrible score, as horrible as my own. But when the man sinks the ball in two putts as predicted, Harriet raises her hands and claps, loud enough to turn his head. He tips his hat at her, and bends down to pick up the ball. He seems equally pleased with himself, but now he walks even slower.

'If you ever get close enough, check out his war medals,' says Harriet. 'He never golfs without them.'

The thought that anyone would wear their war medals to golf makes me laugh. But Harriet looks at me sternly.

'What's wrong with that? He has very limited time left to make use of them.'

Actually there *is* something caricaturistically warlike about Matthew. Watching him play is like witnessing a re-enactment of battle. The forward lean of his body. The upturned collar on his green coat. The golf clubs being carried, ends up, like rifles. His lack of height, and the way he moves sluggishly across the ground, give the illusion that he is knee-deep in mud.

'Matthew's been coming here for as long as I have, even longer probably,' says Harriet. 'Except he never pays.'

'What do you mean he never pays?' I ask.

She points her club up and out to the left. 'See that hole in the fence over there? At the top of that ridge? Entry and exit.'

I look over at the fence to find it's not so much a hole as a chewed-up gash in the wires. I try to picture Matthew pushing himself through it, like a newborn through the birth canal, head first and completely oblivious to the onlookers.

'Matthew thinks Whistles ought to be free for all, like Medicare,' Harriet explains. 'He's not the only one, by the way.'

She looks across the canal, at the other people advancing slowly down the course. 'There's that man too. And that one over there. They've always played here for free. You can call it an unspoken agreement.'

'A course for the people.' I laugh.

'In a manner of speaking. If you think about it, it's how golf got started in the first place, isn't it? All that time ago in Scotland. It was just a bunch of villagers on a wedge of public land between the sea and the farm, taking a chance with a piece of rock and a rabbit hole. If you strip away all the embellishments people have since put around it, that's what it is.'

Harriet bends down, flicks away the twigs on the ground so that there is a clear radius around her ball. Then, planting her feet in position, she scoops the ball unceremoniously into the air, at just the right trajectory for it to avoid the bunker and land on the other side.

'It must be sad for them,' I say, once we've watched her ball hop merrily onto the green. 'I mean, to think that this place will be gone.'

'What does it matter how they feel?' Harriet says, exchanging her wedge for a putter. 'There isn't a thing left to do about it.

Just ask the boy about the petitions and the council meetings. The fundraisers for a bid in the Federal Court.'

'The boy? You mean Josh?'

'Yes, it was Baby Josh who led the charge on all that, and failed. Actually, don't ask him about it. He's still brooding, no doubt taking it all very personally.'

Harriet turns the sole of her shoe upward to dislodge a chunk of grass clippings. 'Apparently his great-grandfather was a greenkeeper here. Ever seen the painting in the clubhouse? He did that, way back when.'

In the distance, a machine throttles; someone on a ride-on mower is weaving through the trees on his way towards the shed.

'Anyway,' says Harriet, 'where is that ball of yours?'

We move to the canal side of the fairway, roughly within range of where my last shot landed. The sound my iron produced upon hitting the ball resembled the throaty honk of a goose, and, according to Harriet, I'd hit the ball with the hosel instead of the club face. Now we are in the long grass, searching for the ball that the hosel dispatched, trying not to trip over the hidden logs.

At last Harriet finds it, calls out to me. She is almost at the water's edge, where the reeds rise high beside her. There would hardly be room to place both feet properly on the ground to make the shot.

'Forget it,' I say. 'I'll just drop a ball over there and take the penalty.'

But Harriet is dissatisfied with my plan. 'No. You've taken far too many drops already! Just get over here and try it, will you?'

Up close, the lie is even worse than I thought. An old tree stump is concealed in the grass, not more than two feet in front of the ball. Unless I got some height on the ball, it would go no further than that. I suggest to Harriet that I might avoid the stump by hitting the ball sideways onto the fairway. It won't take me any closer to the hole, but it will at least put me in a better position for the next shot.

'Play it safe if you like,' she replies. 'But don't you think you might just clear the stump if you aimed straight and scooped a little?'

'Harriet, when has my ball ever done anything to plan?'

'You're close enough for a nice little up-and-down,' she says, ignoring me. 'One shot onto the green, one putt into the hole, and you've made par, haven't you?'

Having stopped counting my strokes some way back, I suddenly realise she's right. She has been counting for me.

'I think a par would be optimistic, Harriet,' I tell her.

'It's what Ballesteros would do. That is all I'm saying.'

Not knowing who Ballesteros is does not diminish the clarity of what she means. There is no way around doing what she wants.

Reluctantly, by the water's edge, I set myself into position. My feet are sinking into the mud. Harriet instructs me to bend my knees low. 'Don't aim for the ball,' she says. 'Aim for the spot just in front of it. That's how the physics work.'

Holding back my breath, I lift the club up in the air and let it come down. But halfway through the swing, something in me hesitates. I suspect it won't go to plan. I should have lined up better, the way Harriet has taught me. The angle doesn't seem right. The only thing to do now is to abort the swing and start afresh.

I let the club fall loose to the side, my body twists, but I find out too late that my feet cannot follow as they are stuck in the mud. Before I can correct myself, the balance has tipped against me. I fall backwards and, with a splat, end up sitting in the cold slimy bog like a toddler in a wading pool.

'Harriet!' I cry, after recovering from the initial shock. 'It's all your fault!'

The woman barely flinches. 'Falling on your bottom wasn't part of my instructions, as you'd recall.'

'I don't think I can get up.'

'Oh, it's just a bit of mud. Come on and hurry up.'

A great deal of slipping and squeaking later, I manage to scramble back onto my feet with no help from Harriet. I'm covered in a sticky muck. There is nowhere to wipe my hands but on my jacket, where two claw prints now give the appearance that I've been attacked by a bear.

'Alright, thank you, I'm ready to go home now.'

Harriet says, 'You didn't touch the ball. It's still two shots to a par.'

She comes over and, perhaps finally feeling some pity, picks my club off the ground and hands it to me. 'Here, you can go home after this.'

For the second time, I'm forced to set myself in position under Harriet's watchful eye. I swing the club quickly, no more concern for what might transpire. But it turns out to be a good hard swing. The ball elevates cleanly off the ground, arches forward, well clear of the stump, and flies through the narrow gap between the trees in front of us. It lands on the edge of the fairway and keeps going like a shooting star, showing off as if it were powered by its own engine. It doesn't stop until it has pierced the edge of the green. Miraculous, even considering the length of the putt still ahead of me.

'Now,' says Harriet. 'To the green.'

She walks ahead, me shuffling behind her like a wet mop and wishing this day were over so I could shower and change.

On the green, she gets down as low as she can manage and reads the break for me.

'See? Downhill but cuts to the left.' She indicates the path with the blade of her hand. 'Gentle is all you need. Don't be fooled by the distance. Do not bring the putter back too far.'

Shivering in my wet clothes, I line the putter up, squinting at the imaginary line. I know as well as Harriet that hitting something gently is harder than hitting it hard. The ball darts out too fast, I think. It will overshoot the point at which it should start to trail down to the left. But something seems to call it to attention, reminding it to correct its path. It must be a small dip in the ground, a slight blemish where someone might have dragged on their putter or pushed the toe of their shoe into the ground. The greens at Whistles are always supple and foam-like, changeable with every movement of the golfer. This time, it has worked in my favour. The ball slows, drifts to the left, as slowly as syrup towards the rim. And when it finally reaches the flag it spills, however reluctantly, into the cup.

It's only moments later, when I have run out of breath, that I realise I've been jumping up and down in my swamp clothes, shrieking with disbelief. A par. My very first. Every nerve in my body is alive with the unexpected delight, the satisfying bliss of arriving. And if this is what a par can bring, then what must it feel like to have a birdie or better?

People must have been watching me. A man on the other side of the canal is motionless as he stares aghast in my direction. Harriet is also observing with some astonishment. Clearly she is not used to this lack of decorum. Her electric buggy is so unimpressed it is already some way ahead of us, tracking towards the next tee.

'Sorry,' I say to her, wiping mud from my mouth. 'Was that too much?'

'There aren't any rules about that,' is her bland reply.

To finish the hole herself, she walks over to her ball, gets down again to examine the angle.

'When I was younger,' I tell her, 'I knew someone who took so much enjoyment in golf that I thought he was odd. He never really made sense to me.' I don't know why I am still talking. My heart is in my throat. 'I haven't thought about it for years. But it seems less odd to me now, how a thing like this can become important. I know just how he felt.'

Harriet rises, her eyes darting intently between her ball and the cup. She seems to know exactly how she must approach the putt.

'Shoosh.'

10

Bebe asks, 'When is Uncle Terence coming to stay?'

Her legs are dangling from the kitchen stool like a pair of stuffed Christmas stockings. Now and then, she looks over at the eggs cooking on the stove, pinches her nose at the smell. Inevitably she will refuse to eat them, especially the part she calls *egg yellow*. But I will place them in front of her all the same, hoping that one day she might have a more Pavlovian response.

'Mama,' she says again. 'When will he come?'

Every morning, the same question.

'Not yet,' I say to her, trying to focus on what the breakfast-show people are saying on the TV. 'Another month.'

'A month! How many sleeps is that?'

'Thirty.'

Bebe drops her lower lip, brings hands to cheeks in astonishment. To a six-year-old this must sound like an eternity. Anything more than three sleeps would.

Lately, I've started to reference dates by their proximity to Terence's arrival. Even when I'm at the supermarket, I'll think: this carton of soy milk will be bad by the time Terence is here, or these dips will last a week after he's gone. The other day, I was looking through a book on the most intriguing women in history, and when I got to Gertrude Bell, the only thought that crossed my mind was: how odd that Terence's flight should be landing on the same day as her birthday.

The idea of Terence is, to Bebe, a simpler construct. To her, he is just someone who shows up at the house every so often, bearing gifts, which makes him rather endearing, even important. Now she turns over the number in her head, in her mouth – *thirty* – before reaching for the Coco Pops.

'Go easy on that,' I warn.

'I know. Too much sugar,' she replies mechanically.

She has learned to be aware of the malice lurking in the foods she prefers, not just the sugar, but the food dyes and the trans fats and the long list of preservatives described in three digit numbers on the packets. Her habits have not necessarily improved as a result of this awareness; perhaps it will dawn on her one day, like puberty.

For now, the brown cereal spills liberally into her bowl. With a spoon, she begins to stir it into the milk, clockwise only, until the milk also turns brown. Then, as always, she stirs in the opposite direction, in the hope that the milk will become white again. It's this second part that never ceases to fascinate her: the inability to reverse the situation. There seems to her no logic that something so easily achieved cannot be undone.

'Do you think he'll bring me any presents?' she mumbles, as if to the milk.

'Yes, maybe he will.'

'Mama, do you want to know a secret?'

I've dished out the eggs and put them in front of her. She pushes the plate away, her arms forming a circle around her cereal. She doesn't notice that her hair has fallen into the milk, both the same shade of brown.

'Me and Dad, we have already told Uncle Terence what I'd like him to bring me.'

'Really? That isn't very polite.'

'You don't have to be polite, he's our family.' With her index finger, she dabs her gum where a front tooth is missing. The milk has left a mark on her chin in the shape of a teardrop. 'He is going to buy me a doll with black hair and brown eyes in a riding outfit and long boots, one that looks just like you.'

'But I don't ride horses.'

'You can if you want to. You would look beautiful in riding clothes.'

'Thank you, sweetheart. Now eat your eggs and we'll be off to school.'

On TV the weather girl is talking about how exciting it is to be in Waikerie, South Australia, this morning. There's a group of kids packed in behind her, looking half asleep and holding up signs that say *Famous for Fruit* and *Population: 2722.*

The town takes the cake for the most adorable street art in the world, the presenter claims, as the camera swings to the left and zooms in on a large rubbish bin made to look like an orange, complete with stalk and leaves on top. This is the heart of citrus country, she explains, though ordinarily the fruits don't grow quite so big. She covers her mouth, laughs at her own cleverness.

I have a vague recollection of reading about her, in one of

those gossip magazines that seem entirely devoted to small-screen people. She married young, to a television producer who was the reason for her semi-fame. He was good for her career but bad for her self-esteem. He drank, she ate, he cheated, she purged. And, as sure as the sun rose from the right and set to the left, she filed. She was striking out on her own and, armed again with her maiden name, forging a path into the weather segment. That was the gist.

And now, at a citrus belt beneath an overcast sky, things have taken another turn. Listen, she tells the camera as the ad break beckons. A quick announcement to the fans, to those slow ones who have not checked their Instagram. A new ring is on her finger, on the finger that matters. The camera does a close-up of the sparkling bauble, fragments of light multiplying through the generous prism. The people behind her gush, applaud. An entire future is flashing again.

'Can we go to Waikerie for a holiday?' The lure is too much for Bebe, who cannot disengage the jewellery from the location. 'This place looks so awesome.'

'We can if you like,' I say to her.

She misses the noncommittal tone. 'I can't wait! Can we go next school holidays? Is it far? Is it close to Tasmania?'

'Not exactly. They're in different directions.'

'Oh.'

'We're talking about two different states.'

This is somewhat difficult, and Bebe pops her lips. 'What's different *states*?'

More than a year at school and the kid still has no idea how the world is arranged around her.

'Why don't you ask Miss Astin when you get to school?'

Bebe thinks this over and says, 'Alright,' but in a way that means she won't.

Again, I push the plate of eggs towards her. She winces, pours herself another serve of cereal.

'You should give the eggs to Dad,' she suggests, helpfully.

'He won't eat it.'

A pause. Her spoon hovers over the brown milk, dripping. Whatever she wants to say next has been in her head for some time.

'Mama, why does Dad only have those milkshakes from the boxes? How come he never eats what we eat?'

'He eats sometimes. He eats in moderation.'

She does not know the word.

'It means less,' I explain. 'Less than the full amount.'

'Why? Is moderation a good thing?'

'Yes, I guess it is.'

This does not seem to resolve her curiosity; it has opened up more questions. She cocks her head, chews, thinks.

'Then . . . should I eat less too?'

She means this in earnest, but still she sucks at the delectable sludge in her spoon.

'No, Bebe. I wouldn't change a thing about you.'

'Why not?'

'Because. Everything you do is perfect already.'

At this, she straightens herself, a vast smile appearing around her clenched teeth. I might as well have handed her a medal. As with every compliment she receives, she will store this away like a precious trinket, one that she might bring out from time to time to play with and admire. Every nicety the world offers has always been taken seriously by Bebe so that, whenever criticised, she is able to recall a previous praise or flattery in order to counter any prevailing negativity of the situation.

The other day, when Adrian corrected her spelling – it was one of those words kids find awkward, *where* instead of *were* – she was quick to remind him that she'd been the recipient of the class spelling prize the week before. She was not defying Adrian's correction, merely suggesting in her own way that she was better than the mistake she had committed. This, I think, demonstrates a certain sensitivity to her own shortcomings, which worries me somewhat. Perhaps she gets it from Adrian.

And there he is at last – Adrian – entering the kitchen, looking smart in a checked shirt and a jumper with elbow patches. He will go to work today, it seems.

He plants a kiss on Bebe's head, makes a smacking sound to which she giggles.

'Morning,' he says to me. I know from the way he runs his hand around my waist that he is still thinking of last night – of the way he told me to turn off the light before pulling me to his side of the bed and putting my hand on his penis. It was already hard, and I stroked it close to the tip, where I knew he wanted me to. His fingers were digging into me and his breath was circling in the dark. I was so tired, but I let him make love to me until the last morsel of him was spent and he fell into a sound sleep.

'Well,' he says now.

'Well,' I say to him, 'would you like some food?'

He removes his hand.

'Adrian, you should have this.'

He sighs at the eggs which, by now, have turned into cold, indigestible muck. He moves away to make the coffee.

'This weekend,' he says after a while, as the water boils. 'We don't have any plans, do we?'

'I told you, we are going to Peter and Louisa's house in Flinders. We're driving down on Friday.'

'Really?' He seems to have no recollection of this whatsoever. 'What for?'

'She invited us, remember? She's throwing a party for Peter's birthday, in true Louisa fashion.'

'That sounds like torture.'

I can't agree more, but I was also the one who accepted the invitation. Diplomatically, I say, 'I thought you liked them. Don't you enjoy their company?'

He shrugs. 'I don't have any objections to them. But a weekend away together?'

'Nevertheless, we've said yes. You know what Louisa's like. I couldn't have declined even if I wanted to.'

'Primrose, I was really hoping to get away this weekend.'

'We're going to Flinders, aren't we?'

'Sorry, I meant just me. Some people from the faculty are talking about a fishing trip.'

'Really. Fishing.'

He grinds the coffee, then he says, 'I need to get away to clear my head. You should understand that. Why can't you go to Flinders without me?'

'I'm not going to face Peter and Louisa by myself.'

'*Face* them? It's just a party. You're not going on trial.'

'Exactly, Adrian, it's a party, so why can't you come?'

'I'd just prefer to do something that doesn't require so much effort and civilities. Simple as that.'

'With people from the faculty.'

'Yes. I already said that.'

'Still, it sounds terribly mysterious. Tell me, who are these people from the faculty?'

'Primrose, what exactly are you asking me?'

This whole time I have been staring at his back, wondering when he might turn around to face me. Now I don't think he will.

'Anyway, you can't, Adrian. Not this weekend. I am not going to Flinders without you.'

He looks out of the window, silent. The colour of his jumper is bleached by the light coming in. He doesn't bother to make the coffee.

Quietly, Bebe slithers off her chair and goes over to him. Like a fish to the earth's tremors, she has always been sensitive to his agitation. With her arms around him, she digs her head into his side. She has done this before, countless times.

'Please, Daddy. Let's go with Mum.'

He lets her dig into him a little more, feigns injury, then smiles. She giggles as he brings her ponytail up to his mouth and kisses it.

'Fine. Flinders it is,' he says eventually, sighing. 'When was the last time we went away together?' There's a blankness in his eyes as he adds, 'It must've been years ago.'

'The summer before last,' I remind him.

He thinks it over, firmly forgetting.

*

The summer before last, on a night in Low Head, where the Bass Strait drank from the mouth of the River Tamar, Bebe crouched down by the window of the holiday rental as the last strokes of the sun sank beneath the water. When were they coming? She wanted to know, her small body rattling with hushed excitement. She had no interest in the food laid out on the floor – some cheese and biscuits, and cherries we'd picked up from a nearby farm.

Adrian came to sit down next to me on the carpet. He opened a bottle of wine and poured it into tumblers. Outside, a single streetlight came on and cast a frosty sheen over the driveway. Together we waited. Hours seemed to pass before small shadows finally emerged, delicate babushkas with turned-out, quivering wings, coming up the incline.

'Fairies!' Bebe cried. 'Tasmanian fairies!'

Her nose was pressed against the window; a fog repeatedly formed and dissipated on the glass in front of her. One after another, the penguins marched up the driveway towards the hedge that ran along the side of the house, and dived into the thick of it, very efficiently. No doubt they had done this a thousand times before. The parade lasted less than a minute, but long after we lost sight of them we stayed by the window, listening to them chirping in their nests.

The next day, Adrian was driving us through straw-coloured country towards Bellbuoy Beach when he opened the sunroof and said to me, 'Poke your head up, I dare you.'

It was late in the afternoon, and the sky was divided into pink and white and blue, like a national flag. He had a boyish look on his face – that entire week he had been so wondrously ebullient. 'Come on, it'll be great. I'll slow down for you.'

Bebe was asleep in the back and the road was deserted for as far as the eye could see. I gave him a kiss, got up on the seat, and stretched up into the open air. I could hear him laughing as the wind swung at me.

He told me to hold on, and the car swerved along a gentle climb to the top of a hill, then started to coast down the other side of it. He held up his hand to me and I took it.

Hold on, he told me again, and hit the accelerator. The car was going faster and faster as it headed down towards the bottom of the hill. It seemed to be skating on ice. I yelled out for him to slow down, but the car seemed to speed up even more as it rounded another bend. I opened my mouth to scream, to laugh, but the air was coming at me so quick that I thought I might stop breathing altogether.

Gasping, I got back inside the car.

'You're awful!' I cried, punching his arm.

And Adrian, who was obviously pleased with himself, pulled me over and held me to his chest. He was still weeks away from his troubles. He drove on like the wind.

Now, in the kitchen, he scrolls through the messages on his phone and coolly slides it back into his pocket.

'Look, I've got to go,' he apologises, not quite touching me as he brushes past.

'Okay,' I tell him. 'Go if you need to.'

'I'll see you later, alright? I'm not sure how long I will be.'

To my relief, he doesn't launch into an explanation about

the essays that are waiting for him to grade, or the extra lectures that must be prepared ahead of the next semester. He takes nothing with him as he heads out of the house, not even a coat.

There are two ways to get to Bebe's school. The first is a kind of Pac-Man route through residential streets and the occasional zebra crossing. The other takes you on a bow's bend along the beach to the playground with the wooden ship. From there, it's another two blocks down North Road to the primary school at the foot of the church.

The way along the beach takes twice as long, but Bebe gets to see the black swans that love to shelter by the bluestone sea wall. The swans are wild yet carefully monitored, each fitted with a collar around its neck, white for the females and black for males. Bebe has always worried that they might be strangled by the collars, which is why she and I invariably take this route to school so she can keep an eye on them.

Her attentiveness has not always been rewarded. Once she made the mistake of getting too close and the birds set on her in a frenzy; they chased her all the way across the sand and did not let up until she scrambled over the top of the sea wall back onto the footpath. Now she doesn't dare to go near them, though in her mind she continues to play the role of a mother figure, a sort of distant guardian who telegraphs her love from afar.

Today the swans are floating like driftwood on the calm water, dispersing out to as far as the furthest boat in the marina.

They are not alone. There is a group of swimmers in the water with them, heading towards the shore in front of the yacht club. Their dark, wetsuited arms pull at the ripples in slow, methodical strokes. Bebe is entranced by the scene, or perhaps merely by the way the swimmers have encroached on the territory of the swans.

'Are you sure they're not sharks?' she worries.

She watches as the swimmers make their way through the swans, each stroke more human-like as they near the shallows. In time, the first swimmer rises out of the water, a seal's glisten on his back, and tills through the wet surf onto the beach.

'That's Peter!' Bebe cries. 'Look! He's not a shark!'

The man's feet sink into the sand as he walks up the beach. He looks back at the water, at the other swimmers who are yet to arrive. As if impervious to the cold, he has begun to unzip his wetsuit and strip it down to his waist. The torso that emerges is the same shade as the sand.

'I don't think it's him, sweetheart.'

'It *is* him. I'll prove it.' And before I can stop her, she raises an arm in the air. 'Hey! Peter, over here!'

Her voice punctures the morning quiet. The man looks out in our direction; maybe the sun is getting in his eyes. A fleeting moment of hesitation. He waves back.

Bebe turns to me, vindicated. 'Told you.'

'Come on, we've got to go.' I grab her by the sleeve and pull her along. 'It isn't him.'

'But Mama, he waved.'

'He only waved because you waved. People'll wave just to be polite sometimes.'

'What? No, it *is* him,' she insists.

'You're wrong.'

'It totally *is* him! Why do you have to say it's not?'

'Because,' I say to her, losing patience, 'Peter would never go swimming in the ocean in the middle of winter.'

At this rate, we will be late for school. But we are late most days, and Miss Astin, the Year One teacher, has got used to this. She will simply smile as she receives Bebe into the circle of children already seated on the carpet, and gently suggest that she add something to the morning prayer.

The morning prayer is a daily ritual at the school. The children start by thanking Jesus for the birds and the trees, then take turns to identify things in their lives they would more specifically like to pray for. Most of the children will mention their mums and dads at this point, or that upcoming holiday up north. One of the kids likes to pray for Wednesdays. For unknown reasons, he loves Wednesdays the way most people love the family poodle.

According to Miss Astin, Bebe has never once shared her thoughts in this spiritual setting. Why is the child resistant to the idea of praying, she wonders, when she is so willing to engage in all other parts of the curriculum? The school does not mind that we are not Catholic, she assures us. There are many families from other faiths here, some who are from none. But perhaps Bebe's refusal to participate in religious reflection reveals a deeper obstruction. Is she reserved about expressing her feelings at home, for instance? Does she worry excessively about the welfare of a particular family member?

The school keeps meticulous records on the progress of its students. If one were to peruse Bebe's file, they would find there an array of information about her love of art, the size of her vocabulary, her aversion to subtraction. They might even find a passing mention of the amount of lunch she eats or discards, or the first time she went from one end of the monkey bars to the other unaided. But her file would not contain the reason for her reserve at prayer time, because even Bebe herself does not know why. That is to say, she does not know on a conscious level, and for a child her age it's the same as not knowing at all.

We are good at keeping secrets, Adrian and I. Not just secrets from each other but, for more righteous reasons, from Bebe. We have not told her anything we suspect would do her harm; she knows nothing of Adrian's illness. She does not know that his absence from her first day of Prep was not on account of a work trip but for chemotherapy. Equally, she is oblivious to the fact that Adrian did not shave his head last year to raise money for cancer research, that the months he spent in hospital were not due to a really bad flu.

All of this active deceit has been reasonably easy given Bebe's naiveté. Even easier are the passive things, the subjects on which we can simply choose to remain silent – like the not-insignificant chance of the cancer returning, and the plan I have laid out for us to leave this dreary town if it should.

But is everything really as watertight as we thought? As time goes on, you have to wonder. Perhaps Bebe knows abstractly that we have lied to her, or at least have omitted information of significance. Could that be the reason for her silence at prayer time? Does it occur to her that the verbalisation of a wish might turn a latent fear into something more robustly real? It is possible that our lies have only a certain shelf life, that one day – sooner than we think – she will know everything.

'Mama,' says Bebe as the wooden ship comes into sight. 'What will you do today, when I'm at school?'

'I don't know. This and that, I guess.'

The opacity of the answer troubles her. She takes my hand and squeezes it. It hurts.

'At school, Miss Astin is talking to us about *occupation*,' she says, pausing to make sure I understood the word. 'We had to tell the class what the people in our family did for work. I said Dad was a teacher at the big people school. But I didn't know what to say about you.'

'I'm a mum. I stay home. You could have said that.'

'Hmm,' she considers. 'Yeah, maybe.'

Her feet are dancing in small steps over the footpath. She's playing that game where she must avoid the cracks in the concrete so as not to be electrocuted. For a moment, this seems to consume all of her focus. But soon she grows tired of it, her movements distracted by some thought that seems to be churning in her head. She gazes up at me. 'Would you like to know your fortune, Mama?'

I give her a nod, going along. And she turns over my hand, the one she has been holding, and examines my palm. The child believes she can see things in the stars.

She says, 'You won't stay home today. You won't clean the house.'

I pull my hand away from her, place it behind my back. 'Sweetheart, that's not what fortune-telling is about.'

'But that's what it says, in the lines of your hand. You can't stay home by yourself today. You will go to Ripley to visit your parents. You will catch the bus.'

'My fortune says all that?'

'It does.'

'That's incredibly specific.'

'It has to be specific. Otherwise you will end up doing things you are not allowed to do.'

'You're a clever girl, aren't you?'

But there is no chance of buying her off with a compliment. Not this time.

'You can't go against your fortune, Mama. Do you understand? It's the rule!'

'Okay, fine. If you say so.'

'Do you promise?'

'I cross my heart.'

'Do you swear?'

'I will even catch the bus.'

She raises her eyebrows, grins at me as if every detail has been arranged just so. Now she walks ahead of me, no longer needing to be hurried along.

A group of joggers wearing leg weights whizzes past us, past their own short, broken breaths in the thin morning air. We can hear music pumping out of their earbuds. Inspired, Bebe launches herself into a gallop.

'Come on, Mama. Can you race me?'

She has reached the wooden ship. She's taking a shortcut and heading straight through the empty hull. Far behind us now, the swans have turned to specks of shadow over the water.

A cluster of swimmers are treading up the beach; lost among them, the man who arrived first.

'Come on, Mama,' I can hear Bebe shout.

By the time I start to run, I can no longer see her. Like a fluttering sparrow, she has disappeared around the corner.

11

From the bus stop on Newton Street, it's a half-hour ride up the highway to reach my parents' house in Ripley. The bus stop happens to be right outside the old Comet, though at no point did these two constructs coexist. The bus was rerouted here a few years ago, and the Comet had disappeared a few years before that. Only people like me can still make the connection.

It seems that I've never managed to wander too far from the Comet. Even as life moved determinedly along the path of work and marriage and motherhood – still the same town, the same neighbourhood, the same side of the highway. I suppose it's a kind of fate at work, since it certainly has not happened by design.

The Comet, on the other hand, has transformed itself beyond recognition. Nowadays, it is not one but two premises: a patisserie that sells cakes sitting on gold doilies, and a florist known for doing minor celebrity weddings – footballers and such. What used to be an interwar-era shopfront is now an interwar-era shopfront with six levels of luxury apartments on top, the floors stacked above one another like neatly organised drawers. Stringy succulents drape Rapunzel-like from the balconies. Small dogs bark through windows.

The florist does not have carnations today, a pity because my mother has always preferred the cheap, hardy varieties of cut flowers. The girl in the shop suggests a bunch of pampas grass, pink and feathery, a romantic cloud of sneeze-inducing irritants. Politely I decline and settle for buying the roses, which I know will invite a lecture from my mother on thriftiness.

Next door in the patisserie, the man packs a slice of cream-filled sponge cake into a paper box like it's a pair of opera gloves. Will I be eating it soon? he enquires as he fusses over the ribbon around the box. If not, it is best to refrigerate as soon as possible.

The cake is for my father, who, unlike my mother, does not suffer from type 2 diabetes. He will eat it with a cup of Longjing tea, brewed to the colour of peridot, and make remarks about the coincidence of East meeting so perfectly with West. Although he may not elaborate, this is his way of positing a larger view about the world. More specifically it is a lament over why two countries, the United States and China, cannot get along with each other.

In recent years, he has narrowed his interest in international politics to the Sino–US relationship. The fact that he lives in neither country has not diminished the importance he attaches to the issue. What happens at the macro level, he thinks, will always set the tone for how people behave towards each other everywhere. The whole history of love and hate is made in this way. It is how September 11 forced all Muslims into a single, detestable category; how Pearl Harbor led to the legitimisation of internment camps that deprived Japanese Americans of their basic civil rights.

My father is old enough to remember Nixon's visit to China in '72, and Deng Xiaoping's reciprocal visit seven years after that. When I was young he talked to me often about these events, not so much the politics that went on but the curious details which stuck in his mind as being peripheral yet important. First Lady Pat Nixon, for instance, had worn a long red coat all through those wintry days in Beijing. The colour was significant, not only because it stood out in a sea of navy and grey, but because of the auspiciousness of the hue that said more for diplomacy than anything that could've been said in actuality.

Later, at the age of thirty, my father had watched on television a Kennedy Center gala that Jimmy Carter threw in honour of Deng's visit. It had not been easy to find a television that day and he'd had to watch through a neighbour's window. The gala had included an array of American artists he'd never heard of. The one he remembered most vividly was John Denver singing 'Rocky Mountain High'.

There is no more room for song in the modern political era – he thinks this is the pivotal problem. Someone ought to play a tune before the whole world descends into a raw-knuckled brawl, one in which no winner can be called.

At the bus stop, a woman glances at me, smiles between darkly painted lips. She is wearing a T-shirt that says *Don't force Mother Earth to kill.* Her hair is up in a turban; only her grey roots are showing.

'I hope you don't mind,' she says, referring to the cigarette she holds in the same hand as her takeaway coffee. 'I think I am downwind.'

We are the only people waiting for the bus, which has at last materialised in the distance. She takes a sip of her coffee, winces before returning to her cigarette.

'I remember this place back when you could get coffee and toast for three bucks, and the coffee tasted better.'

She is gesturing accusingly at the patisserie. Perhaps she thinks, by the look of my extravagantly packaged dessert, that we might share a common complaint. 'A nice Chinese family used to run this place. They're gone now.'

Gone.

Isn't it strange to hear yourself talked about in this way?

I could have taken her order once: sat her down at one of our tables and brought her coffee topped with a foam love heart. We could even have chatted. She seems like the sort who might've asked for my name, my age, the whereabouts of my school. Perhaps she even heard me play on the keyboard.

Then the bus comes, and the woman must drop her cigarette, stamp it out with her foot. Her shoes are monk-like, sewn together with indigo fabric. I can see the outlines of her toes, shaped like a bird's claw.

On the bus we find ourselves the only passengers. She can sit anywhere she likes but chooses the seat across from mine. We are forced to watch each other sway like metronomes as the driver makes the necessary turns onto the highway.

Sitting down, she shrinks to the size of a bat, her loose clothing wrapped around her like wings. She is incredibly thin, but thin in that prunish way that suggests younger days lived in a larger size. After a while, she produces a piece of paper from her bag, nudges it towards me.

'Here is something for you to ponder. Please, take it.'

Suddenly I think I *have* seen her before, though not in the Comet but outside on the street: a bygone version of her passing out flyers to people who tried to walk around her.

The picture on the piece of paper is of bushfires and fleeing marsupials, rainbow parakeets scattering over a red sky. A helicopter hovers but appears to serve no purpose. *Climate emergency,* the blocky red letters say. *Totally preventable.*

'I draw all these myself,' she explains. 'They really speak to people, I find. More so than paragraphs on a page.'

'I can see that,' I say to her, reaching for words. 'The message is quite strong.'

A flutter of vanity escapes her. She searches in her bag and takes out another.

'Here's Uluru, blown up to make way for the next coal mine. You probably think it'd never happen. But never say never.'

More people get on the bus and she distributes her flyers among them. In here, all audience is captive. Her bag, it soon becomes clear, is a cornucopia of political agitations. Out of it pours picture after picture of doom and injustice, everything from fracking to planning laws to refugees and Aboriginal deaths in custody. No subject seems to have escaped her scrutiny, her artistic manipulation.

She watches as people sit down, as they choose to look out of the window instead of at the flyers in their hands. Does it bother her? If so, she gives nothing away. She smiles as she drinks in the scene. This is no more to her than observing the behaviour of mammals.

Another stop, and her attention returns to me. 'This one, I think, will speak to you in particular.'

She hands me a picture of five people standing against a wall as if in a police line-up. Some of them have dark skin and curly hair, others are Asian-looking. They're wearing placards around their necks saying *Not Aussie Enough*. One of them has a tear running down her cheek. The others are simply frowning.

'We are going backwards as a country. Fifty years of progress and now the dial is turning again towards intolerance. What do you think about it all?'

'I have no complaints,' I reply. Everyone around me is silent, listening. 'I think that on the whole people are kind and generous to each other.'

A look of surprise from her. She must have assumed I would possess some special knowledge on the subject, and now I have let her down.

'That might be true as discrete observations,' she prods, 'but what about us as a collective?'

'What can I say? I mean, I truly believe this is a place of good people.'

'Mmm, I do too, don't get me wrong.' She has straightened her body, taking time with every word she utters. 'The goodness of people is not in dispute here, but unfortunately, sometimes, people and country can be two very different things. You can't tell me some of the rhetoric from the conservative Right doesn't seem ominous to you.'

'Look,' I say, 'I understand that racism is an issue, I do. But sometimes I wonder if it isn't counterproductive for people to be reminded of it so often.'

Now she frowns just like the people in her picture. Perhaps she thought my agreement with her on the matter was guaranteed. And all I've given her is placid ignorance.

She shuffles in her seat, still frowning. It's clear what she wanted from me: a first-hand story of injustice, some vivid recollection of prejudice being thrown in my face. But why would she expect me to share such things with a total stranger? And on a bus, no less, while surrounded by other people?

I'm trying very hard not to look at her, but she seems unable to accept this stalemate.

'I can see you're uncomfortable,' she says, as the bus finally makes the turn into Ripley. Infuriatingly, her tone is not at all apologetic, merely diagnostic. 'I'm just not entirely sure which part of this situation you are uncomfortable with.'

'The truth is I don't think about it much until people remind me I'm a target.'

'Oh, is that how this has made you feel?' She is confused. More than confused, she is taking pity. 'That's very regrettable.'

No more to be said, she shrivels back into the folds of her clothes, braids her fingers together.

I get up to press the buzzer. My parents' house is still two stops away, but it would be better to walk.

My mother and father had bought their Ripley house in the nineties, for its time a cheap purchase in a cheap neighbourhood.

But even so, with interest rates in the teens, we could not afford to live in it. Instead we rented it out to various transient families like ourselves while we dwelled above the Comet in a one-bedroom apartment, where the living room was able to serve as an extra bedroom. My parents often like to remind me of this detail in our history, as if to say that everything I have now, I have too easily. I think they forget that I was right there, living the same life with them.

When retirement finally brought them home to Ripley, they immediately set about filling the house with stuff. All those years spent dreaming about living in one's own house got to them. The garden became a jungle of orchids and begonias, ferns and philodendrons, until my mother discovered she was a gnome person. Then the garden beds quickly fell to an infestation of Disney characters.

Inside the house, the rooms became snug and cave-like, packed with filing cabinets and op-shop knick-knacks, compact discs and old books. My father purchased furniture made to imitate the mid-century style. My mother, who objected to the aesthetic, bought rococo furniture, which was more to her liking. Perhaps she'd thought that a baroque fainting couch was enough to obscure a faux-Danish lounge, or that a gold armoire could sufficiently distract visitors from the adjacent plywood bookshelf. In the end, the house became two competing dynasties of taste, a warring metaphor for the two people who inhabited it.

As usual, no one answers the front door. I walk to the back of the house and look through the kitchen window to find my father at the dining table, taking a screwdriver to his laptop. The table is no longer used for dining but to accommodate tray upon tray of documents he finds difficult to part with – mainly utility bills, and instruction manuals for various appliances around the house.

'You didn't call to say you were coming,' he says as I slide open the door. He's not being reproachful, just indicating a preference to be warned in the future. 'Your mum's gone out.'

'That's alright.' I set the flowers and the cake on the kitchen bench. 'I made a promise to Bebe I would visit, that's all.'

'Next time you should bring her.'

As usual, he is talking to me in Shanghainese, and I to him in English. Over the years we have developed a habit of communicating bilingually, since he has always insisted on making use of our native dialect, in case it should die with him.

'Where is Adrian?' he asks, as if to make sure he isn't about to walk into the house.

'At work, of course. Where has Mum gone?'

'Yoga.' He gets up from his chair and walks over to examine the cake.

By yoga, he means the twice weekly hatha lessons my mother takes with her friends down at the seniors club. She's always pestering him to go along, but he tells her that old people look ridiculous when they stretch.

The older he gets, the more he seems to believe the world around him to be ridiculous. His friends, for instance. His wife, certainly. And, perhaps a little more with each day, his only child.

Years ago, when I told him I was marrying Adrian, it did not particularly thrill him. It was firstly to do with the way he found out – he would have much preferred to have had his opinion sought before a decision was made. But, more fundamentally, he had doubted Adrian to be good marriage material. This he never explained fully, noting only that there was an element to marital success and failure that tended to run along family lines. Wasn't Adrian's brother Terence well known for being a bit of a Romeo? He actually used the word, *Romeo*.

It's clear that my father has always believed Adrian would leave me, one way or another. And, over time, his conviction has only grown stronger. I sometimes wonder if all fathers give up a little on their daughters when they marry, or at least they give up on the idea of protecting them, of being able to protect them. I think that is what has happened between us, because whenever we discuss my life now, he is no longer interested in seeking agreement. He merely says what he thinks, take it or leave it.

'How is my Bebe?' he asks, cutting the cake with a knife and placing a piece, dripping with cream, into his mouth.

'She's fine. They've made her a hyena in *The Lion King*.'

'What?'

'Hyena. In the school musical.'

He shakes his head, as if something is very out of order. 'Bebe, a hyena? She's playing the bad guy?'

'It's considered one of the main roles. She's thrilled about it actually.'

'Cute little girl, a hyena.' He makes a tooting sound. Something delicious in his mind has been spoiled. 'She's too good for that.'

He goes to the stove to boil a fresh kettle of water. From the cupboard, he takes two mugs and throws a liberal amount of tea leaves into them.

He has left a newspaper on the bench, with huge headlines about the trade war between China and the US. One of them says the two countries are increasing tariffs on each other after a breakdown in negotiations. Another talks about the US move to place Huawei on its blacklist.

The dirty dishes in the sink look dry, as if they've been left there overnight. You can tell last night's meal wasn't a fancy affair, small bowls of this and that, probably rice and steamed eggs.

'Tell Bebe I've got her a new trumpet,' my father says, flicking a hand at the black case on the floor, by the fridge. 'I promised her I would teach her, as soon as her front tooth grows back. You can look inside.'

The smell of valve oil is what hits me first as the case is unlatched, that charred metallic twang that has always been my father's signature scent. For as long as I can remember, and even before I can remember, he has played the trumpet. It's the only hobby in the man's life that has outlasted smoking.

Every year, on Anzac Day, my father is at the local park before sunrise to play the Last Post. The residents there have come to expect it, just as they've come to expect that he will be there every Saturday, by the bike track, to play his music for the crowd. He has become somewhat of a local identity for this reason. Sometimes people film him on their phones and post it on Facebook like it's a cute animal video.

At the park, my father is more in his element than

anywhere else in the world. He plays all sorts of music there, ranging from classical to big band to modern. But what he plays most often is music from the movies. *Star Wars*, *Home Alone*, *Harry Potter* and the like. This, he observes, triggers the same reaction from everyone, no matter their age, gender or ethnicity. It triggers laughter and good humour, friendliness; it is a psychological phenomenon which affects people uniformly. And this is the reason he devotes his time to such an exercise. It isn't to provide entertainment. It isn't even some ploy to embarrass my mother, as she would suggest. It is, he says, to insist on and reinforce the commonalities between people in a society that is continually at risk of being fractured.

The small trumpet he has purchased for Bebe reminds me of a toy kitchen, something that has all the appearance of being the real thing. Though it is real, of course – more real than a toy – in the sense that it will produce the right sounds at the right pitch when the right keys are pressed.

'I didn't know you could get these in baby size,' I say to him, marvelling at the goldenness of the instrument, the milky, ivory-buttoned keys.

'Of course – eBay has everything.'

'It's very nice, Dad.'

'Leave it here. I will give it to her myself.'

I can picture how this will happen. He will bring it over to the house. She will sling her arms around him, kiss him on the cheek. She'll make him believe that she will apply herself to the learning of the instrument so that one day they might stand side by side in the park and perform a duet to the crowd. He is so gullible when it comes to her charm, the way he used to be with mine.

Now he makes the tea, wipes down the bench in front of me and places the mug there.

'I don't think I can stay for long,' I explain, not without a pang of guilt.

'You have been very busy lately.'

I nod.

'I don't understand,' he says. 'How does someone who has no job keep herself busy all day?'

'If you really want to know, I've been going down to the golf course.'

There is both thrill and regret in the offering of this detail. It is sure to rile him. He would never approve of golf as a way of occupying one's time.

He looks at me, shrinks me to a child. 'Tell me this – why does an activity which lacks any utility have to take up so much time and space?'

'That's a leading question.'

'I'm not in court. I'm allowed to ask a leading question.'

'You're assuming that it has no utility.'

'But does it? I can't see any, whichever way I look at it.'

'People seem to enjoy it, even want to devote themselves to it. It can be a meditative experience.'

'Meditative? That sounds like luxury, not utility.'

'I guess it's a different thing to different people.'

'For you, what is it?'

'Perhaps it's the proportions.'

'Proportions, as in the size?' He's dismissive, as if something so banal cannot legitimise anything.

'It's about how things become relative. On the course,

everything is so large that you can be as small as you like. And if you are small, then every thought in your head becomes insignificant, negligible. I'm not sure if I can explain it properly.'

My father drinks his tea, chews the leaves in his mouth. 'You're right. I don't think you explain it at all.'

'Anyway, I don't play at one of those posh clubs you despise. The people at Whistles . . . actually they are just like you.'

'Like me?' He bats a hand, unable to believe.

'It doesn't matter anyway. They're closing the course down. Things are coming to an end.'

'What will happen to these golfers who have nowhere to play?'

'I don't know. I suppose they will go somewhere else, or stop playing. It's not that complicated.'

'What will you do?' He's not talking about golf anymore. He means something broader, life-related.

'I thought I might start writing again. I've been thinking about it, but I haven't worked it out.'

He's halfway through the cake, crumbs falling as he dusts his fingers. 'But you hate to write. Isn't that why you quit your job?'

'That was different. I was writing for *Criterion*, for a business publication. It was completely irrelevant.'

'I don't believe you mean that. It was a legitimate thing to write for.'

'I wrote about stocks and companies and profits.'

'No, you were writing about what you believed to be right or wrong within a particular context, the context being the big rich cats who bullied the mice. You were writing politics. Everything is politics. You had a point of view which you were able to express to people. You took a meaningful position on things.'

'Nobody cared, Dad. They were just words. Who remembers anymore?'

'The point is you had a purpose, not to mention a career of your own. You should always have that. And why? So you can be an independent person. A person should always be that, no matter what. Otherwise you must be shackled to someone else, you give up your power.'

'Dad, stop telling me this.' Without meaning to I have raised my voice. 'You don't know me at all.'

He has told me the same thing many times, always rather biblically, as if reading text from a stone. But he understands it much less than he thinks he does. He has only a theoretical idea of why I left my job, an assumption that is consistent with the reason women often stop working. To look after children, to make the home, to reprioritise life. I have let him go on thinking this. And even though he is not a feminist, he has held it steadfastly against me. I've never had the urge to explain it to him properly. Come to think of it, he's never asked me to.

These days my father's tune has changed a little, not in the substance but in the hypothesis. Where he once valued my independence because of his suspicion that my husband might one day leave me, he now argues for it on the firmer basis that my husband might simply expire.

What if he dies? Is what my father is really trying to say. These are the unspoken words that we both know to exist between us. *What if you are left with a shell of yourself, emptied out by a man who is no longer here?*

Sometimes, when I think about this train of thought coursing through my father's head, I can see what a disappointment I must be to him. It is sad to think we have come to this, that I cannot even prove to him that I've married the right man.

'You can go if you need to,' he says, two cups of tea still steaming between us. 'Don't let me keep you.'

I wait for a while, to see if he will change his mind. But he does not look at me, only at the dancing leaves in his cup.

Eventually, I gather my things, touch him weakly on the arm.

He says, 'Children should have their own lives.'

12

Peter opened his atlas – the same edition that everyone at school had for geography – and found the map of the United States on page 123. He pointed to a spot on the east coast. New York.

On the page it didn't look any more remarkable than the other towns around it: just a slightly bigger dot, and a slightly bigger font. All of the east coast was coloured in the same lovely green which, according to the legend, indicated a low-lying shoreline stretching all the way from Maine to Miami. It seemed to me that Peter could have pointed to anywhere on that part of the map and convinced me it was New York.

As for the west coast, that was a different matter. The west was a crumpling vastness of topographical changes, full of deep furrows and towering summits. There was a madness about that side of the country, where mountains seemed to rise straight out of the sea and rush to gain ever more altitude as they tumbled unrelentingly towards the brown heart of the Rockies.

Looking at a map of America – of the way the different colours fought for attention, and the names of towns and cities jostled for space – it somehow made more sense that the people there should disagree with each other so often, why everyone got so worked up about the OJ Simpson trial, the Rodney King incident. Which seemed to me a perfectly good reason why Peter should not go there, even as he said, 'When you come to visit me, we will take a road trip, from here to here.'

He was running his finger from New York to Chicago, where he had always wanted to watch a baseball game at Wrigley Field – ever since he was six, when he saw an aerial poster of it hanging on the wall of his dad's house. It was the colours that struck him: the redness of the infield, the green turf mowed to a lattice pattern. Also the thought of people eating American hotdogs.

We were at the dining table in his house, a vase of banksias at one end and us at the other. The table was an old wounded thing, full of marks made by the bottoms of burning pots. Donna preferred furniture that told a story about how they'd been used. Almost all the furniture here had lived a former life in someone else's house, with someone else's family. What Donna liked to call history was really just damage, Peter believed. Some people rescued injured animals. His mother did the same with things made out of wood.

There were 800 miles between New York and Chicago, said Peter, already leaving the metric system behind. There was a chocolate town along the way called Hershey; we could stop over there if we found it interesting, or further along in Pittsburgh. Either way he would take me on a detour to see Frank Lloyd Wright's Fallingwater. Had I ever seen a picture of it? His dad Robert had been there and said that it was the aesthetic pinnacle of American architecture, that nothing fused nature and man more gracefully than it.

'So, what do you think? Will you come to see me in June?'

It didn't sound like a real question, more of a confirmation.

By June, Peter meant the northern summer, before the start of his academic year at Columbia. He'd be properly settled as a New Yorker by then, well acquainted with the city under Robert's guidance.

It had been Robert's idea that Peter should join him in New York and, once the idea was floated, Peter did nothing to sink it. At first, Donna had tried to talk Peter out of it, but the more she tried the more it seemed to cement his resolve. He had a lot of catching up to do with his father, lost time that only a country far away from here – far away from Donna – seemed capable of returning to him.

Sometimes Peter seemed to forget that I had two more years left of school, that I had none of the freedom that he now possessed. He assumed that things, even people, could just fall into place around him; maybe it was because for him, they always had.

In reality I knew that it was far easier for him to stay here than for me to go there. Several times I'd wanted to ask if he must follow through with this whole plan of going, but in the end I always held my silence. It never seemed like the right time; it never seemed he would give me the right answer.

When I talked to my friend Agnes about Peter, she'd tell me in no uncertain terms that he would never come back. Why would anyone prefer little Melbourne on Port Phillip Bay over culture and art and history and politics, all of which had been assembled in abundance on the banks of the Hudson? No, it was plainly clear, even for someone who had never been there before. We were all steeped in American culture. Going there was like going home. She was certain that he would not come back. No offence to me.

Agnes was the only one I had told about Peter. She thought we were, in her words, a 'perishable' thing, because everything that happened before the age of twenty-one was. No one knew what they were doing at our age; it was the blind leading the blind. That cliché about monkeys typing madly at the typewriter – that was us. Anything that came out legible was purely accidental, highly suspect.

'I'll ask my parents if they'll let me go,' I said to Peter, looking at the invisible line he had traced over the map. 'I promise.'

Peter smiled, as if everything had already been arranged, and kissed me on the bow of my lip. 'I'll be waiting for you.'

We went out onto the terrace, which was decorated with Donna's topiaries in alternating shapes of balls and pyramids. She spent a lot of time out there, trimming the regrowth with a pair of clippers. The ivy that grew all over the house received the same attention, but she did that with the help of a man in overalls – he at the top of the ladder, she instructing him from below. Together they had made the ivy look geometrically spontaneous, if such a thing was possible. It was beautiful to look at, the entire house shimmering as the wind blew.

Upstairs, Erin was playing a Westlife CD, which Peter said he hated but I thought he secretly enjoyed. He picked up a putter that had been left against a planter and walked down onto the lawn, barefoot. He had, several days earlier, fashioned a golf green of his own there, which was to say that he had dug a hole in the grass and placed a plastic flower pot inside it, both to maintain the shape and to make drainage possible. Now he placed a ball on the grass and putted it towards the hole. The grass was too long and the ball travelled unwillingly. He made it harder for himself by placing the ball so far from the hole it hardly seemed worth the trouble. But each time he did not succeed, he brought the ball right back to the same starting position and tried again.

Over and over he tried with the ball. He seemed to extract satisfaction simply from the repetition of the task. I sat down on the steps and wondered how long he could keep going.

It was the last week of February and school had been back for a month. So far the year 2000 had been everything that other years hadn't. All of January he and I had been together, lazy and free, slow and wasteful. All of February I'd spent counting the minutes to the 3.30 bell, then rushing out to spend those precious hours after school with him, before the daylight dwindled and my parents began to worry about my absence.

In March, Peter would leave. But in the meantime, he said he would wait for me at the school gate every afternoon. He said he would sit on the bonnet of his car and smoke a cigarette like a character out of *Grease*; he would put enough gel in his hair to make it pouffe up high in the front. Of course, he was only teasing about that part, but he stuck to the essentials of what he had promised. Every afternoon at the school gate, there he was.

Now, in the backyard, Peter threw his putter to the ground. With eyes wide open, he watched the golf ball navigate over the grass like a tiny hamster.

'This is it. Watch it go.'

He was electric with confidence. And finally the ball reached the lip of the cup and dropped cleanly into the hole. It was like watching the fall of a villain at the end of a movie. Peter's fist punched the air.

'Yes! Did you see that, Primrose?' He ran a victory lap around the lawn, then another, and another. His arms were up. 'Birdie on the eighteenth. Mark that down!'

Erin poked her head out of her bedroom window, considered the spectacle of her brother down below.

'Shut up, Peter,' she called out. 'You're being weird! Primrose, tell him he's being weird!'

Peter dropped to the ground, turned himself onto his back. Quick, exalted breaths rose and fell in his chest.

The sky above us was a limitless blue; it seemed neither near nor far from us, impossible to judge. When older people told us we had our whole lives ahead of us, this was perhaps what they meant – a vast, disorienting emptiness through which we must travel by our own estimation.

Peter lifted his chin, looked at me over the top of his head: an upside-down view of me and the world in which I was held.

'Everything about this makes sense,' he said, pure joy dissolved in his voice.

He was just an outline of a boy etched in the grass, ready to vanish.

*

In August, Peter sent me a postcard from America. There was a photo of a house on it, a house that seemed to grow horizontally out of a green wood. Water flowed through the house as it streamed down the mountain in tiered, fountain-like steps. And the house was so still, so settled in the shade of the trees that it seemed to have gone to sleep forever.

I'd never seen a place like it before, and it made my hands tingle, my head hot, knowing that from now on I could never unsee it, no matter how much I would like to.

Peter had not written much on the card, just a few words to say that Robert was right about the significance of the architecture, that it was a truly contemplative experience to be there. He would make an effort to see more of Frank Lloyd Wright's work if he had time.

If he had time.

How would he spend it otherwise? Presumably with new people he would meet in new places he would go. Did he wish that I had been there with him? He would've written so if he did. He would always be honest with me, I thought. And if he did not feel something to be true he would not say it.

Some time later, another postcard arrived. This time it was a cornfield in Linn County, Iowa, which called for the atlas. Like New York and Chicago, it was found on page 123, some way west of the state border with Illinois.

Peter wrote that after he drove to Chicago, friends had convinced him to drive further on. He was glad he did; he was awestruck by the endlessness of the cornfields, the size of which he could never have imagined. They were beautiful and, in a way, very majestic. But did we really need all this food?

He would drive on for another day and play golf (he did not say where or with whom) before heading back to New York in time for college.

A distant yet curious fact about Iowa that no one ever bothered to notice: in the province of Shanghai, the word was used to convey a message of pain in the local slang. Not the pain you inflicted, rather the pain you felt. Said flippantly, it was on par with a passing complaint. With more gravitas, it was capable of expressing great suffering. And how fitting that it was now, at the point of looking at a postcard of a cornfield, the very heart of agricultural Iowa, that I should become determined to cry.

I let myself cry in a way that foolish girls in the movies did, in a way that I knew I was better than. I couldn't think of a single good reason Peter had sent me this postcard. There was nothing remotely beautiful or wondrous about the cornfield, which was merely monotonous, and so green that it must have been drunk on herbicide. I thought it was either some kind of joke or his way of proving to me that, by going beyond Chicago, by extending the bounds of this road trip he had always planned for the two of us, he had moved out of the sphere in which we were together.

From there, another year passed. It's too casual to dismiss such a length of time, to reduce it to a shortcut, but that was how time happened at that age, not day by day but in one fluid stroke. Now it was 12 September 2001, and I woke up to the ringing phone by the side of my bed.

'It's five in the morning,' I told Agnes.

'You'll want to see this,' she said. 'Turn on the TV.'

Bob was staring at me from the floor. My arm was sticky where he had been licking. Perhaps he had wanted me to wake up too. His ears were oscillating like a pair of satellite dishes.

The remote was missing and I had to get out of bed to press the On button.

'Which channel?'

Agnes snorted to indicate that this ought to be obvious. 'Any channel.'

She could not believe we had slept through the most significant event in world history. I could hear her eating breakfast as we watched an interview with a security expert on an American network, about the likely motives behind the attack. He looked like he had hurried to put on a suit; his hair was ridiculous. The anchor was asking him about Al Qaeda. He nodded and said it was still early days, that no one had claimed responsibility, but, yes, the most likely suspect was Al Qaeda, and therefore Bin Laden.

'I knew it,' Agnes said, even though I was pretty sure she had never heard of either name.

At school, no one had ever taught us a single thing about terrorism. No teacher ever spoke to us about the tension in the Middle East or about Islamic extremists. Once or twice in the past, my dad had mentioned it after reading certain reports in the newspaper. It was not a one-dimensional issue, I remembered him saying. A human conflict was not a boxing match that ran on a stopwatch. Who was right and who was wrong depended a lot on where you started to look at the problem and where you finished. It was entirely your choice, this 'where' that would form the basis of your belief. And therein lay the difficulty.

I didn't know what he would say on a day like this, but Agnes was sure that George W Bush would now drop a nuclear bomb on Iran, or maybe Iraq or the UAE. That was what the US had always wanted to do, wasn't it? This seemed like a good justification for it. The more she talked the more it became apparent that Agnes was deliriously lost to this geopolitical vortex. She sounded really wound up about the prospect of a nuclear winter in the Middle East.

When we were in Form Two, Agnes changed her name by dropping a handful of letters from Agnieszka. Even though this had seemed like a minor alteration, she was a different person. She got a lot more confident after that and seized on every opportunity to debate people about seemingly random propositions. Propositions like: are Tamagotchis ruining our lives? Will IBM one day take over the world?

Agnes didn't care about the answers to any of these questions. She was just one of those people who thrived on conflict. Why else was she doing two history subjects for our final year at school, one on colonialism and imperialism and another on revolutions?

'Agnes, do you think he would've been caught up in it?' I asked.

She had to process this before realising who I meant. 'What the hell, Primrose! Is that all you can think about at a time like this? *Him*?'

'I'm just trying to figure out how far the university would be from the World Trade Center. I think it's on the river, but everything in New York seems to be on the river. It's so confusing.'

'Primrose? Listen to me. Are you listening? You and Peter don't owe each other anything.' She stretched out the word 'anything' so that it took her three times longer than usual to say it. 'You were sixteen, he was eighteen, the whole thing lasted about three days, who the hell's going to remember any of it by the time we're thirty? Now, can we please get ourselves back to the bigger picture of a World War III?'

As Agnes had never made any secret of her doubts about Peter and I, she felt vindicated about the way things turned out. It was not that we were impossible, she'd say. It was just that our differences outnumbered our similarities. Sure, we had some things in common – a faint connection in our ancestry, some resemblance in the provenance; perhaps we were like birds drawn to the same migration route. But scratch beneath the surface, and look at the divergence in more pragmatic terms – level of wealth and means, friendship circles, social mobility et cetera. His family was old enough to be considered old money. I still had the whiff of being freshly off the boat. In the end we were two very different people made up of very different parts, driven by dissimilar socio-economic forces. She made us sound like cars, but I got what she meant.

The channel changed at Agnes's end, but we were still watching essentially the same thing. The footage being replayed over and over from all different angles was of the second plane flying into the second tower, the red impact that was quickly followed by plumes of black smoke, and the gasps of the onlookers behind the cameras as they realised what was really going on.

'I think I'll write him an email,' I said.

'Do what you want,' Agnes replied. She was lost in the footage.

I turned on the computer. Bob laid his head on my lap as I typed the only three words I wanted to say to Peter. *Are you alright?*

But as soon as I sent it, I wished I hadn't. Regardless of whether he replied, I was sure I'd made a fool of myself.

It had been nine months since I'd heard anything from him. Last Christmas, he had emailed me to say that everything was going well for him and that, even though he always thought he would study law, he now wondered if it was best to get a business degree. He had talked to Robert about it but he still had time to decide, he supposed. He wasn't going to worry about it too much.

At the time, he said he and Robert were playing a lot of golf at a course called Bethpage Black, where conditions were so challenging that there was a sign warning people of it. That seemed a good enough reason for him to go back day after day. His handicap was lower than before but not nearly where he wanted to be, so he was working on it.

I didn't write back to him after that, and that was where we left it. I was exhausted from writing all those long emails to him, the ones that took hours to craft because I was trying to make them sound exciting and worth reading. In reality, he knew what life was like here, he had lived it himself. Everything that I could tell him, he would have already observed in person.

I didn't want to write anymore. It was better not having to confirm to him that I was still living the old life, putting on my uniform every day, doing my homework, working at the Comet.

Towards the end of our correspondence, we stopped saying things to each other as if we were together. We just kept it civil and friendly, not very meaningful. It would have been clear to Peter that I was never going to visit him, and he didn't say a word about it.

I'll ask my parents if they'll let me go, I had once told him, when he'd had his finger on the atlas, his head tilted expectantly towards me. So why didn't I ever ask?

The honest truth: I didn't know why. I seemed to excel at doing things without reason.

Later that day, at school, Erin said, 'Don't worry, Primrose, Peter's fine. My dad called us to say that he's not even in New York right now. He's decided to take some time off. I think he's travelling around Canada.'

She looked like she'd been crying earlier and then put on makeup to cover it.

'Thanks,' I said. 'I did email him but I guess he doesn't check it all the time.'

'Yeah, he's pretty terrible with communication these days.'

Mr Cunningham, our physics teacher, had wheeled a big TV into the room so everyone could watch the news coverage. He was looking around at the walls and asking himself where the power socket was.

Some of the boys were sitting on their desks, flicking through a copy of *The Age* and discussing it deeply. I had never seen them do that before.

'Primrose, not sure if you know this,' said Erin, 'but Peter's with someone else now.'

'I know.'

This was a lie, and I didn't tell it convincingly.

'Oh, that's good,' said Erin. 'I just wasn't sure if he'd told you. Actually she seems really nice. She's Canadian.'

'I'm happy for him, honestly.'

'Okay. Great.' Erin smiled, and as she headed back to her desk, she gave me a tiny wave as if we were saying goodbye for the last time.

Mr Cunningham turned out the lights, fiddled with the antenna on top of the TV. For once, he did not have to demand our attention. Everyone had already lowered themselves into their seats and shooshed each other into silence. Nothing but the perished towers seemed to matter anymore. By the time the world was right again, the year would surely be over. And with it, high school, leaving no trace of us behind.

13

When you google the address of the Loy house in Flinders, a number of things come up. The first is its physical location, an innocuous spot at the tip of a headland that juts into the sea, not far from the blowhole. The second is a government site which lists the house among historically significant buildings protected by state heritage laws. No photos are provided, but a short description gives away its age – built in 1888 – and the neoclassical style to which it pays tribute.

It is only by the third item that you learn about the fire. A news article from twelve years ago states that a blaze triggered by an electrical fault had destroyed much of the southern wing. The house, which had been in the hands of the prominent Loy family since the 1950s, was in need of significant repair.

That summer when Peter and I were together, he had mentioned the place to me. It was bought by his grandfather, who had hoped it would consolidate a certain status for the family. Having established a sizeable wealth, he didn't believe he should be regarded any differently from a respectable white person. But he understood very well that he was, and he was comfortable with the idea of buying his way out of it.

The Flinders house has a name – Homer – which Louisa makes fun of because of the Simpsons reference. Outside of that, she does not seem to find Homer remotely funny. It is clear that she feels a certain isolation when there, which has always given me an impression of a kind of outpost, a far-flung colony in a storm-battered sea. Often, she has also complained that Peter is overly devoted to Homer's restoration. This does not sit well with her; she thinks money could be better spent elsewhere, also time.

Louisa prefers home to Homer in a way that conjures images of evil stepmothers in fairytales. To her, home on Fairwater Avenue is light and expansive, recently refurbished and readily approved by trendy people on Instagram. Homer, on the other hand, she describes as antiquated and cavernous, dark in the winter and tomb-like in the summer. There's nothing to do there but stare off, over the cliff, as if you're in some Gothic novel. And she is no Jane Eyre.

Yet Homer now emerges in the distance like a stallion in bronze, riding high on the hill, winning the sunlight at every angle.

'It's magnificent,' I find myself saying, staring at it. 'Is there another word for it?'

We are on the main road, looking for the turn-off. Adrian considers my question, squeezes my hand.

'Old-fashioned,' he offers. As usual he is amused by my attraction to the classical. 'It looks like something an archaeologist has dug up.'

'What's an arkologist?' Bebe asks from the back seat. She has been eating a muesli bar, and makes a muddle of the word.

'Someone who searches for lost things. Artefacts buried in the earth.'

'Like a tomb raider?'

'Yes, like Lara Croft.'

Adrian slows the car as we turn through a set of wooden gates and begin the winding climb towards the house. The land all around is covered by long wisps of hay, punctuated only by a small outbuilding with bleached timber and a roof that has collapsed in the middle.

'Peter tells me he keeps all his art here, paintings he actually enjoys looking at,' says Adrian. 'He hates the modern stuff Louisa puts up at home.'

'And what does Peter enjoy looking at?'

'I don't know. Old landscapes, I think.' Adrian laughs. 'Probably *The Hay Wain* type of stuff, the kind you like. Who knows, maybe you two have more to talk about than you think.'

'He's a hard person to talk to.'

'I haven't found that. In what way is he hard to talk to?'

'He doesn't say much, for a start.'

Adrian produces a short, inward laugh. 'Maybe you're the one who's difficult to talk to. Have you considered that?'

He means this as a joke, but adds, 'I'm not sure you should have said yes to this weekend.'

We proceed through another set of gates, this time more decorative, a wrought-iron display of flowers and birds mid-kiss. We must be close to the house now and the landscape has become greener, more formalised. There is a garden on the right, divided into walled sections of reflection pools and citrus trees. An olive grove covers the hillside on the left like wool growing on a sheep's back. A hedge of roses lines the driveway. As we go around another bend, the house comes once more into view, looming large in the near distance.

Bebe rolls down the window. She peers out at the house, at the vines trained in the shape of obelisks, and the library of Grecian columns that guard the front door. Her fingers are perched over the window; she lets her nose grow cold. 'Where are all the people?'

In the afternoon, no one wants to go outside because a gale has started to blow. Louisa guides us into one of the rooms for champagne and what she jokingly calls pointless socialisation.

What is modestly referred to as a room is more of a theatre, with a dome-shaped ceiling that gives you the feeling of being enclosed in a bell jar. There are big doors which lead out onto a terrace overlooking the sea. We can hear the waves tossing in the distance like great sheets of metal being shaken out. It's a long way, but a fast drop, down to the edge of that water.

'I told you so,' whispers Louisa, sneaking up on me. 'Perfect place for a murder–suicide, don't you think?'

She does a belly laugh for dramatic effect, fills up my glass. Each movement expels a waft of her scent: gardenias and something musky like patchouli. Her hand is full of shiny rings that she has stacked tightly over her fingers, reminiscent of the long-necked women of certain Burmese tribes.

'It's beautiful here, Louisa. I can't believe you don't think so.'

'Please. Do I look like a fucking lighthouse keeper's wife to you? I'm a city person, you know that. When I look out the window, I'd like to see a couple of sexy joggers with sixpacks and sleeve tattoos. Here, you're lucky to get a frumpy old dude down on the rocks, chucking a fishing line at the water.'

She finishes her drink, and looks at her glass quizzically, as if unsure of how it had emptied.

'Anyway, it's Peter's birthday and he loves this place more than life itself, so I'm happy to put up with it for one weekend. Have you been mingling? I'll introduce you.'

She flutters her fingers at a large, red-haired woman who is resting by the wall, beneath a painting of chrysanthemums. The flowers yawn out of a vase into a plume of crimson and gold, dressing her head in a garish hat. The illusion is lost as she walks over to us.

'This is Marin,' says Louisa.

And Marin says, 'Don't tell me. You are Primrose. You have been mentioned and discussed before.'

'Really?'

'Yes, yes. It's always Primrose this and Primrose that.'

I must look puzzled. Louisa puts her hand on my shoulder. 'Primrose is the only interesting person I know.'

If this is true, she has never told me so.

Marin blows air out of her mouth. 'Well, sure, no offence taken by Marin.' She is drinking what appears to be whiskey, the ice cubes in her glass tinkling. 'Just don't expect me to sell you any more of my pieces in the future.'

Louisa chuckles. Now her hand is on Marin's shoulder. Marin, she explains, is not just an old friend but also the artist responsible for the large egg sculpture I would have seen in their garden back home, as well as *Melting Ice-cream No. 4* by the pool and the androgynous Venus de Milo in the gazebo.

Apparently Marin is known around town for her use of stainless steel, usually in bright colours and finished to a mirror shine. The egg, for example, is an intense magenta, gloriously polished to a blinding glare, accessorised with a crown on top, sitting askew. *Do you think it's hard-boiled?* That's usually the kind of conversation that ensues when people see it for the first time.

Indeed Marin herself has all the air of being slightly whimsical and misplaced. Her hair is a tumbleweed of frizz, a flaming red rebuttal to the neutral tones of the furnishings all around us. She is wearing a sort of kaftan that is best suited for holidays in warm climates. And while everyone else shivers, she seems to have brought her own weather. Perspiration has added highlights to her face, bringing out the pinched cheeks, the vacancy of her forehead.

'So, what do you think of *this* house?' she asks me, looking around. 'It is very classical here.'

'I think it's wonderful,' I tell her.

But Marin is not satisfied. 'In what way wonderful?'

'In its lines and its symmetry, I guess. But mostly just in the fact that it's here at all, that it hasn't fallen into the sea.'

'Oh, I agree! It's a feat in and of itself.'

I can see Louisa rolling her eyes.

After a long sip of her drink, Marin adds, 'It's not exactly my oeuvre, sure, but I am an admirer of all genres of creation. To me, this house is the earth itself. That rich terracotta hue – like it's just come out of a kiln – is so very tactile. It reminds me a little of Petra.' She is talking at me but looking at Louisa. 'You ought to tell Peter what you think of the house. God knows he won't get any approvals from Louisa.'

Then she links arms with Louisa, her lips squished together, teasing: 'You look so sour here. What's wrong?'

'Stop it,' Louisa snaps, freeing herself from Marin. 'Peter doesn't give a shit what anybody thinks. If he loves it, he'll love it regardless. That's the end of the story.'

With that, she surveys the room, suddenly seeming bored with the guests she has assembled here by her own accord. 'I need a top-up,' she announces, before drifting away on the tips of her shoes.

A chorus of laughter rings out from the couch, where two couples have been sitting for the past hour, watching something on their phones. Whatever it is, it has sent them into a fit of revelry, a relay of high fives. Earlier, they said their names were Bridget and Greg, Eve and Lawrence. Now I can't remember who is who.

Over by the fireplace, Adrian is talking to Peter and another man wearing a plaid shirt and corduroy pants. Adrian looks over at me, raises his chin as if saying hello. The fire beside him is seeping out of the cinders in small desperate puffs. I don't know why no one bothers to put more wood on it. It's freezing in here.

Bebe, it seems, has made friends with a dark-haired girl in a leather jacket and combat boots, a silver stud on one side of her nose. How old is she? Maybe ten, eleven. Too young to be allowed a piercing on her nose. Together the two of them have settled among cushions on the window seat, engrossed in a game that requires a lot of hand gestures.

Marin transmits a motherly look, says, 'Helena. My daughter.'

Bebe is shrieking with delight as Helena demonstrates a set of actions with her hands, lots of fists and scissors, followed by a cymbal clap of the palms.

'They're putting a spell on us,' explains Marin. 'Helena thinks she's a witch, that she can create her own magic. Healthy sign of an active imagination.'

'They all seem to believe in their own brand of magic,' I say.

'I think my Helena has fallen in love with your daughter. She's always wanted a little sister, ever since she watched that movie about that girl in the ice palace. What was it called? Never mind . . . Danny, my husband, he probably wouldn't mind another child either, but I'm way too old. My ovaries are a restricted zone now.'

She laughs, and there, in her mouth, a sign of her age: a missing molar in the upper gum, a weeping pink mass in its place.

The man in the plaid shirt, who must be Danny, is summoned by her laughter. Rubbing his hands together, he swaggers up to her. His arms are barely long enough to circumnavigate her waist.

'What's so funny, darling?' he asks, starting to laugh with her. His face is very red from drinking.

'I was just telling Primrose about dried-up prunes,' Marin says. 'Not you, just me.'

Danny kisses her on the ear. 'Don't be silly. You're lovely as hell.'

She seems to be melted by his words, and directs his kiss to her mouth. Her hands are a clam around his face.

Into her lips he says, in a whisper, 'And very fuckable.'

And, suddenly, the rain. A storm upon the windows like rubber pellets. The two couples on the couch move in for a better look, just as Bebe and Helena run away in a burst of overdramatic screams.

Either Lawrence or Greg says it's not rain but hail. The other one agrees. Just look at the ground over there, he points out. It's piling up already.

Eve and Bridget press their cheeks to the glass, looking sideways in astonishment. It is hail, they say together, giving off little shivers to demonstrate how cold the sight of it makes them.

Then one of them says, 'Look! There is someone down there!'

She is pointing to the bottom of the olive grove, where two figures on horseback are riding furiously towards the main road. Now even Marin is looking, dragging Danny along with her.

'Are we expecting more guests?' she asks, hungrily, as if enquiring what's for dinner.

'How very regency period,' Bridget or Eve exclaims, perhaps because of the horses.

'Positively Austen-esque,' the other one adds. 'Mr Darcy, here he comes.'

'Or Willoughby.'

'Yes, this is very Willoughby!'

Then comes Peter's voice. He doesn't need to look out the

window; he isn't even looking at any of us. 'The local riding club has a licence to cut across our land, that's all.'

Dinner is a casual affair, a buffet of cold and warm things, some of them vegan for Helena's sake, ordered in by Louisa. We fill our own plates, sit down together at one end of the long table in the dining room. It's a great ship of a table, built to receive a convoy of dignitaries. Three chandeliers hang above it, a constellation of reflections and refractions in constant flux.

Tomorrow, for Peter's birthday, we'll have to dress up like debutantes, Louisa reminds us, apologising. It'll be proper catering and we'll have to use napkins and cutlery laid out in the proper way.

All this is said to tease Peter as well as to emphasise the trouble she is going to for him. She reaches over to stroke the side of his neck. He strains his face into laughter, before leaving the table to fetch more wine.

Is he embarrassed by the fuss she is making? Since dinner began he has been to the cellar three times. He's drinking too much. Most people at the table seem to be.

Inebriation is the reason that Greg and Lawrence have been discussing Trump's re-election chances for the past half-hour, even though the US election won't be taking place till the end of next year. The two of them are more or less at the same end of the political spectrum, but each is trying hard to distinguish himself from the other.

'If an election were held tomorrow he would almost certainly win again,' says Greg, who I now realise is the taller of the two, tanned and athletic, a friend of Peter's from his golf club. 'So far Trump's exceeded all expectations. Wall Street is up and the trade war sits well with the working class. His only enemy is time, too much of it. Almost eighteen months to go till the election: that's a long time for him to screw something up.'

Lawrence dismisses this. 'What could happen? As long as he does well on the economy – which he is, through the tariffs – people will forgive everything else.'

'Still, geopolitically you can't rule out the chance of military action in some form. It doesn't look likely now, but next year, who knows?'

'A war in 2020? How exactly could that come about? If it's the South China Sea you're thinking, no one wants to be all in on that.'

'I don't know how.' Greg seems frustrated by his own unknowing. 'One simply gets a feeling, that's all. Black swans, you can call it.'

'In any case,' Lawrence says, 'if there is going to be a war, it will undoubtedly favour the incumbent. Nothing puts a shine on the commander-in-chief quite like a pile of dead bodies. Am I right?'

Lawrence jiggles the collar that has been buttoned stiffly around his neck. If it's comfort he's after, why not release a notch or two?

Earlier he mentioned he was a partner at a firm specialising in employment law, which I think must mean he represents big corporations in unfair dismissal cases. Even though he is talking to Greg, his eyes are dashing around the table as if inviting others to join in. Eve, meanwhile, has been nodding her head at everything he says. Each word he utters seems to reveal her innermost thoughts.

'I don't want to oversell a Democrat slogan,' Lawrence continues, 'least of all one from Clinton, but – *It's the economy, stupid.* A trade war is the only war Trump needs to win to get re-elected in 2020. And he's going to win it.'

Peter puts down his fork, looks at Lawrence. 'Suppose he doesn't win it, the trade war, then what?'

'I'm sorry?' Lawrence lays his hands flat on the table, and puts on a dramatic display of disbelief with flabby cheeks and bulging eyes. It wins him a few chuckles around the table.

'Well, there's no evidence as yet that the tariffs are working,' says Peter.

'I would dispute that.'

'Dispute it if you want, but you won't find much economic data to back you.'

'That kind of thing takes time to flow through, Peter.'

'So while we're waiting, let's suppose for a minute that he doesn't win this thing. All you're left with is what? A unilateral trade policy that has not only consolidated the position of your enemy but damaged relations with all your traditional allies.'

'Hear, hear,' Marin cuts in, raising her glass drunkenly.

'Here we go,' says Greg, rubbing his hands together, getting ready for a fight.

Peter says to Greg, 'You said earlier that you don't know what will happen next year. But surely we can make a calculated guess at what things might be like in 2020. The past informs the future, doesn't it? It's logical to assume that a man who actively seeks out the friendship of autocrats and dictators will increasingly undermine the democracy that elected him. Also reasonable to assume that a president who won't condemn the alt-right movement will continue to divide and fracture his country. All of that, in an election year, can only mean violence on the streets. That much is written on the wall.'

'A crystal ball, Peter,' says Greg. 'Wish we all had one.'

'It has nothing to do with clairvoyance,' now Adrian says. 'It's just history repeating itself. Despite appearances, humans have very limited ability to reinvent themselves.'

Peter nods. 'People have always been capable of being bad when they are given the all clear by an authority that condones or even encourages the behaviour. Remember the Milgram experiment? And how willingly people gave those electric shocks to others when instructed to do so? It went a long way to explain how Nazi Germany came about, and how it could happen again, anywhere in the world.'

'One thing I don't understand,' says Marin, her eyes not altogether focussed, 'is the golf! How can someone like Trump, a man so egotistical, be so devoted to pushing a little ball around on a green field? How does he find the time in between looking at himself in the mirror? Can somebody explain that to me?'

'Even dictators have hobbies,' Danny says, patting his wife's shoulder as if she has grown fur there. 'Kim Jong Il was obsessed with Hollywood movies, I hear.'

'Mussolini played the violin,' Peter adds. 'Stalin loved the piano.'

He shuffles in his chair, bothered, unable to be still. The way the light strikes only one side of his face makes him appear sallow, tired. He was very quiet all day. It's the wine that's making him talk now.

He didn't say a single word to me as we arrived in the morning. He greeted Adrian and exchanged pleasantries, even held Bebe's hand and led her to the kitchen when she told him she was hungry. But all the time he pretended I wasn't there, like I was just an empty shape of air blown in through the door.

At times, Bridget and Eve have circled him, each wooing his attention in her own way – Eve clumsily touching him on the arm at every opportunity, Bridget fixing her hair, playing coy. It occurred to me then, watching them, that Louisa may have been telling the truth all along about the door that was open in their marriage.

Somewhere in the house a clock chimes. Louisa stretches out her bored arms, strums Peter on the back.

'I just wonder why we spend so much time talking about America,' she whines. 'Why are people so obsessed with that country?'

'Yeah,' agrees Bridget. 'Shouldn't we care more about what's happening here at home?'

She has a habit of touching her hair as she talks. Her eyes are always somewhere above her. 'I mean, haven't we just had an election ourselves?'

'Oh Lord, the conservative miracle!' Danny scoffs. 'That's no less depressing a subject. I still have trouble believing people voted that government in.'

'That's the problem with this country,' Lawrence says, tasting his wine. 'All the deluded Bolsheviks who can't process the fact they've been abandoned by the proletariat.'

'Who me?' says Danny, looking around. 'A Bolshevik?'

'Yes, you, Danny,' Lawrence replies.

Marin touches her husband on the arm, her bosom pooling over the table. 'It must be the corduroy that gives you away, my love.'

'Well, better a Bolshie than a bigot, I suppose,' sighs Danny.

To which Lawrence says, 'So everyone on the right is a bigot? Now who's profiling?'

'I think most of that lot in Canberra wouldn't be ideologically opposed to bigotry.'

'Quite frankly, I'm sick of hearing that. There is a difference between being bigoted and being patriotic. A tough stance on immigration doesn't equate to racism.'

'Really? Have you ever seen a family of blonds holed up on Christmas Island?'

'What I really object to these days,' says Marin, tapping a finger on the table, 'is all that far-right nonsense about the country being overrun by spies. I don't need to have my intelligence insulted, thank you very much.'

'Wait,' says Lawrence. 'Are they insulting your intelligence, or are they just warning you of an existing reality?'

'The former, I should think.'

'But you have heard about that MP in Western Australia, surely. The one who conveniently forgot to declare his affiliation with several Chinese-linked organisations.'

'Oh, it was silly of him to forget, but does that really say something about where his loyalty lies? He served in the army!'

'Exactly. A Chinese-born captain in the Australian army, and presently a state member of parliament.'

'What are you really trying to say?' asks Danny, suspiciously.

'Simply that it doesn't hurt for us all to be more alert. Because – and I mean no offence whatsoever – some people have a greater propensity for supporting the CCP.'

'I'm not sure what I'm listening to here,' says Danny.

'Chinese people spying for the Chinese government. It's not exactly the stuff of science fiction. It's just a fact we must contend with, unfortunately.'

Danny throws his hands at his face, wipes his eyes with the corners of his palms. He can prolong the argument or change the subject. Perhaps wanting neither, he resigns to being mute.

Peter touches Lawrence on the shoulder, gives him a shake. 'You need to stop, Lawrence. You've had too much to drink.'

'Peter!' cries Lawrence, as if suddenly waking to the presence of his host. 'You didn't think I was talking about *you*, did you? That's not what I meant at all. You've been here all along. You're an Aussie through and through. But what about the ones who just got here on a visa? We can't just go on blindly trusting everyone. Times have changed.'

Lawrence rubs his face so hard we can see flakes of his skin settle over the table. 'I'm not sure if I'm making sense, but I have a point.'

Louisa snorts. 'You're being a dick, Lawrence.'

'No, I'm not.'

'You so are,' Bridget insists. 'You're offending everyone.'

And Eve says, in a conciliatory tone, 'You know, it's such a grey area, isn't it?'

Lawrence blinks repeatedly as if that might help him decide what to do. Then he says, 'Primrose! Were you born here? No? Then help me out. Am I being offensive? Are you offended?'

Everyone is looking at me and all I can do is look at the old paintings on the wall. The torment of Prometheus. The seduction of Leda.

'What!' Still Lawrence protests, looking around. 'I'm simply consulting her since, obviously, more than any of us, she is actually the subject of this discussion. What's wrong with having an open conversation? Why can't we say anything anymore?'

Finally, Peter gets out of his chair and says, 'Lawrence, dinner's over. Go to bed.'

Then the room is in motion. Peter moves away from the table. Bridget starts to clear the plates and Eve stands up to help. Marin yawns, drains the rest of her wine and hands over her glass.

Where is Adrian? His phone was ringing at some point during the conversation. He must have left the room to answer it.

Everyone is trying to avoid looking in my direction. One by one they are shifting away from the table. Helena has gone over to the fireplace and laid herself down on the rug, the top part of her body concealed behind an armchair. Only her legs are visible, black lace-up boots pointing outward, like an expired ballerina.

Realising no help is forthcoming, Lawrence angles his arms to lift himself up, and slinks across the carpet. At the door he rests, retches drily before disappearing into the corridor.

From under the table, Bebe emerges into my lap. It is well past her bedtime and dark shadows hang beneath her eyes. She curls her fingers, demanding my ear.

'What is it, Bebe?'

'Mama, am I Chinese?'

'Go play with Helena.'

The light above us is flickering, just enough at this late hour to trick the eye into believing there is life on the wall. Sirens gliding over the water, half woman, half bird. Nymphs and fauns in the sacred groves, gathered in embrace. These are the paintings collected by the Loys of past generations. The fraction that survived the fire.

It sends a chill through me to think what this room must be like once we have all gone to bed. Ghostly creatures stepping out into the dark.

14

I wake the next morning in the darkness before dawn, to the smell of ashes in the fireplace. I get out of the bed, creep through the door and down the stairs on the tips of my toes. In the front hall, the glass ceiling peers down like the bottom of a boat, giving the sense that the house had sunk into the sea while we slept. There isn't much light, barely a shadow anywhere. Sending my fingers out in front of me, I head down the corridor, an interminable length of it, before reaching the kitchen.

At last, a light switch after much fumbling. I can see last night's dishes piled high in the sink, leftovers scattered over the bench. All I wanted was to get a drink of water, but now my head is swimming, my hands are hot, as I survey the mess and consider the prospect of cleaning it all up.

That familiar pleasure rises from the pit of my stomach. Each breath I extract from this room is filled with the thought of the satisfaction. What would Elaine say if she were here?

The dishwasher cannot accept all of the dishes at once, so the filthiest get a turn, the rest I do by hand. One by one, the dishes drown in the milky detergent, a baptism of sorts, before emerging clean and slippery, anew. Is it possible I have been here in my dreams, doing exactly this? I rinse everything twice and stack the plates on the drying rack in neat rows of eight.

My hands are hurting, but the benchtops can't be left in their current state. I wipe them down a number of times, paying special attention to the red wine stains made by the bottoms of half-drunk bottles. As to the floor, it is filthy enough to need two rolls of wet paper towel just to get rid of the superficial dirt. I do it, gladly, on my knees. And, not finding a brush anywhere, I use my fingernails to scrape away the scum collected in between the tiles.

An hour must have passed to achieve all this, although it still seems very early by the time I'm finished. No one else in the house has got up. The sun has not risen. By the sink I pour myself a glass of water and drink it all in one go. I don't remember ever being so thirsty.

There are ways to get lost in this house which do not exist in most. One turn can lead to another, then another, until you cannot remember what happened five corners ago.

From the kitchen, I somehow come to the end of a corridor with a window that looks onto a wide open space. By now, the sky is as clear as washed glass, and off into the distance, a yellow smear oozes over the end of the land. Anywhere else, this would be a promise of fine weather. In this part of the country, it means nothing.

Unlike the gardens that are visible from other parts of the house, there are no flowers here in neatly laid out beds, nor fruit trees trained by espalier. It's just a field of woolly-tipped fountain grass, and a tiny statue of a girl in arabesque, her dress combed by a seaward breeze.

I sit down on the window sill, contemplating the view and how long I can rest here before someone comes searching for me. Then I hear a creak from behind. I look around. A door has come undone, revealing a slice of warm electric glow. At first, I think someone must have left the light on overnight. But footsteps approach from the other side of the door and a shadow emerges. The door creaks again, widens.

'Oh. Morning,' says Peter.

He must see the white terror draining from my face. 'Don't worry, this house is not haunted.'

The air from the room behind him carries a whiff of old paper and upholstery. Inside, a blanket drapes over a green couch, lit by a lamp beside it.

'Did you spend the night here?'

He doesn't answer, but I think he might be wearing the same shirt from last night. He's still doing up the buttons.

'Would you like to come in?'

'Right now?'

He shrugs. 'Why not? Since you're here, you might as well see the best part of the house.'

He stands aside, lets me into the room, then goes to the window to open the curtains. The room is much larger than the glimpse from the door suggested. There is a bookcase along one wall, with a ladder that can be pushed across it. In the middle of the room is a round table with three clawed feet, the kind that would normally have a vase of flowers on it but is now holding only a bunch of work folders, some open, some shut. There is a desk by the window, with more folders and a laptop on it, and a cockatoo lamp pluming over everything like a dancer, reminiscent of the girl outside.

I wish I'd got changed. It seems inappropriate to stand here with only a cardigan to pull across my nightdress. At least I should've worn shoes so I wouldn't have to stand here on his rug with one set of toes covering the other.

'So,' he says. 'What do you think, Primrose?'

He points behind me, where scrolls of Chinese paintings drape down the wall, each lit from above by its own lamp. They are a series of landscapes, done in a wash of ink and colours, mounted on silk-like paper that has browned with time. They look like the sort of thing that once belonged in an imperial household, ruminated over by men in long gowns and women with bound feet.

'Who painted these?'

Peter takes me closer, his hand pushing into my back. All the paintings contain vertical passages of Chinese calligraphy, finished with the imprint of a red seal.

'Zhang Daqian,' he says. 'They called him the Picasso of the East, the greatest Chinese artist of the last century.'

The night's sleep is still in his voice. He clears it, goes on: 'Believe it or not, he was a brilliant forger too. No one knows how many ancient Chinese masters hanging on museum walls today are actually his counterfeits. I like that about him, the fact that the line between real and replicate is very blurred in his view of art.'

From left to right, as if by logic, the paintings travel from earth to the heavens. Waterlilies pink as newborns, a pair of mandarin ducks swimming by. A scholar reading beneath a peach tree in season. A forest of pines halfway up a mountain. A lone temple at the end of a perilous pass, a pilgrim at its gate. An archipelago of mountaintops, obscured by a sea of blue-green clouds. Then the sky, an entirety of sky in the blue and black of a storm, a wound of light striking through it, the shadows of pines begging from beneath.

'They're beautiful,' I say to him. 'They're a lot more than that.'

'It took me a very long time to collect all of these,' Peter says. 'They were not always in the obvious places. And once I found them, I could only imagine them here in this room, all to myself.'

He crosses his arms, lets his head fall to one side. 'When I was little, I saw these in a book on the shelves at home, and I liked them straight away. I thought that if the people in these paintings could talk to me, they would sound just like my ancestors. Silly, I know.'

'I don't think it's silly at all, Peter. It's not a fantasy but a fact that you came from these people.'

He gets very close to one of the scrolls, scrutinises it as if admiring a new discovery. When he was younger, he'd had the same look of concentration when he came across things that gripped his interest. An old movie in a far-flung language. A new gadget that made some small aspect of life easier. And, once, an old golf club a neighbour had put out on the nature strip, which he took home and rescued, rudimentarily, with steel wool and wax.

'This is the Yellow Mountain,' he explains, pointing at the behemoth that descends in deadly cascades towards the river beneath. 'See the recluse? Standing by the water, beneath the willow.'

He is referring to a figure dressed in a robe and sash, gazing towards the midriff of the mountain and stroking his long beard. What might he be thinking? And why does he not direct his eyes to the summit?

'Solitude is a constant theme in Chinese art. It's symbolic of spirituality and virtue and harmony with nature. My dad was always fascinated by the role of the recluse in these paintings. I think it spoke to him, because he never wanted to be with my mother or with us or anyone who ever had the slightest desire to be with him.'

He seems almost surprised by what he has said, like it was a slip of the tongue. It draws him to a pause and he says nothing more about the paintings. All the light contained in his eyes seems to waver. I don't know what happened between father and son in the years since Peter left to go to America. But Robert now lives in the past tense, that much is clear.

Eventually Peter says, as if this has been the heart of the matter all along, 'Primrose, about last night. I'm sorry about the conversation at dinner. Lawrence is an idiot when he's drunk. I'll talk to him today, now that he's sober enough to listen.'

'I didn't mind. I didn't know why everyone at the table assumed I should've had a reaction.'

'Because it was rude and inappropriate. Unfortunately

certain people's politics still require everyone to be swept into discrete racial definitions. It was ignorance compounded by intoxication. I don't want you to take it personally.'

'It might sound odd but I don't even know how to pin down the offence he has committed. I'm sure he is wrong but I can also see how other people could think it is perfectly okay. To be honest it only puzzles me. None of it actually bothers me that much.'

'Really? It certainly bothered me. Surely you and I are not that different. Are you really not affected? Not even in principle?'

'I think people have a right to speak their thoughts. Without freedom of thought, you have no democracy, right? Isn't that the contract?'

'But you are allowed to react to what other people think and say. You can tell people what *you* think. That is also part of the freedom.'

'I don't do that anymore.'

'Do what? Give an opinion?'

'React to people. I think it's only at the moment you react that you give them a way to become dangerous, because then they become part of the conversation. The more things are talked about, the more they become legitimate. Everything can be talked into becoming logic.'

Peter frowns. Something in what I said troubles him. He seems unable to decide what to do with his hands.

'Primrose, this isn't high school anymore, where the best students stay quiet and listen to the teacher. It's real life.'

'I know how real it is.'

He exhales. 'You haven't changed. Still guarding all your thoughts, not letting anyone near them. What are you saving them for?'

'Peter, stop talking like you get me.'

'I'm just saying that I know you care about this.'

'I care about it enough to ignore it, so that the rot can only fester where it is, that it's not given the room to spread.'

'But it spreads *because* you choose to ignore it. People like Lawrence need to be taught that there is a difference between a political ideology and a race of people, that their objections against one cannot be allowed to contaminate their view of the other. They've got to be told in plain language that an entire ethnic group cannot be put in front of the firing squad because of tension between two countries.'

'That's all very sound in theory but when has that ever dictated the terms in reality? People have been generalised into friend or enemy based on ethnicity in every conflict in the world. Prejudice begins with it. Strip away everything and you are still left with this fundamental core that cannot be eradicated. It can only be contained, to some extent, if you're lucky.'

'Is that what you really think?'

'I do. People will always look at me and question whether I'm as Australian as my passport says.'

'I don't think that's true,' Peter says, considering. 'I don't believe people would look at me that way. I *am* the same as everyone else in this country. I'm pretty convinced.'

'Of course you are.'

'What is that supposed to mean?'

'You've always insisted on being the same as everyone else.

I mean, this house, those European masters hanging in the dining room. You're dressed head to toe in someone else's culture. You've bought your way out of being who you are.'

'That's not what I'm doing.' He takes me by the arm, pulls me towards him. 'I know exactly who I'm supposed to be, Primrose.'

'Are you sure?'

He tries to compose himself, but cannot conceal his indignation. 'I'm always sure. Now you have to take back what you said.'

'Take it back? *Take it back?* Now who's in high school?'

'I'm not joking, Primrose. Take it back.'

'I will not do that.'

There's blood in his eyes, an anger I haven't encountered before. We have backed ourselves against the wall. The tremor of his hand is the only thing cutting through the impasse between us.

Moments go by in silence. He is still holding on to me, but his gaze is slipping away, as if, with each second, he is growing more embarrassed of his own insistence. It fills me with the sour taste of regret to think how my words might have hurt him.

Then he drops my arm, and watches in amazement as the tears slip down my face.

'Don't cry, Primrose. Why are you crying?'

'I don't know,' I say, trying hopelessly to clear the tears from my cheeks. 'It's so last century to cry.'

Then he touches the fabric of my dress, my collarbone, my skin. He brings my mouth close to his, too close, and all the details of his face is lost in a blur. I am shaking uncontrollably, my body a trembling mess against his. He kisses me, steady and determined on the lips, taking in the salty taste. The years, I think to myself. They haven't changed him.

In a moment, we will have to let go of each other and pretend none of this has happened. But for now, there is only safety, warmth, in this corner of the house where the lost end up. I let him take my hand, kiss it, hold it up to his face. He looks at it, intently, surprised. It's still red and raw from the work in the kitchen. He asks, 'What have you been doing to yourself?'

Quickly I draw him back to me, put his lips to mine so that I can drink in the closeness of him before it is gone. He lifts up my dress and touches me in the triangle of my legs. His fingertips are cold, every small movement vivid. Through quickened breaths he grows hard against me, and I have to bite down on his shirt to keep myself quiet as he pulls away my underwear and puts himself inside me.

The hurried rhythm of him takes over; I am no longer trembling.

I was wrong – the years *have* changed him, changed *us*: everything more urgent, more exquisite somehow, than before. Maybe it's because we know now that nothing can last; we know this because nothing did.

I tighten myself around him, trying to hold on as he drives me against the wall.

The light through the window is playing tricks on me, flickering as it beckons me to open my eyes to it. The morning outside – when did it ripen into such a blinding shade of coral?

Elsewhere in the house people seem to be stirring. Small voices. The clanging of utensils. Am I imagining the footsteps coming down the corridor? Could it be Adrian? Could it be Louisa? All of a sudden it seems so brutally real again that we are not alone.

'Peter?' I don't know what it is I'm asking.

Breathlessly, he searches for my mouth. He must think I can give him air. 'Don't, Primrose. Not yet.'

A panic grips me. Even as I lay my lips on his skin, it is Louisa's voice that runs through my head. I can't stop thinking about all those stories of hers, about the other people entangled in their marriage, even about Eve's and Bridget's flirting yesterday. Is there any truth in what she says, or is everything a figment of her imagination? She could be lying; equally she could be telling the truth. And if it were all true, then who am I and what is my role in all of this? What are we doing together? What am *I* doing?

I cannot extricate myself from this train of thought.

Peter slows himself. 'Do you want to stop, Primrose?'

His face is burning against mine. We are still tenuously linked, afraid of the smallest movement. The smell of him is the same as always, of summer in the night-time.

'I don't think I can do this,' I say to him, finally.

He lets out a sigh, and moves away. He says, 'Sometimes I wish you would take back everything that happened.'

15

Temperamental June weather is the reason nothing has been planned for the day. Everyone is left to decide for themselves, Louisa declares. As long as they are back in time for the party tonight.

The men depart first, leaving for a local winery owned by one of Greg's friends. Louisa, too, wastes no time in herding Bridget and Eve into the car with lists of last-minute errands she cannot run all by herself. As they leave, they discuss the scent of the candles they will buy, and whether they need new earrings to go with their dinner outfits. From the driver's seat Louisa blows me an apologetic kiss, as if to say I could've come if I didn't have Bebe in tow.

Marin suggests a walk to the blowhole at Elephant Rock, where there are plenty of snails and starfish in the rockpools for the children to explore. A set of steps by the edge of the property will lead us down to the bottom of the cliff, she points out. From there – since the tide has gone out – we can simply scrabble our way over the rocks to our destination.

So we are the last to set off, with Helena darting out ahead, her skinny legs ruddering over the gravel towards the olive grove. She's wearing the same black boots as yesterday, and black stockings with ladders in them.

Bebe tries hard to keep up. 'Wait, Helena! It's not fair. You got a head start!'

We walk through the olive grove towards the steps. The trees are convenient for Marin, who must hold on to them to stop herself from rolling over. Again, she is dressed in a kaftan designed to shroud her robust figure. But with the breeze coming at her, you can still see the largeness of her breasts, the quivering sack of her belly.

'Mama!' Bebe shouts from ahead. Her face is lost among the trees. 'The house gets smaller every time I turn around.'

'Of course, sweetheart. We are moving further away from it.'

'No, silly! The house is moving further away from *us*.'

By the edge of the olive grove, the cliff awaits. The steps that Marin mentioned are no more than crude platforms hewn into the bluff, each one an ambitious drop from the one above. They have not been made with any consideration for safety, but if someone is determined to get down from here, this is the only way.

'Should we really do this?' I ask Marin, concerned.

'Don't worry. I've done this before. It has been tried and tested.'

She offers to lead, and surprises with her agility.

'I do this every time I visit. It's simply the best thing about being here.'

Helena follows, then Bebe. I keep watch at the back.

For every step, we must get on our bottoms, slide our bodies down to the next level, dust our hands off and go again. This set of actions we repeat for what seems like an eternity. The whole thing feels like a leap of faith, though leaping, you warn yourself, is the last thing you should do.

By the time we arrive at the rocks below, Marin is a woman reborn.

'I just love it here,' she shouts over the waves.

The wind is fierce. She drags the salty air into her lungs, opens her arms out to the strait. Perhaps she imagines herself a high priestess upon the black, scarred basalt.

'Imagine being out here for a millennium, pummelled by the surf. Don't you feel jealous of these rocks?'

Helena rolls her eyes, grunts. 'Mum, that's so cringe.'

'But why, poppet? Why should we assume we've drawn the long straw just because we're humans?'

In the distance, Elephant Rock is just a dark outline against the sun that is not done rising. It looks exactly like an elephant, its body half submerged in the water as if taking its bath. In high spirit we begin to trek towards it, clambering over rocks, the crunch of crustaceans beneath our feet.

But the animal that seems so near we can get to it in minutes turns out to be too cunning for our patience. Funny how we never fail to fall for nature's chicanery. Half an hour later, and halfway there, the kids call a stop to our progress.

'What's wrong, Bebe?' Marin asks.

'It's too far. My foot hurts.'

Helena says, 'What's the point of getting there anyway?' She's squatting over a rock like a marine bird. 'Can't we just, like, look at it from here?'

'Determination, poppet!' cries Marin. 'Commitment! Fortitude! How else are you going to learn the meaning of these words?'

'Maybe we can stop for a rest,' I mediate. 'Then we can see if we'd like to keep going.'

Forlorn, Marin looks away at the elephant. 'Alright, I guess I am outvoted.'

The sand inspires the girls to a snowball fight of sorts. Giddily, they hurl it at each other, colouring the air between them in a beige smog. It goes on and on until Helena screams at the wrong moment and ends up with too much sand in her mouth. Her face convulses, she sticks out her tongue and hurls her body at the ground as if violently ill. Bebe laughs, falls backwards, kicks up her feet.

'I've been poisoned!' cries Helena.

'No, you haven't. You're just pretending.'

'What do you mean? I'm actually dying.' The girl gets up, hobbles away on the sides of her feet. 'Sayonara.'

'But Helena,' Bebe calls after her. 'Where are you going?'

'Over there.' Helena points out towards nowhere. 'I need to look for an antidote.'

'Can I come? Please?'

'Hmm, okay, but hurry up or it will be too late for me.'

We watch them link hands and march out over the rocky ledge towards the white, flowering waves. Even together, they seem so helpless against the uninterrupted ocean.

'Don't get lost!' Marin calls out.

Helena turns, gestures at the wide open space around her. They'd have to walk a long way in any direction to be out of our sight.

'Come on, open your eyes, Mum,' she shouts, walking on.

Marin adjusts herself on the rock as if she is trying to get comfortable on a saddle. 'Serenity,' she says to me. 'It was good for us to split up for the morning. There's only so much of Louisa I can take.'

'I thought you guys were good friends.'

'Oh, we are. But it's mostly just because she buys my art.'

This bluntness is unexpected, even from Marin. I say to her, 'I think most people would find Louisa quite captivating.'

'I'm an artist. It takes a lot for me to find someone captivating.'

She has an air about her, of judgment and constant evaluation.

'Sure, Louisa's tonnes of fun and throws lovely parties, but I'm opinionated about people who have big social lives. That tends to come about only through orchestration. It can reveal a person as contrived and insincere. Do you agree?'

'Well, she does throw lovely parties.'

'No, Primrose, what do you really think?'

'What can I say? She lives across the street. They happen to be people who live across the street, that's all.'

Marin is unimpressed, and she isn't ready to let go of the topic. 'If you ask me, it can be quite uncomfortable to be around the two of them. It makes no sense that they are together. A lot of empty space between them, if you know what I mean. It's like they are living on separate islands and they're managing their marriage via remote control. Don't you think?'

'It might just be that they are unconventional people, that they don't live by the same rules.'

'I don't understand.'

'Well, some people have alternatively exhilarating lives that others may not be able to understand.'

'What do you mean *alternatively exhilarating*?'

Marin seems offended by my use of the words. She seems to think that only she could deserve such a colourful description.

'I just mean . . .' I try to explain, mumbling. 'All I'm saying is that, I was given the impression they have a kind of open arrangement with each other.'

'*Open arrangement?*'

'Why is that so implausible?' I ask. And is it really possible that Marin is hearing of this for the first time?

She looks at me like I've just failed a test in simple arithmetic. She's trying to suppress a laugh.

'Don't kid yourself, Primrose. I've known Louisa and Peter a long time and I've never heard of any such thing.'

After a moment of contemplation, she adds, 'Louisa is someone who will always want to have possession. Beyond that, I'm not certain what she cares about. And as for Peter – who knows what the man wants. Not this, it would seem.'

She waits for a flock of gulls to pass overhead, then – 'Sometimes mistakes are made. People lose their way and they marry wrongly. Believe me, those two are just regular people with a regular set of marital problems.'

She bends down and picks up a seashell from the ground, rolls it around in her palm. It is the size and shape of a rosebud, intensely red.

'See this? This I find captivating.'

As she considers the shell, she strains her face as if creating a mental sketch of how it might feature in her next work of art. Then she stores it away in the folds of her kaftan. When she looks at me again, she is clean and ready to move on.

'What about you, Primrose? How is your husband?'

'How do you mean?'

'Louisa told me he had cancer.'

There is an abruptness in this, or perhaps it is in her choice of words. Most people talk around the cancer. They might use words like *sick* or *ill* or *unwell*, but never the word that goes to the root of the issue. But Marin has said it casually, like she's used to saying it all the time.

'He's better, for now,' I tell her. 'It's one of those unpredictable things – you're fine and you're fine until maybe one day you're not. Please don't mention anything around Bebe. She doesn't know about it.'

'Fine. Of course.' She nods and then, in return, offers: 'I had a stroke a few years ago.'

Why do people think that two tragedies can neutralise each other?

'Now there is a fifteen per cent chance of my having another one,' she continues. 'If it happens again, I don't think it will be as kind as the last one.'

'Doctors have a probability for everything. Adrian has been given one too.'

Marin pulls her legs into a lotus position, in so far as her body will allow it.

'Most people I talk to think it's rather academic. They think:

fifteen per cent, that's so slim a chance it's negligible. But look at it another way: what would they do if they knew there was a fifteen per cent chance of being killed by a car today? They would stay home, wouldn't they? They would bunker down until the day was over. So how can it be negligible to know that the same probability applies not just for one day but for the rest of your life?'

Her kaftan billows; she tucks it between her legs and goes on. 'I always wonder how people feel after surviving a disaster. Not just an illness but a plane crash or an earthquake, anything along those lines. What I mean is, do these people see it as a lucky escape or, alternatively, do they see it as an omen that sooner or later will come true?'

'I think it depends on the person and their beliefs. It's up to the individual how they interpret it.'

'You're right. It's up to the individual.'

Marin closes her eyes and all I can see is the red eyeshadow she has put on to match the colour of her hair. I can't quite imagine a blood clot in that spacious head of hers.

Turning towards Elephant Rock, she inhales. 'Everyone should be made to be out here once a day. Just to feel how insignificant they are in the scheme of things.' Her belly wriggles before the sound of her laughter travels. 'Try to throw any bullshit you've got out there, it'll just throw it right back in your face. As an artist, I can never create anything of value unless I recognise the scale of the world around me. It's essential for each person to appreciate how they fit within the order of things, how small their troubles are within the grand design.'

'But human nature is faulty. I think most people have a tendency to look inward rather than out.'

'They've got to resist that. We all do.'

We can see the girls in the distance, bent over a rockpool, fishing with their arms. Helena finds a crab, which she dangles by one leg next to Bebe's face, letting it swing like a pretty earring.

The sun is right above us now, though we find ourselves in shadow. The shadow is cast by a tree that has cantilevered out of the cliff like a diving board. It should not be able to survive in such a manner, but it does; it thrives.

Marin reaches up towards the sky, expels a breath and looks back at me as if she has absolved me from some pre-existing ignorance. I am reminded of her statue – the crown-wearing egg – beaming its hot pink glory at the world.

'I'm very intuitive, Primrose,' she states in a tone of uncompromised certainty. 'I have an ability for presage, some people might say. It's the basis of my work. I can look at a person or an object I've never seen before and understand them in their entirety. Would you like to try?'

I want to laugh. 'That's very kind, Marin, but I'm already seeing someone for that.'

'I'm not talking about something you can get from a psychologist's couch. I'm talking about an image of you. How I would see you as a work of art.'

'Like a painting?'

'No, I never paint. I sculpt. It's the realest form of interpretation.'

Again, the egg statue comes to mind like a glaring vision

of an anti-god, summoned into existence by the blood clot in Marin's head.

'I see you on a ship,' she says, conjuring. 'You have something around your neck. A rope, but not just a rope. A bird on the end of it. Yes, a dead bird.'

'Marin, that's incredibly macabre.'

'Not macabre. Intriguing. My art always comes from intrigue.'

'I don't want to be your art. I'm sorry.'

Now Marin's the one who laughs. 'Primrose, you are missing the point.'

The wind throws sand at us; the sun has gone behind a cloud. Where are the girls?

We hear a thundering wave and turn to find the water frothing over the rocks where a minute ago it was dry and unthreatened.

The girls. They were standing right there. Now we can't see them at all.

We get up onto our feet, but that unspeakable fear that afflicts all mothers stops us. Images of disaster flash before me. Helena thought it impossible to be lost out here. So where can they be?

The wave retreats, a white sheet being dragged reluctantly back out to sea. But still no sign of the girls.

'Bebe!' I call out.

'They must be hiding,' Marin says. She's now running out after the wave.

'Bebe! Please!'

'Look, there they are, behind those rocks! For God's sake, come out of there!'

They emerge from where Marin is pointing, from behind a rock the size of a tombstone. They must have been huddling behind it as the wave came in, clinging to each other, wet as lambs caught in a spring rain.

'Mama!' Bebe calls, waving her arms. She is running towards me and I am running towards her. 'Did you see? We almost died!'

It shocks me to find that she is not at all upset. There is only a look of boastfulness in her eyes, satisfaction at an adventure completed.

'Don't ever say that again, do you hear me?'

She seems confused. She has no idea what wrong she has committed.

'Listen to me.' I take her face into my hands, hold tightly to her gaze so that no matter how hard she tries she cannot look away. 'Dying is not a joke. We are going back to the house.'

16

In the evening, we gather in the dining room, the men in tuxedos, the women in dresses that reach the floor. A jazz song, full of saxophone and double bass, is playing from somewhere in the ceiling. Rose-scented candles have been scattered all around the room. Now and then, someone is reminded to step away so they are not set on fire.

Floral displays tower over the dining table: clouds of daphnes and polyanthus and dahlias underscored by fern fronds and eucalyptus leaves and, more intriguingly, the arthritic branches of dormant fruit trees. The table does not need these embellishments, being already laden with candlesticks and crystal glasses, and ornate tureens in which the bread rolls are ceremoniously exhibited.

'It's a bit over the top, am I wrong?' a woman I don't know says to another. When I walked into the room, her densely sequined body was the first thing I saw.

'You're not wrong,' says her friend. 'Dahlias are not even in season, this time of year.'

'It has Louisa written all over it.'

The friend agrees, and proceeds to take a video of the table settings.

The women are among the dinner guests who arrived in the afternoon, business-looking people from Peter's side and a trendier set from Louisa's circle. The business people immediately went around the house looking for the room with the strongest mobile reception, while the others enquired about the supply of beverages and argued among themselves as to who would be doing the driving at the end of the night.

Now everyone is descending on the two waiters in white jackets who have silver trays balanced on their fingertips –

'Are there more of those mini caviar things?'

'Is this the gluten-free version of the wasabi shrimp?'

'Is there trout in the salmon mousse? I taste trout.'

'Sir, please don't smoke that in here.'

Adrian finds me through the crowd. He is dressed in a black suit and a white shirt, which could have gone well with a tie if he wasn't so averse to formalwear. He hands me a drink.

'You look amazing,' he says. 'Refreshed.'

'Thank you. I'm sorry I fell asleep.'

In the bedroom earlier he came up to me as I stood in front of the mirror and unzipped the dress I had just put on for dinner. I turned around to look at him, and all I could see was his hair falling over his temple.

'I feel I've been a terrible person,' he said to me.

'What makes you say that?'

'I've been detached, to say the least.'

'Have you?'

'I want you to know that I'm trying very hard to get my shit together.'

'Adrian, you've been nothing but perfect.'

The lie felt as real as the truth.

I thought about the wave which had threatened to take Bebe in the morning, the absence of her over those primitive black rocks. I wanted to tell him about it, but telling him would do nothing but multiply the terror, so instead I kissed him on the cheek and he kissed me back on the mouth. Then he started to undress me completely. We lay down on the bed, him on top of me. He pressed his hand into my skin as if he were trying to mould something out of my flesh.

'Adrian, do you mind if we don't do this right now?'

He was perplexed, and waited for me to change my mind. He had lines on his face I'd never seen before, a two-stroke frown cut deeply into his brow. Eventually, I closed my eyes and fell away into a shallow sleep. When I woke up, the room was dark and I was alone.

Now, in the dining room, he says to me, 'You haven't missed much. Only vacuous social discourse.'

A bell rings; we are asked to find our seats. At the table, people have begun to move the little white place cards around –

'I hate to sit with my back towards the door.'

'Move her away from the flower arrangement, she's allergic.'

'We'll just squeeze in next to Louisa, if that's alright.'

On account of all the shuffling, we end up in the middle of the table; directly beneath us, Bebe and Helena have set up camp to avoid interacting with the adults. We can hear Bebe's singing as Helena calls her to attention.

'Peter seems a little withdrawn,' Adrian remarks as we watch him come to the table and sit down among people who are eager to talk to him. 'He was like that all day, when we were out together. Do you think he is unhappy about something?'

Adrian's arm is resting on the back of my chair, but I feel as though it is strangling me by the neck.

'I don't know, Adrian. I would be the wrong person to ask.'

'But honestly, it's not just him. It's everyone here. They're all behaving so tediously. If they're not talking about stock prices they're "commenting" on each other's hypoallergenic puppies. I mean, aren't dogs even allowed to shed a single hair anymore? I'm glad we go home tomorrow.'

Then something occurs to him. He takes out his phone and opens up an email to show me.

'By the way, good news. Terence has had a change in his schedule. He'll be coming early.'

By chance or design, Eve sits down next to me and, next to her, Lawrence.

'How are you enjoying this weekend?' Lawrence asks, overly civil.

'It's been lovely, thank you.'

'Oh that's wonderful.'

It is the first time he has said anything to me all day. He has a smile larger than his face can comfortably accommodate.

'It was such a pity you could not join us at the winery.'

'Yes, pity.'

'They had some magnificent vintages I hadn't come across before.'

His lips are very dry, and the driest parts are stained by red wine. The evening being young, Eve has decided to move his glass away while he's not watching. She fills a clean glass with water and settles it in front of him.

Around the room, champagne flutes sing as Louisa gets up to make her toast. Everyone hushes, transfixed by the bold splashes of graffiti across her silk gown. She plays with her earring, promises not to sing like Marilyn Monroe. People laugh, glasses are raised. She and Peter are at opposite ends of the table. She walks towards him, and he meets her halfway, kisses her until she bends. A round of claps and whistles. The formalities are done.

The food that comes to the table is like the food of hotels, served on gold-rimmed plates and with sauces that pretend to be art. Everything tastes like butter and salt, gravy and thyme, drowned in the smell of candle wax. Casually, Adrian touches me under the table, like it's just a form of communication. I have to keep drinking to distract myself. Maybe, in a moment, his phone will ring and he will cease to touch me. I wish it were ringing now.

'Primrose,' says Eve, attempting chitchat. 'Bridget and I are very intrigued by you. Do you want to know why?'

'I can't imagine the reason.'

'Oh, you're so modest.'

She giggles like a teenager. I have never seen a botoxed lip up close until now. It is wonderfully seductive, pearlescent, like a well-fed caterpillar.

'We wanted to know why you are so adored by Louisa,' she says. 'She usually judges everyone, but not you.'

'If you find out why, I'd love to know too,' I say.

She giggles again, in a way that suggests she does not believe she will ever find out. Lawrence puts his arm around Eve's shoulder, leans into the conversation.

'Actually, your name is very familiar,' he says. I noticed earlier that he was squinting at my place card. 'Li. Primrose Li. Why is that?'

'I can't say I know why.'

'I'm usually very good with names.'

'He is,' agrees Eve, dusting Lawrence's lapel and giving him a peck. He is shorter than her at standing height, but sitting down he is suddenly her proportional equal.

'You must have me confused with someone else,' I say to Lawrence.

'No, I don't feel that's the case,' he replies. 'Let's see. Have you ever worked in the law? Maybe we've crossed paths professionally.'

I shake my head.

'Still, I think I must've seen your name in a very specific context. Have you worked in human resources? Corporate affairs? Some type of media job, perhaps?'

'Many years ago,' I answer reluctantly.

He closes his eyes, then opens them again. 'Of course, now I remember reading you! Didn't you used to write a column in *Criterion*? Wow, that's amazing.'

He studies me in mild disbelief. What exactly is amazing to him? I guess it must be the disparity between the woman in name and the woman in person.

'For some reason, I can't picture you,' he says, backing away to get a better view. 'You've been so quiet all weekend.'

Eve adds, 'You've said nothing at all to give that away. Here we were, thinking you were the silent, stay-at-home type. Of course, I don't mean that in a bad way. Aren't we all stay-at-home types!'

'I'm not offended,' I say to her.

'Well, that's wonderful, Primrose. It must've been fascinating work. I was watching a movie the other day. What was it called, honey? It was about a bunch of reporters who were investigating this murder of a girl and ended up exposing a whole series of murders done by the same psychopath.'

'No, honey,' Lawrence stops her. 'She wrote about the corporate sector. Different kettle of fish.'

'Oh,' says Eve, a little disappointed.

'Your columns were quite strong, I seem to remember,' says Lawrence, turning again to me. 'The entire publication took a very hard line against Big Business, didn't it? Some of your ideas . . . I mean, they bordered on utopian. Did you guys really think that social conscience should be legally enforceable and written into the Corporations Act?'

'It was a long time ago, Lawrence.'

'But for a time, corporates were quite worried about people like you. How the hell were they going to factor the good of society into their profit-making decisions? They thought it was nuts. Surely you remember.'

'I remember that they needn't have worried. No one could've ever messed with the business lobby.'

'Still, you had a few politicians singing your tune.'

'A few, but never enough.'

'Is that why you don't write anymore?' he asks. 'I'm sorry, is that too personal a question?'

'There were a lot of reasons. But, cutting to the chase, it was a little tiring to have a view about everything, take a position for or against. It took its toll, I guess.'

'Nevertheless, Primrose,' says Eve. She is rubbing me on the arm, talking to me as if she knew me long ago. 'You were very impressive.'

Very late in the evening, a plan is hatched to visit Lost Cove the next day, before everyone heads home. Lost Cove is the golf club that Peter and Louisa belong to, a short drive down the coast from here. Everyone knows it by the lighthouse at the end of the course, a historic landmark that the club members adoringly refer to as the Final Pin. Greg, who is also a member there, is the one who suggests the idea of going. To that, Louisa says, 'How fun, let's all go.'

By now, most of the other guests have left, veering out into the night like space rovers over a dark moon. Only a handful of stragglers remain, either spread out semi-conciously over the sofas in the sitting room or smoking outside in the cold.

Bridget and Eve suggest that, while the boys play a round, the girls have lunch in the clubhouse. Marin snorts, counts herself out. She can stay behind with the children, she offers. Danny links arm with her in solidarity. Lost Cove, he says, is not exactly their milieu.

Adrian is not so sure either.

'Come on,' Greg says to him. 'I'm allowed to bring one guest. What's troubling you?'

'I didn't bring my clubs.' He doesn't have any.

'They will have some you can borrow,' assures Lawrence.

'I would only slow you guys down.'

He detests golf, but for some reason is not prepared to say.

'Nobody ever says no to a round at Lost Cove,' Greg insists. 'You're coming.'

In this way a foursome is formed. Greg and Peter, Lawrence and Adrian.

All the time Peter says nothing. It is possible that having spent the night mired in frivolous conversation, he has forgotten to keep track of how much he has drunk. He raises an empty bottle. One of the guys in white jackets approaches quickly and replaces it with another.

Bridget tells everyone that Greg is planning to join the PGA Seniors Tour, just as soon as he turns fifty in a few years' time. She does this while playing with the watch on his wrist. He has been training hard and has been on the course almost every day, she laments. He hardly has time for his children, aged five and eight, which has left her drained – a single parent, for all practical purposes.

Greg denies he has been neglectful. She pulls her hand away from him, and between them a hushed argument ensues. Strangely, the argument is not over the golf but why their children had not been brought along for the weekend. There is some mention of a nanny, of a mother's need for reprieve, and of an untimely ear infection, the cause of which cannot be determined. It ends with Bridget doing what she habitually does, combing her long hair back through her painted fingers. Greg coughs under his breath. The matter is put on hold.

Louisa brings up a new subject: Lost Cove has been through a redevelopment. She says the clubhouse has gone completely 'green'. But exactly how this compensates for the environmental impact of maintaining a thirty-six-hole course, she does not know.

Lawrence rolls his eyes. He doesn't want to upset people with what he thinks about climate change. We better talk about something else, he warns, before he gets himself into trouble.

The subject shifts quickly but lingers on golf. Greg and Lawrence have booked tickets for the President's Cup in December. The International Team is in a strong position to take the Cup from the Americans, they think. And how fitting it would be for that to happen again at Royal Melbourne. How long ago was the last time? Lawrence wonders. Greg thinks it must've been in the nineties.

On account of my golf bag, I know the answer to be 1998. But it hardly seems to matter whether I make this clarification, so I stay quiet.

All the sandbelt courses are magnificent in their way, according to Greg, but Royal Melbourne has something truly special. He has only played there once, by invitation from a friend, having himself been unsuccessful in obtaining a membership. He thinks it is the greens which set the course apart from the rest. Only the most accomplished golfers can truly overcome them. It has to do with the way the sand granules interlock, and the particular height to which the grass is cut that produces the quickness of the surface. So firm are the greens that you could probably play basketball on them if you wanted to.

Louisa clicks her tongue at me, grins. 'Hey, Primrose, tell us what the greens are like at Whistles.'

Adrian is surprised. 'You've been playing golf?'

Lawrence chuckles to himself. 'Whistles. That's a public course, isn't it?'

A wink from Louisa indicates that it is all just harmless fun. No one seems to be expecting me to say anything. And why should they, given the precedent I set for myself last night?

Maybe it is the light, the dimness of it now that the candles are flickering on their last reserve, but everyone's faces are swimming, distorted by their own shadows.

'Louisa,' I say. 'Have you ever knelt down on a green and placed your palms on the grass?'

'What?' She screws up her face. 'No, I don't believe I have. Why would I do that?'

'Well, I have, at Whistles. Sometimes I put my hand on that grass and I think I could go right through it, right down into the soil, into the earth beneath.'

'Primrose, what does that have to do with anything?'

'You asked me a question and I'm trying to answer it.'

Bridget giggles, then Eve.

'That sounds really insane, Primrose,' says Louisa. 'I warned you about Whistles, didn't I. Don't say I didn't.'

'All I'm trying to say is that the green at Whistles is not hard and compacted, furiously fast the way people seem to like it. You definitely *cannot* play basketball on it. The Whistles green always feels like it has been rained on overnight and the water stayed too long, the soil grown too fat. It's no more than the swamp it was always meant to be. It doesn't pretend to be anything else, and nobody who goes there pretends it is either.'

Everyone is looking at their glasses now, turning them by the stem in deliberate, small rotations. Louisa frowns as if she is not quite sure what just took place. An uncomfortable silence is left to take over the room.

By now it must be very late, so late that the morning will soon be upon us. I think everyone is waiting for someone else to get up and declare the party over.

Then Peter leans forward on his elbows and says to me, 'I heard that it's being closed down.'

Maybe he remembers the day we were there together. Younger versions of ourselves.

'Yes,' I tell him. 'It's closing.'

It's almost dawn when I go to sleep, dreaming of my familiar wheat field, the harvester that harvests me, the dance of my dying little body. But that is only at first, because after a while everything changes. Suddenly nothing hurts anymore; it feels like comfort, like rest. I ask myself why, look through the teeth of the thresher for the reason.

Outside, things are different. It is no longer a vast field of wheat in which I am the stranger. Instead it is Whistles, and the sun is rising joyfully over the trees. There are golfers by the canal, a woman who might be Harriet. No one has their clubs; everyone is holding spades and pitchforks, bent over the land provided free for their use. And even Elaine is there, somehow peering out from the ether, astounded by all the things I never said but she at last sees for herself.

Then the woman who is now more clearly Harriet puts down her tool, drops to her knees and starts to dig. She calls out to the rest, holds up in her hands a small white-feathered chick so pure it is like fresh snow on a winter's branch.

For a moment, the length of which I cannot measure, I feel a life transformed; only light and grace surround me. But then I wake, and the first humanly thought that occurs to me is the same as always. I turn myself around, wonder if Adrian has made it through the night.

17

Louisa is wearing sunglasses as she sips the green vegetable juice she has ordered for lunch. No one has seen her eyes all morning. She says that, after the last two days, her face is taking the day off.

We are sitting in the main restaurant of the Lost Cove Country Club, next to a plate-glass window that overlooks the length of the eighteenth hole. The eighteenth begins lower than it ends. Golfers trudge uphill towards us, four at a time, in what looks like poorly rehearsed military moves. For people in the restaurant who cannot judge distance in golf yardage, it must feel like being forever in the firing line as one ball after another is lobbed at the green.

The restaurant is filled with men in sports jackets, women in knee-length dresses. When we first arrived, the manager politely pointed out to Eve that she was wearing a tube top. This was a non-tube-top type of place, he explained, even if it was a fetching one by Gucci, with expensive jewellery to match. Then he offered her a club jacket. It was a squarish men's jacket, with brassy buttons and a crest on the pocket. Eve pouted at it, her lips looking like a squashed apricot. But she did not have the option to decline.

In the middle of the restaurant, a silver anniversary lunch has been unfolding over a long table. With the toast made, a cake in the shape of an open seashell is being sliced into sugar-conscious slivers and distributed on tiny little saucers.

'Talk about death by a thousand cuts,' Eve says. She's still annoyed about the jacket.

'It looks delicious,' says Bridget, ogling. 'I think it's hazelnut praline.'

'Yuck. Hazelnut.'

'Look, there's even a pearl in the middle. How beautiful. I saw one just like that at Pierre's.'

I can't bear to hear Bridget talk about that cake. All morning I've had a splitting migraine, and now each one of her words seems to be plucking at the pain like a small pulse of electricity.

When we drove away from Homer earlier, I turned around to look at Bebe through the back window. She was standing in the driveway holding Marin's hand. The way their figures bobbed up and down as the car travelled over the gravel made me want to faint.

Was I alright? Adrian asked. He was driving but placed one arm across me so I wouldn't topple over. I told him I was fine. He said I could be coming down with something, to which I replied that everyone was likely to be worse for wear once this weekend was over.

This seemed to put Adrian in a bad mood.

I asked him what was the matter.

He said to forget about it, it was not a big deal. He was

driving very fast to keep up with Lawrence's car in front of us, but he was talking very slowly.

I knew he was not looking forward to the golf, which he felt he'd been pressured into. He'd never cared much for the game, especially when it came to all the etiquette and rules about what you couldn't wear and how you mustn't behave. Still, I got the feeling it was a roundabout way of raising a grievance with me, because I'd been going to Whistles all this time and hadn't said a word to him about it. Did this qualify as a secret of the kind that one spouse should not keep from another? To him, it must.

Then he said abruptly, 'Bloody hell. What is he doing?'

He was referring to Lawrence, who was driving one of those big show-off Range Rovers in front of us; the car looked like a rhinoceros on steroids. Lawrence must have been trying to make a point about his engine, which was a certain number of cylinders. He had pointed this out to everybody before we set off. Each time the road swerved, the car flew out over the road markings like it was in a police chase.

'That man is nuts,' said Adrian. He slowed down and let Lawrence disappear into the blue country beyond.

Now Louisa waves a hand in front of me. Her rings sparkle.

'Primrose, are you with us?'

'Yes, sorry. I have a headache.'

'You should get one of these.'

I wish she would stop stirring the green juice with her straw. To the waiter earlier, she referred to it as 'her usual detox' and he knew straight away what she meant.

'It's called the Triple C,' Louisa explains to me. 'A Cucumber Can-Can. Do you want to try some?'

'Please don't say *can-can* to me right now.'

'Well, suit yourself.'

Louisa is wearing a dress with two different sizes of polka dots. It looks pretty on her, but the sight of those dots is starting to test my sense of balance. They make her seem both near and far at the same time.

You can tell the four men at the next table have been looking at her, even as they carried on a conversation about the quality of the golf being exhibited on the eighteenth, the techniques and strategies of each golfer as he came up to the green. They seem to know the names of all the golfers and to be able to provide assessments on whether they've improved since the last time they played.

Louisa says, 'Guess what's the thing that Cove members hold dearest to their hearts?'

She is not really interested in having us guess, and immediately throws out a string of clues for what isn't the answer. It is not the lighthouse, though officially that is what the club would have you believe. It's not the bent grass greens or the couch fairways, said to be among the best in the country. And it isn't the views over the cliff, or the historic clubhouse built from local stones a century and a half ago.

Eve points to the foyer. 'Must be those trophies in the glass cabinets.'

Louisa shakes her head, drops her hands onto the table.

'Okay, I will tell you.' She uses her fingers to corral the secret, whispers, 'It's the showerheads in the men's locker room.'

'You're kidding, right?'

'No, I'm dead serious.'

Bridget confirms this with a little nod. 'She's right. It is the showerheads.'

'But I don't get it,' says Eve. 'What can be so special about showerheads?'

'They're huge. They come down from the ceiling like big umbrellas, the size of manholes. I mean, literally big enough to hose down a circus elephant.' Bridget explains this while making a circular motion over the table linen. 'They're relics from the thirties. To get the right water pressure, they had to put in special fittings or something. And the drains had to be twice the standard size too, so that they don't clog up. Apparently you can't find them anywhere but here, and you can imagine the monthly water bill.'

Louisa adds, 'When they were upgrading the clubhouse to be eco-friendly, the matter of the showerhead was put to a vote by the male members. The fuckers flat out refused to downsize.'

'But why?'

'Who knows.'

'I think a lot of them thought it would be like metaphoric castration?' offers Bridget in earnest.

Louisa snorts. 'A lot of Napoleons around here. Anyway, the ancient and sacred club rules decreed that any plumbing works would need to be approved by a special majority of seventy-five per cent. In the end, they barely got two votes to rub together.'

'What about the showers in the women's room?' I ask.

'Okay, for starters, the women's locker room has only

existed for ten years, considering the club didn't allow women members before that. The girls were just so grateful they were allowed in that they never even bothered to campaign for showerhead equality. They have those wall-mounted ones that you can adjust the angle on, which is nice for them since no one wants to get their hair wet.'

'That is a ridiculous story on so many levels.'

Louisa puts her mouth around her straw, takes a tiny sip of her juice. 'Facts are often ridiculous.'

The waiter interrupts with a platter of breads and anti-pasto, and promises to bring out the fries in just a minute. Louisa looks at him, then at the food. She makes an unsavoury noise.

'I can't eat any more after this weekend. Let's go do something fun.'

Bridget is suspicious. 'What do you mean?'

'Yeah,' joins Eve. 'After your showerhead story I'm not sure exactly what fun would entail in a place like this. I'd rather stay here and vegetate.'

Louisa raises one eyebrow so we can see it over the rim of her sunglasses. 'No problems. You know me, I never offer an invitation twice. Primrose and I will go.'

She grabs me by the wrist, pulls me out of my chair.

'That's fine by me,' says Bridget.

Eve concurs. 'I'll just be here, eating the fries and wearing this jacket.'

Feebly I protest, 'This *something fun* . . . Does it have to involve leaving the table?'

'Come on, Primrose. Don't be a bad sport.'

I can see Eve waving at me, mouthing a little *byee* as Louisa drags me across the restaurant, past the booking lectern and out the door.

From the back of her car Louisa gets out a driver, some balls and tees. I can see Lawrence's car nearby, glowing in the sun like a hot meteorite, parked over two spaces.

'I don't want to play today,' I say to her. 'Do we have to do this?'

'It's not what you think. Come with me.'

Since we are both wearing heels, we must go barefoot across the practice green, down an unofficial track that runs along the eighteenth, risk being hit by oncoming balls, before diving into a thick bushland which looks very deliberately placed to keep people out.

Louisa is ahead. 'Don't worry, I do this all the time.'

'Why is that not a comfort?'

'Ha-ha.'

We weave along a dark tunnel of melaleucas, the soft carpet of their leaves underfoot. The air is moist and salty. The intensity of the darkness changes constantly with the density of the canopy. All around us, things we cannot see are hissing and fluttering. I start to worry there might be snakes. Then it occurs to me they'd be hibernating in the winter.

The sound of the sea grows closer. We are heading towards the edge of the cliff, that much is clear.

'Pretty amazing, isn't it?' I hear Louisa say. Then, as I emerge from the darkness into full light, I see her standing on a rock the size of a beach towel. The only thing separating us from the merciless drop is a small lip formed by the white trunks of dead trees.

'Isn't this a bit dangerous?'

'Only for whoever is down there.'

She bends to plant a tee in a gash in the rock, and places a ball on it. Her skirt is a parachute. Her hair swims over her face.

'Here we go.'

She stands up, faces the water, does a stretch. Then with her club she takes a swing at the ball. It flies into the air and drifts to the left, carried by the wind that is blowing across us. It's impossible to judge its distance. Nothing around it, neither the sky nor the ins and outs of the coastline, gives any perspective. At a certain point, the ball can no longer sustain the height, and gives in to the long descent. Our eyes follow it all the way down, until it drops soundlessly into the rolling, iridescent water and disappears without a fuss.

Louisa throws down the club, plants her hands on her hips.

'That's pretty much the only thing I love about golf.'

Her nose casts an angular shadow over her face. She adjusts her sunglasses, then her dress. 'It's like watching Wile E Coyote being run off a cliff.'

'There are some minor similarities.'

'Now your turn.'

We manoeuvre around each other in the small space between staying alive and falling. Rocks dig painfully into my feet. Suddenly Louisa grabs my arms, laughs hellishly and shakes me around.

'Are you crazy, Louisa? Stop it!'

'Relax!' She's still laughing. 'Do you think I'd actually push you off a cliff?'

'I'd say that falling right now is a distinct possibility.'

I pull her arms off me. She retreats, nurses her wrist as if I've injured it, and pulls a face. She says, 'Just so you know, that was a trust exercise. And you've failed miserably.'

We walk away from each other, swapping places. The rock is hot to stand on; it takes getting used to. I put a ball down where Louisa did. There is nowhere else on this rock that could have accommodated the tee. It's as if someone left a single fissure in the formation specifically for our use.

I can see the lighthouse to my right, a faint mark in the distance that could be Homer. There is a small wedge of beach down below, the waves leaving the sand more pristine each time they retreat. I steady myself against the wind.

Louisa says, 'Do you feel like the king of the world right now?'

'More like the woman who turned to stone.'

'Which one was that?'

'Just one of my father's cautionary tales from when I was little. Man goes to war, man gets killed in battle, woman weeps so hard she turns to stone, right on the top of a mountain, forever waiting for him to return.'

'Oh. That old chestnut.'

'I used to think he was just warning me not to marry a man in the army. Now I think he was actually saying: should any man leave you, do not turn to stone like that other woman.'

'Sensible advice.'

'I agree.'

'Wait,' Louisa calls to me as I ready myself with the club. 'I forgot to tell you this part. Before you take that swing, you have to think of something that you really, really hate.'

'What do you mean?'

'Come up with something you completely despise, like income tax or shoulder pads. Pretend the ball is the embodiment of that. Then swing the club and do your worst.'

I try to think, and when I'm ready I take a big swing at the ball, send it out like a startled bird into the blue nothing ahead of us. I have to squint in order to see it in the rays of the sun.

'Ouch, that's spectacular,' Louisa says. 'You really have been practising.'

We watch the ball inevitably perish into the great spectacle of nature below us.

'Doesn't it feel truly cathartic?' Louisa asks.

I look down at the ground. We have four balls left between us. I set up another and hit it cleanly out into the air. Everything is easier when you don't have a target in front of you to reach, when the ball can just about land anywhere to equal effect.

'Can I hit another one?'

'Be my guest.'

My head throbs. I dispatch another ball with a ping, then another.

How is setting flight to all your theoretical hatred meant to feel? If this is catharsis, as Louisa suggests, then why does nothing feel lifted? My head hurts even more than before, and the pain is radiating all through my body. Everything hurts so terribly that a raging symphony has started to play between my ears, timpani being pounded.

All the balls are gone, I realise as I look down again. I don't even remember hitting the last one.

'Can we go back?'

I step over the narrow path, get myself past Louisa.

'Sure we can go back. But are you alright?'

'I don't know. I don't think so.'

'Primrose, you're breathing like you've been for a run or something. You're acting strange.'

'Haven't I always been strange?'

This time I am the one who leads us back into the dark womb of the bush. I can hear Louisa picking up the club and running after me. She stumbles over something, curses to herself.

'I don't understand why you're snapping at me,' she calls out. 'Didn't you have fun?'

'Not everything is about fun, Louisa.'

'Then what is it about? Tell me. What is Primrose Li all about?'

We must be halfway through the tunnel by the time she catches up to me, halts me by the arm. 'Wait, Primrose.'

There is a smiling crescent of light above us, as weak as a waning moon in the night.

'I think I know what's upsetting you,' she says. 'Why you've been acting so stressed out.'

'Do you? How?'

I'm swallowing my words, swallowing the fear of what she might say next.

'It's Adrian, isn't it?'

Let her think that. She's halfway to being right.

'I'm sorry, babe,' she goes on, crossing her arms. 'I know what he's up to. I saw him in the garden the other night, after dinner, talking on the phone. It was pretty obviously not a colleague or a friend or anything like that. Tell me, how long have you known?'

'I *don't* know.'

I find myself looking at the trees, at the mottled darkness. 'Until he admits it himself, nothing is true or untrue.'

Louisa licks the tip of her lip. 'Don't you want to find out? Get to the bottom of it?'

'It's not a priority of mine to find out.'

'Why isn't it?'

'Because I wouldn't leave him when he's trying so hard to put himself back together, when Bebe still has so much growing up left to do. I would happily let Adrian do whatever it is that he needs. And if there is some hope or motivation he can draw from another person, then maybe that person should be allowed to exist, to be there for him.'

'Mmm,' Louisa says. She has relaxed her stance ever so slightly. 'Well, I'm happy for you if that's your plan. I really am. You and Adrian make so much sense together.'

Then she smiles, a little too benevolently. 'You're a better woman than me, Primrose. I'm not sure what I would do in your situation, but probably not that.'

I shut my eyes, try to stop a breath from escaping. 'I'm sorry, Louisa. I can't talk to you about this anymore. You and I are so different. Sometimes I have no idea why we're even friends.'

'There you go again,' she says, scoffing now. 'It was just

a compliment, Primrose. Why can't you ever stop being so bloody serious?'

A pause between us. I can't see Louisa's eyes, only the distorted silhouette of myself in those sunglasses. But something changes in her: the way she uncrosses her arms, ruffles her hair. Her voice is as even as the air around us. She says, 'Okay, if you really want to know why we're friends, I'll tell you. I find you very interesting, Primrose.'

'Yes, so you've said.'

'By that, I only mean that I find myself questioning who you really are. See, all this time, you've let me barge into your house unannounced, and you've listened day after day to all my talk, and I've never been able to get anything out of you. What is keeping you so quiet? Are you shy? Are you empty? Or just a bit dim? I've realised, as time goes on, that it's none of those things. It's because you just don't like me. No matter what happens, you just don't. That seems worth looking into.'

There is a lump in my throat. 'Is that why you're always around? You're trying to make me like you?'

'Of course not,' she puffs. 'I don't give a fuck if you don't like me, if I have one less person liking me. It's completely unimportant. It's just that sometimes I can't get over *why* you don't like me. That, maybe, is less unimportant. I think, slowly, I am getting to the bottom of what you are hiding.'

She must be able to see the colour rising in my face. The silence between us is torturous, full of insects. Louisa's expression is blank, frozen. It feels like a trap, like she is baiting me to say the wrong thing. Then finally, she covers her mouth, stumbles back on her heels. She's laughing to herself.

'Come on, look at you.' Her usual voice returns, the same Louisa as always. 'For God's sake, Primrose, cheer up.'

And before I realise it I am walking again. Half walking, half running, away from her. Maybe she is still talking, but I cannot listen to another word. The trees disappear behind me, Louisa too. She's making no effort to follow this time.

Then I am running at full speed up the hill, past a group of golfers on the eighteenth. One of them is trying to operate a gadget on his wrist; his friends are telling him which buttons to press. They look up, confused at first, then enraged by my intrusion. One of them shouts, waves at me as if swatting at a fly. But there is nothing they can do but wait, as I make my way up that hill.

Finally reaching the top, I realise I've dropped my shoes somewhere along the way. I run across the green, towards the restaurant. But a group of staff in uniform are standing at the entrance, watching me questionably. I change course, head for the car park. Without shoes, they'd never let me inside.

The asphalt in the car park is baked, burning my feet with each step. Lawrence's car is right in front of me, its great backside sticking out two feet from the rest. Almost out of breath, I stretch my arm to reach it; I cannot go any further.

Something heaves right from the middle of me. My body shivers against the warmth of the car's metal. It is not just warm but boiling hot. For a moment I think I will faint from its heat.

I'm glad we are going home tonight. Glad I'll be rid of all the madness from this weekend, that I'll never again have to set foot in Homer or the Cove or any such place. How lovely is the thought of home: the running tap in the laundry, the pool house where my rusty old clubs live. My heart is bursting at the thought of it. Then I remember Terence, looming on the horizon. And something inside me begins to heave again.

Someone touches me on the back. I think it must be Louisa, and I try to shake her off. 'Leave me alone!'

Then I hear Peter's voice.

'Are you unwell? Let me take you inside.'

He's still wearing his golf glove; his arm has tanned after a morning in the sun.

'Primrose, what do you need?'

'For you to go away.'

But instead he makes himself useful. He rescues my hair just as I surge forward and let it all come out over Lawrence's car. It's as if everything I have ever eaten has decided to abandon me at once. Then my head clears. The symphony is gone, along with the throbbing. Little white wings flutter over my eyes, trying to carry me away. I want to curse myself for being so weak and useless.

I try to straighten myself against Peter. It must seem pathetic, leaning on him like this, but if I let go now I think I will fall in a heap, and then I'd surely have to endure the drama of an ambulance being called. I close my eyes, wishing I could disappear.

'Please don't tell anyone,' I say into the sleeve of his shirt, into his arm. 'It's too mortifyingly humiliating.'

'Hmm,' he says, as if internalising something else he wants to say.

'Do you think I should clean this up,' I ask, 'before Lawrence comes back?'

'There may not be time.'

'He'll lose his mind if he sees this.'

'Yeah, he won't take it well,' Peter agrees. 'What were you thinking, Primrose? Of all the cars.'

His whole body is vibrating. Every bone jitters with an electric delight. He tries to cover it up with a cough, but nothing can disguise it. The audacity, to laugh at a time like this.

18

On my twenty-sixth birthday, I received an email from Jonathan Lange, editor of *Criterion*. I had applied for a job there a few weeks earlier and now he wanted to have a conversation face to face. Not an interview, he stressed. It was not the kind of establishment that insisted on formalities. It was just a chat, over coffee if I preferred.

I was unfamiliar with the street address he provided; it was all the way across the city and I would have to take the car. I hated driving in weekday traffic.

'What do you think?' I asked Adrian. 'Should I go?'

'Well, let's see. What other jobs are lining up?'

The year was 2009, in the midst of the Global Financial Crisis.

'None,' I replied. 'There are no other job prospects at present.'

I had just lost a job, in fact. I'd been working in a bank doing financial modelling for deals where one company took over another at a price that made the board of directors on both sides pleased as punch. The bank had a reputation for turning average people into millionaires. In reality it was just turning millionaires into billionaires.

People at the bank worked sixteen-hour days and went out drinking afterwards instead of going home to see their families. Sometimes, when the senior people got drunk, they said things to the junior people that made everyone else look the other way to check the cricket score. Sometimes people stayed up all night, searching for new ways and new premises to spend their bonuses. Sometimes they woke up in the mornings to find their lives changed, with a bad marriage ending and a better one ready to take its place.

A lot of people thought it was a nice place to work. And when the stockmarket crashed, the bank even sent out fruit baskets with the redundancy packages.

'What's *Criterion*?' Adrian asked. We were on the bed in our newly rented apartment, and he was looking over my shoulder at the website on my laptop.

'It's business news with a bit of politics. Actually, a lot of politics, to the left.'

'So it's sort of an outlet for corporate activism, going up against the big guys?'

'You could say that.'

'Is this the person behind it all?'

There was a headshot of Jonathan above the main story on overhauling corporate governance laws.

'Yes, it's pretty much a one-man shop. I don't think he can pay me much.'

'Maybe this can be the year you don't worry about money. You have savings from the bank job. Just do what makes you happy.'

'Will this make me happy?'

'Why not? You love to write.'

'But writing business?'

'As long as you have something to say, you can say it through any medium. You'll be great at it.'

Adrian seemed impatient, and reached over to shut my laptop.

Earlier he had taken me out to an Ethiopian restaurant where the food was a colourful arrangement of pastes spread over a large pancake called an injera. We ate with our hands, and the owner of the restaurant, a beautifully turbaned woman named Bathsheba, said the mess was all part of the magic of eating at her establishment.

'Well, then, happy birthday,' Adrian had said as he leaned over to kiss me. We both laughed, trying to avoid touching each other with our dirty hands.

Now the bed wobbled as Adrian got up. We had a cheap mattress with weak springs that made sleeping feel like drifting on a half-inflated raft.

'I have a present for you,' he announced.

'You shouldn't have, Adrian. Dinner was lovely enough.'

'It's only this. I thought it would look pretty on you.'

From the drawer he produced a small velvet box with a gold ring inside. The ring had a ruby on it, surrounded by tiny crystals. It looked almost childishly pretty, like trinkets I used to keep in a cookie tin under my bed.

'Don't look so worried,' he said, half laughing. 'This is not a proposal or anything.'

'I didn't think I looked worried. This is very sweet of you.'

'Put it on. It suits you.'

'It does. Thank you.'

Adrian had one of those longish haircuts that could go either to the left or to the right, and it inevitably landed somewhere in the middle, over his forehead and eyes. This gave him an endearing, comical look as he moved himself closer and gave me a peck on the lips. Then he had that look in his eyes, and he kissed me properly.

He walked around to my side of the bed and whistled at Bob, who was asleep on the floor. The dog ignored him. He bent down and gently lifted the animal. 'Come on, doggie. Time to leave.'

Eventually Bob conceded to the disturbance and steadied himself on his paws. He was so old now that he was only able to create a forward motion by shuffling himself along, very slowly. At the door, he looked at me with one last petition to stay. I knew he could see me as I blew him a kiss, even if it was through the blizzard of his fading vision.

Again Adrian whistled, and snapped his fingers. Out.

The dog bowed his head and agreed to be led through the door.

Left alone, Adrian and I made love under two blankets. It was only April but so cold that the little oscillating heater could not warm one end of the room without neglecting the other.

Adrian was on top. As usual he took great care not to crush me; he put his body to mine in a softly, measured way. He said, 'I've never wanted anyone this way. Do you know that?' Then he tasted the skin on my throat, on my breast, and put my hand on his penis. When he got very hard, he anchored into me and thrust against the spot he knew would render me weak with desire for him.

Soon, having two blankets over us seemed excessive. He peeled one off in a quick motion, like it was a big band-aid; it was funny the way he did it. Everything went according to plan after that. That was the thing about making love to Adrian: it was always reliable and predictably nice, like Adrian himself.

'I love being here with you, living together,' he said after we were done. I rested my head on his chest and he held me for a while before sitting up and turning on the TV.

The late night news was on. We had missed the main segment and it was now the tail end of finance. The stock-market had fallen another 3 per cent but economists believed Australia would narrowly avoid a recession. Our banks were well capitalised and the resources sector continued to do well on trade with China. One analyst from the Sydney office of an American bank suggested that our smallness would save us. For better or worse, he added, we were not the United States.

The sports news was dominated by golfer Ángel Cabrera's win at the Masters. He had won the green jacket in a playoff against the more popular Americans, Kenny Perry and Chad Campbell. Now the Argentine was being touted as a hero of the golf world, in a true rags-to-riches story that crossed class and cultural lines. Apparently he did not grow up dreaming of golf; he dreamt mainly of food.

'That's all very well,' said Adrian, 'but you can hardly hold up golf as some equal-opportunity advert.'

Adrian felt disdain for sport in general, golf in particular.

The whole history of the game was clouded by racial and social divisions, he seemed to think. He said Augusta National, where the Masters was played every year, had operated for decades on the basis that golfers were white and caddies were black. It wasn't until the nineties that Tiger Woods came along to flip the table, by winning the Masters with a white caddie.

But that was not exactly the happy ending, he added. Caddying, once considered a menial job fit only for blacks, had become a lucrative occupation fought over by the tertiary educated. Which meant the same principle was now being applied in reverse but with the same result. No more black caddies, for all the wrong reasons.

The news was followed by a program on which a panel of US experts discussed the Obama administration. It was almost a hundred days since the inauguration. People were saying that what happened now would set the tone for the remainder of his term, and determine his chances for a second term. Most of the experts thought he had gone out with all guns blazing, but they still worried that *Yes We Can* would prove to be just campaign rhetoric. We would have to wait to find out what it meant for the world five, ten years from now.

While the program went on, I opened my laptop to read the corporate governance article on the *Criterion* site. It discussed the lack of board independence at some of Australia's most recognised companies, the risk of this leading to fraud and malfeasance, and the large base of mum-and-dad investors who were kept in the dark by the opaque structures of the companies they had put their savings in.

'Have you made up your mind about that job interview?'

Adrian asked. He was stroking my skin with the tip of his finger.

'I haven't yet, no.'

'It sounds right for you. Where is the hesitation coming from?'

'I think it could be awkward.'

'Awkward how?'

'I know him, actually.'

'You know this guy? In the photo?'

'I knew him from school.'

'Right. Were you friends or something?' Adrian asked.

'No, he was more a friend of a friend.'

The Jonathan in the photo had hardly changed since I saw him ten years earlier, on that New Year's Eve at Peter's house, on the cusp of the new millennium. He had kept the freckles, and the boyish excess around the face. His hair was the same too, cut so close to the scalp that you couldn't help but admire the perfect shape of his skull. Only his eyes were a little different now, somewhat sunken and dark-rimmed, a hint of an unslept night before the photo was taken.

'I don't see what the problem is, you knowing him.'

'You're probably right.'

'Maybe he recognised you too,' Adrian suggested. 'From your application.'

That was unlikely. I hadn't put down my school details in my resumé. As a rule I avoided discussing high school unless absolutely necessary. Over the years, this had not been particularly difficult. Turned out high school was completely irrelevant once you'd left it behind.

'I'd be very surprised if he remembers me,' I said. 'We only spoke once. At the time he was very upset about the republic referendum. All his friends thought he was going to do something political with his life, and here he is.'

Jonathan did not remember me. He just looked at me in that wide-eyed fashion as if he could not quite put a finger on something.

He invited me to sit down at a round table, over which a stack of newspapers had spilled into a low-lying mound. His desk by the wall had the same disarranged look.

The office was on top of a bridal shop called Style for Life. It sold dresses that were puffy and synthetic-looking, with rhinestone bodices that clinched the waist like torture devices. We could hear their phone ringing through the floorboards, and a woman answering it, announcing her name was Camilla.

Jonathan handed me a plastic cup of water. 'Camilla is great. You'll get to know her well should you end up working here.'

The view out of the window was of powerlines and shop signs, reminding me of being at the old Comet. The place even smelled the same. Old paint over old wood. Meat cooked over charcoal.

'So you did commerce at Melbourne.' He sat down beside me, cradling one knee with dovetailed hands. 'That's where I went, but I dropped out halfway through. I'm one of those people who are allergic to traditional structures of learning.'

'I felt that way too sometimes. But I always got good grades, so I had no excuse to quit.'

'Yes, you did very well there.' He looked down at my resumé. 'The Salomon Barney Prize. What was that for?'

'My honours thesis.'

'And the subject matter?'

'The value of humour in corporate leadership.'

'Intriguing. What's the argument?'

'The argument is that CEOs can use humour as a tool to distract the market from their own poor performance. The funnier they are, the less likely they are to be punished for a failure to do their jobs properly. You can see that from the transcripts of what they say at press conferences, at interviews. They crack a joke, make an adorably self-effacing comment, and the market forgives them. The company share price does not fall, or at least does not fall by as much as it should. Sometimes the market even thinks, *Phew, it's not as bad as we thought*. And the share price rises. If you are charmingly funny, you are excused in a way that others never are.'

'What does that say about us, as a society?'

'That we are too reactionary to the superficial. We ought to be more thoughtful, more astute.'

'I suppose the same observation can be applied to life generally,' Jonathan said. 'People befriend each other on the basis of humour. They get married because they're able to laugh together. Is it possible that humour is just as important as things that are perceived to be more fundamental?'

'Not unless humour has the power to change what is fundamental, which it doesn't.'

Jonathan got up and lowered the blinds so the sun did not shine in his eyes. It was possible that he had had a growth spurt since high school. He seemed taller, though this was merely a guess since, up until today, I had never seen him standing.

'You come across as a very serious person,' he said, neutrally. It was not clear whether he saw it as a virtue or a flaw.

'I like to laugh, but not at things that are too important to be funny.'

'You may need to work on that if you take this job.'

'Does that mean you're offering it to me?'

'I should mention the pay first.' He wrote down a number as if he was embarrassed to say it out loud. 'Sorry, but there's a financial crisis.'

The rest of the year we spent working on *Criterion*'s subscriber base. Our readership grew quicker than we'd hoped, almost tripling. We started to get interest from advertisers. Instead of producing a daily edition, we produced a morning issue at seven and an afternoon round-up by four. People, we realised, wanted to read us even if they didn't agree with us.

Jonathan was invited on a radio program. He talked about the lack of transparency in superannuation funds, the fees blindly charged without member consent, the shady strategies employed to inflate the value of their assets. He was not afraid to name names because he had nothing to lose but the clothes on his back. For this reason he was invited on more programs, TV and radio, to talk about the chicanery and deception that went on in the corporate world. His name became familiar to those who read the business news, who were *in* the business news. He made quite a few enemies, hardly any friends.

Camilla moved from answering phones downstairs to answering them upstairs: 'Welcome to the Criteria, how may we help you?'

It drove Jonathan mad. But besides that, she turned out to be an effective frontline against the throngs of PR people hired by aggrieved companies.

Then Camilla began to answer calls of a different nature, anonymous ones with messages for Jonathan. They advised him to be careful, to watch what he said and to remember his place. Simultaneously, people started calling him a Nazi on social media. They implied he was a fascist who spread lies to attack the free market, the very bedrock of Western democracy. They claimed that his great-grandfather had been in the SS and was tried for war crimes.

The last part was half-true, Jonathan admitted. It was not his great-grandfather but a cousin of his who was the war criminal. By the time World War II broke out, Jonathan's family had been settled in Melbourne for three generations, though being far from the war, from Germany, did not keep them far from trouble. Anti-German sentiments had been brewing since the first world war, and they were getting used to being attacked on the streets for no reason whatsoever, then thrown into a jail cell for un-Australian conduct. Some of the family changed their names. Lane instead of Lange.

One day Jonathan received a package, a swastika made out of cardboard, dipped in red paint. He held it up, then set it down on his desk, against the computer screen. The paint stained his fingers.

'I believe that is the appropriate gift for six generations in Australia.'

The look on his face was more bemusement than anger, but the indignity brought Camilla to tears.

'I really feel bad about this,' she cried. 'I don't know how long it must take for stigma to wear off.'

'I'd argue it never does,' said Jonathan.

'You don't deserve any of this harassment,' she wailed.

Jonathan adopted the stance of a cowboy. He narrowed his eyes and made a gun with his hand, blew at the tip as if it had just been fired. 'Deserve's got nothing to do with it.'

The Clint Eastwood reference was lost on Camilla. She sobbed into her hands, and tears seeped through her fingers, fell onto her lap. 'This just makes me so angry. I wish people could behave better.'

Towards the end of the year, almost Christmas, things took a different turn. Media Company NWC made Jonathan an offer to buy him out. For once, we were the ones who made the news.

According to the NWC board, the purchase of *Criterion* was part of its strategy to diversify. It would bring a fresh angle, a different political flavour, to its predominantly right-wing stable of mastheads.

With the money they were offering, Jonathan could live larger than he ever imagined. His credit card debts would perish into memory. His parents could retire without giving another thought to the life savings lost in the financial crisis. He could even buy them the boat they had always wanted, to sail around the country.

But to all this, he said no. He did not take the offer, not even when NWC guaranteed his tenure as editor-in-chief, plus a shiny new office in a more central location. No terms in a legal contract could ever guarantee editorial independence, of that he was sure. Since when did being owned become synonymous with being free?

Again Camilla cried, this time out of joy, not rage. It was towards the end of the day, time for her to go home. She tidied her desk, knowing that everything that was here today would be here tomorrow. Still sobbing, she walked across the room, hugged Jonathan in the way that mothers hugged their sons at graduation, and hurried out the door to catch her bus.

Jonathan looked at me, pink from Camilla's affection. He ran a hand over his bristle-like hair: 'Fuck it. Can we go for a drink now?'

We went down the creaky stairs and out onto the street. Summer was just beginning and all the shops were decorated for Christmas. We headed to the usual corner, where he bought me a drink.

He shuffled from one foot to the other as we stood at the table. His body was alight with something fierce and hopeful.

'It's a new chapter for *Criterion*,' he said. 'And I wouldn't have got this far without you.'

'I merely follow orders from my fearless leader.'

'See, I wish you'd stop doing that.'

'Do what?' I asked.

'Selling yourself short. You've written some fantastic pieces that you should be really proud of. Stories that have led to public discussions about corporate fairness and financial abuse and law reform. Each of these stories add up, and one day you'll see that the totality of what you're doing is far greater than the sum of its parts.'

A crowd rushed in from the street, young guys in T-shirts and board shorts and flags of Saint George's Cross stuck in their hats. Another crowd, who was already here, greeted them, and the two groups merged at the bar.

A rugby match between England and the All Blacks was about to start on the TV. In honour of this, the guys started to elbow each other, bump shoulders, wave fists. Some of them tried to form a scrum. There wasn't room, and in any case they were too drunk for such an effort. They collapsed in a heap on the floor, laughing as they let people walk unsympathetically over them.

Jonathan drank his beer carefully to avoid ending up with a foam moustache. The rugby crowd was making such a racket that, when he started to talk again, he had to adjust his volume. 'By the way, I remember you now. New Year's Eve. Peter's house. I remember boring you about the referendum.'

'Oh,' I said. 'I remember you too, but I didn't want to say anything.'

'Why not?'

'I thought it was better to start with a clean slate.'

This seemed to catch Jonathan's interest. He scratched his head.

Then he said, after a while, 'I keep telling Peter that he should pay us a visit. But he's always coming up with one excuse or another.'

'I thought he was in the States.'

'He's moved back, didn't you know that?'

I shook my head. 'We haven't kept in touch.'

'I was in the city last month and there he was, walking down Collins Street, all grown up and looking like a proper human being. Turns out he'd been back for over a year and never thought to let me know. We grabbed a drink later, and I got to meet the girl he's seeing. She was wearing this ridiculous dress, all bling and logos. I don't know, maybe he's going through a phase. He's a bit different to how I remembered.'

'Should that be a surprise to you? It's been a long time.'

'You're right. We were all babies back then, weren't we. Now he's working for the family bank, and just started a private equity arm, the one that's bidding for Orion Airlines. I guess they're gonna buy it so they can strip away half its workforce to lift the bottom line. You could argue he's become the enemy.'

'Jonathan, you think everyone is the enemy.'

'I do, don't I?' he laughed. 'Though not all enemies are equal in my eyes. I think I might invite him to our Christmas party, what do you think? Should be fun to relive some more memories.'

The rugby guys had locked arms, started to sing 'Rule, Britannia!'. Every time they got to the part about Britons never being slaves, they shook their heads emotively. Their cheeks wobbled like rooster wattles.

'I've always been confused by that song,' Jonathan said. 'Who ever said anything about making them slaves?'

The game was about to start. The players had entered the field and lined up for the national anthems.

Jonathan finished his drink, checked his phone. 'It's time to go.'

We wandered out into the night, in the direction of the office. It was cold now that the sun had gone down. The street was filled with the smell of restaurants. Crowds of people spilled out of them and swelled over the footpath. It was busy for a weeknight. People seemed to be operating on an elevated level. Everywhere I looked, they were talking and hugging in a festive manner.

Outside the community centre, where a group of boys were doing tricks with flashing yo-yos, Jonathan stopped for a chat. One of them tried to teach him how to drop the yo-yo to the ground and walk it behind like a dog on a leash. It was too hard, and Jonathan handed the toy back in defeat. They laughed as we walked on.

Further down, Jonathan said, 'I hope you weren't upset when I brought up Peter. Is it a thorny subject? I don't know how serious you guys were.'

I shrugged. 'It was high school.'

'That's not a fully committed answer.'

'What do you want me to say?'

'I'm not sure, but I know you froze a little when I mentioned his name. You're not still pining after him, are you?'

He had only said this flippantly, in a way that suggested he didn't expect me to respond.

Did people pine after each other anymore? It seemed like such an archaic concept, to yearn for a distant person when so many alternatives were within easy reach.

'Adrian's a nice guy,' Jonathan added. 'I like him a lot.'

'Yes, I like him too. He's wonderful actually.'

'So will you guys get married or what? I get the feeling it's a sooner or later thing.'

'I don't know. I think, if he asked me, I'd say yes.'

We had reached my car and I had to fumble in my bag for the keys. My fingers were acting stupid, could not be made to work.

Somewhere down the street, female voices were singing 'Silent Night' without any regard for the tune. The high notes fell flat, the low ones cut too sharp. Their voices built, expanded, and invited a chorus of laughter and applause. They took over the night.

'Jonathan?'

'Yes?'

It seemed like the right time to ask him.

'Jonathan, would you be okay with not inviting Peter to the Christmas party?'

He considered this for a moment, and he nodded. He did not ask me why.

19

Terence is greeted in the driveway. He picks up Bebe, kisses her on the forehead. Unprepared for the weight the child has gained since the last time they met, he quickly returns her to the ground. With Adrian, he shakes hands, then pulls him in for a hug. From a distance they look like father and son.

He has brought with him only one suitcase, the size of carry-on luggage. He pushes rather than pulls it, lets it reach the front door first.

'Primrose,' he says on the steps, in a way that makes hello unnecessary. We touch cheeks, kiss into nowhere.

He is very tanned and muscular, showing signs of exercise beyond what is required for good health. The smell of a long flight spent with first-class whiskey lingers on his breath. He clasps my shoulders as if I have done something exemplary. There, in the parting of his mouth, are words on the cusp of being said. But, choosing not to say them, he lets out a simple sigh.

Bebe does not receive the doll she requested, as Terence was unable to find any Primrose-looking dolls dressed in a riding outfit. Instead, she is given a chess set, which she arranges on the coffee table with Terence's help.

The chess pieces are characters from Super Mario, with Team Mario on one side and the villains on the other. She is amused by this unconventional set-up. Terence pretends to argue over which side he wants, but ends up letting Bebe take the side of the righteous.

Bebe considers her moves slowly, Terence rather too quickly. Chess pieces hobble over the board like the hooves of a crippled horse.

'Watch out for the queen,' he instructs.

'That's not the queen,' corrects Bebe. 'It's Bowser Junior!'

'Alright, watch out for Bowser Junior. You're about to leave yourself very exposed.'

'What does *exposed* mean?'

'It means you'll have nowhere to hide.'

Despite this, she wins the game and is rewarded with a head ruffle from Terence. She wins three more times without ever noticing the quiet allowances made by her opponent. While they play, Adrian and I set things down for dinner. Although he is more interested in joining his brother and Bebe at the chessboard, he has made a point of offering to help me. He takes plates to the table, arranges the knives and forks, chooses a Vouvray for the wine.

Dinner is Patagonian toothfish, which comes out of the oven looking snow white, almost translucent. Terence has always said he prefers food that swims in water over those that walk on land. As far as I can gather, it doesn't have anything to do with an environmental concern or a philosophical rejection of animal slaughter. It is a simple matter of taste, of favouring one flesh over another.

We are out of practice as far as eating together is concerned. We stand around arguing over which seat belongs to whom until Terence puts an end to it by planting himself at the head of the table. In doing so, he throws out the balance of the rectangle. This he seems to neither notice nor care about. Plates are re-arranged, and around him we fall into a less-than-ideal formation, Adrian and Bebe on his left, me on the right.

Adrian pours the wine, dishes out the food like this is what he does every night. As for the food on his own plate, he does his best not to let it go to waste. He divides into small morsels the fish, the potatoes, even the lettuce leaves; he moves them around into separate quadrants of the plate and then, as if counting pills, rushes them down his throat, one after the other.

This return to eating is a recent development, which began about a week ago, likely motivated by the desire to avoid any questions from Terence. It hasn't been a full-hearted embrace of food – just a piece of toast here, half an omelette there – though it seems to give Adrian a colour that I'd long forgotten was missing. For a brief moment one day, I even thought the boxes of Life Meal had been miraculously tossed out of the house, forever eradicated, until I found them hiding in the space beneath the stairs, every one of them accounted for.

Throughout dinner Terence talks to Adrian about the people he plans to see while he is in town – colleagues from companies he used to run, and politicians who want to appoint him to various advisory councils. He talks about the successes of the venture capital fund he currently runs in London, and the endless tide of capital flowing in from Asia. But all things considered, he adds, the move to London was a misstep, what with all the vitriol and stupidity plaguing the country over Brexit.

Speaking as an outsider, Terence is quite comfortable with Britain's exit from the EU. Unlike most Canary Wharf types, he does not conform to the view that the break-up is bad for the British economy. He thinks that there is merit in disengaging from the bureaucratic red tape in Brussels, that over time domestic capacity will lift within the country to pick up any slack.

It's not that he particularly cares about the fate of the UK, but he's nevertheless angered by the ignorance of the left, by the fact that after all these years certain factions are still clinging to some utopian concept of Europe being a united whole. He does not believe ethnic and cultural differences across an entire Europe can ever be resolved through idealistic, egalitarian delusions. Just look at what is happening within France.

Adrian disagrees on the economic point, but says that he can see where Britons who voted for Brexit are coming from. There is something to be said for reclaiming sovereignty, for reaffirming a national identity and having a say on how one manages one's own borders.

This is Adrian's way of concealing a fundamental difference between his brother and him. In reality, he believes the campaign was run on lies, that it was the legitimisation of racist attitudes under the guise of patriotism. Brexit, to Adrian, demonstrated an anxiety and self-consciousness that was growing throughout the world, the classic paranoia of being engulfed by enemies, of being outbred by the populace who live beyond the borders.

Yet Adrian says none of this to Terence. And Terence, growing tired, waves a hand to signal a change in subject. He is about to put a lot of money on the line for a blockchain start-up, he says. Next year, he's likely to spend the bulk of his time in Palo Alto.

'I think,' Terence speculates, 'I could be a better American than a citizen of any other country.'

'Didn't you once date a woman from California?' Adrian recalls.

'Date her? We were practically married. Nadine, lovely Nadine. She had a house in the woods, outside Carmel. It was something that belonged on a biscuit tin.' Terence eases back into his chair, fists on the table. He seems temporarily struck by the memory of Nadine. 'Pity that didn't work out.'

He pauses, the silence punctuated only by the occasional sigh as he thinks her over.

Terence has had many women in his life, but not ones who stay around for very long. News of his relationships tend to reach us slowly, having taken place in other corners of the world, at a point in the past, bearing no consequence of any kind. You get the feeling that it is always Terence who ends things, or at least, having committed some error, has made the woman's staying untenable.

Nadine was the last girlfriend we'd met in person. It was years ago. He had brought her to Melbourne for a visit, not long after Adrian and I were married. We had lunch in Terence's apartment, the one he kept on the top floor of the Wilfred for those rare occasions when he was in town.

The lunch was Terence's apology for missing our wedding. At the time he was based in Hong Kong, heading up one of those investment banks that had a bull in their logo. It was explained to us over poached salmon and watercress that, as we had got married right in the middle of a significant and very hostile takeover, it had been impossible for him to fly to Melbourne for a personal engagement. Things had been moving quickly at work. His deal team had needed him to make real-time decisions. So much was riding on the transaction that he could not have left the running sheet in the hands of a subordinate.

After that, Adrian touched his brother's shoulder appreciatively to signify that no offence was ever taken; it was very boys' club and chummy. We were just glad to see him, Adrian said. Who cared if he was several months late, it was good of him to spare the time now. Didn't it always seem like they could pick things up right where they'd left them? And by the way, the salmon and watercress Nadine had cooked was delicious.

Nadine had, throughout this conversation, sat in quiet observation of us. She seemed reserved, contemplative, like someone who lived in the woods. At Adrian's compliment, she merely dabbed her red lips with a napkin and offered us more wine. She looked very slim and elegant in a white cashmere dress, which she had kept spotless during the entire ordeal of cooking us the meal.

After lunch, Terence asked Adrian about his work at the university and whether he was enjoying it, to which Adrian waved a hand as if dismissing a second-rate novel. Teaching was just a job that put food on the table. The reality was that none of his students thought he could impart anything of value, and, reciprocally, he was under no illusions that any of them could ever instil in him a sense of purpose in his career.

As usual, Terence responded by saying that he should have heeded his advice to go into business, and, as usual, Adrian nodded, agreeing a little too reverently.

'But teaching is more noble a profession,' Nadine objected suddenly, to everyone's surprise. She had one of those intensely marled accents sometimes found in the children of travelling diplomats. When she spoke, you could hear all the other languages in her head. 'Don't be like Terence, he is too involved with his money.'

This sounded like a criticism, but Terence laughed it off while caressing her cashmere. The next time Terence was in town he was without company, and we never heard what happened to Nadine.

At the dinner table, Bebe is entranced by her uncle's reflective mood. 'This lady called Nadine, was she nice?'

Terence comes to. 'Warm and lovely.' He gives the child a fragment of a smile. The next part is unnecessary, but he adds anyway, 'Like your mother.'

I get up, begin to collect the empty plates. To Bebe I say, 'It's time to go to bed.'

From Bebe's room I can hear the water running at the kitchen sink, then the voices of Adrian and Terence as they head outside into the back garden, the noise the chairs make as they sit down by the pool.

Bebe wants to read *The Tiger Who Came to Tea*. It never gets old for her, this tale of a hungry tiger who visits a suburban home, and proceeds to eat all the food in the house without ever remembering to devour the humans who live there. Tonight she bestows on the tiger a special name – Terence – an idea so absurd that she barks with laughter.

'Imagine if Uncle Terence really is a tiger. Maybe he's wearing human clothes to cover up his stripes!'

She does not need to look at the words on the page; she knows them by heart. But to delay the bed-going, she splits up the syllables, takes forever to sound out the digraphs. For an unbearable length of time, I must wait for an end to the story of the tiger named Terence. Then, mercifully, the effort exhausts even Bebe. She closes the book, willingly lays her head on the pillow.

'Mama,' she says, rubbing her eyes with the sleeve of her pyjamas. 'Why don't you like it when Uncle Terence visits?'

I stroke her head, kiss her on the temple. She forgets to wait for an answer and, without having to say a word, I reach for the light.

20

The last time I saw Terence, just over a year ago, he was getting up from his piano, moving away from me without a word. We were in his apartment at the Wilfred, which had windows that overlooked a square. The voices of the people below travelled up to us as if by telephone. A woman was telling a child to be careful with his ice-cream. Someone was being asked to move a step to the right and smile for the camera.

The piece of music which sat on the piano was Beethoven's Sonata No. 30 in E major, the third movement. The composer's instructions: *Andante molto cantabile ed espressivo*. Slowly. Sing it with great feeling. With expression.

When I arrived at the apartment earlier, Terence had greeted me with a kiss on the cheek. I could feel that he was in the process of growing a beard.

'Primrose,' he'd said, and with one arm out and the other not quite touching my waist, showed me in.

The transition from the artificial lighting of the corridor to the unobstructed sunlight in the living room put my lungs in a bliss. All the air was spinning out of my body and I felt I must sit down.

'How are you?' Terence asked.

His eyes ran over me. He must have noticed I was having trouble forming my words, so he responded to what he supposed would have been my answer. 'Don't think that way, don't think anything,' he said. 'Nothing bad is going to happen to Adrian.'

But something bad was already happening to him, and Terence was a liar for saying otherwise. If he had sat with Adrian in the hospital for the past three months, he would not have said such a thing.

Each morning the nurse would come into the ward and write Adrian's blood results on the whiteboard, like they were a benchmark he must try to exceed the next day. But each morning, the numbers told the same story. Despite the chemo, the disease was multiplying where other living cells languished. The chemo was only killing the parts of him that were good enough to keep. The doctors were starting to talk about other options, alternatives with acronyms that sounded like codes for nuclear testing sites. And while all of that was being worked out, they told Adrian: get out of bed once in a while, exercise.

Exercise in a ward that you could not leave meant only one thing, and I watched as Adrian went around and around the corridors, in a rectangle, past all the other rooms in which people were either dying or getting better or anything in between. He went clockwise some days, the reverse on others. It became a habit of his to run a hand along the wall as he went, the scratching sound made by his nails a small distraction from the tedium. The wall was covered in purple flower decals, someone having decided this was the visual solution to misery. I never knew I could hate a colour so much.

In Terence's apartment, I sat down at the piano, not because I wanted to play it but because it was the closest thing to the door. A part of me felt safer there. It was as though, had I stepped deeper into the apartment – even to where the couch and coffee table were – the balance between us might be broken.

That was when I first noticed the Beethoven on top of the piano. I looked at the key, at the sixteen-bar progression that opened the piece, and remembered how the notes sounded years ago when I had played them myself.

Terence came over, handed me a glass of red wine which I had not asked for, and again told me there was nothing to worry about.

'He once broke his leg,' Terence said. 'Adrian did, when he was little. He'd climbed on top of a mini-van and tried to be a hero. Came down hard over the concrete, fractured in four places. He had to have two surgeries to set it right again.'

He was shaking his head pleasantly at his brother's antics. I wondered what the point of the story was.

'My point is, he is very resilient,' said Terence. 'He's going to be absolutely fine.'

He sounded like a salesman as he said this, like he was vouching for the quality of something he had cobbled together in a workshop. And when he finished saying it, he came closer and sat down next to me on the piano stool, the length of which made it necessary for our hips to touch. Not knowing what to do, I drank the wine, all of it, and put the empty glass down on the floor.

'I think you're holding up very well, Primrose.'

As he uttered these words I could feel him examining the side of my face, and I understood from this that he would soon try to touch me with his hand.

'I don't know you well as a person, but from everything I've heard, you've been very good to Adrian, very strong for him during this time. I'm grateful to you for that. I really am quite pleased.'

It was strange, the way he said that. He made it sound like I did everything for *his* sake.

'You should know, Primrose, that I do think very highly of you. You are easy to be fond of.'

'Thank you,' I said to him. I tried to change the subject. 'Adrian's so happy that you've made the time to be here, when your life is elsewhere.'

'Don't mention it.'

'But it needs to be mentioned, because you being here . . . it matters a lot actually.' My throat was warm from the wine and my voice seemed to evaporate.

'Ah, yes, this thing that matters a lot. Well, now would be a good time for you to tell me about it.'

He put his hand on my leg then, where the hem of the skirt abandoned the skin. He rubbed it slowly, back and forth, and the motion of him doing so made the slight shift of his hand towards the centre of me seem innocuous, accidental.

None of this was surprising to me, because he had done the same thing a day ago, when we were both at the hospital. We had been sitting in the small, purple-coloured kitchen in the ward so that we could talk without Adrian hearing. One of the bulbs in the ceiling was broken and the room was half-lit. I was trying very hard to convey something to him that was important, something that, before saying it, I had rehearsed a number of times based on what the doctors had told me. I was almost getting to the point when Terence said in a peculiar manner, 'Would you like a favour from me, Primrose? Is that what this is leading to?'

There was no other way of putting it. I nodded.

It was then I came to realise this was going to cost me something, because that was when he first touched me on the leg. But instead of retreating, I let him keep it there, and I tried as hard as I could to act as if I had not noticed. It wasn't the right time to create a situation. Drawing attention to this would only stand in the way of achieving what I wanted, needed. It was better to dismiss it and pretend it was not happening at all, and to keep on talking and to make sure I was heard.

Minutes passed like this in that sterile kitchen, of me talking and of Terence touching me. Then he suddenly collected himself, stood up and said, all business-like, 'Why don't you come by my apartment tomorrow? We can talk properly there.'

Therefore the reappearance of his hand on my leg was not a surprise to me. By now I was prepared; in a way it was easier to know how everything was going to play out.

'Talk to me, Primrose,' said Terence. 'Whatever is on your mind.'

I felt distinctly like a woman on a stage being given the signal to begin the second act. And the second act required me to start all over again, so I started at the beginning. I explained to him that Adrian wasn't going to get any better without going down an alternative path of treatment. After three courses of chemo, everything still stood against him. I told Terence about the biopsy results, and the particular mutations which complicated his situation.

Terence grew impatient and pinched me lightly on the surface of my skin.

'You've got to break it down for me,' he said. 'The bare facts, stripping away all the medical speak. I have enough contempt for doctors as it is. Just tell me in plain English what is the problem for which I can be the answer.'

I imagined that this was the way he talked in his work, surrounded by note-takers as his hands gesticulated a large-scale crisis into a tiny, crystallised solution. He seemed like the kind of person who thought that for every complex way of solving a problem there was an equal yet less complex one, that everything which did not take you from A to B in a straight line was a detour.

'Alright, Terence,' I said to him, as directly as I could. 'It's money. We need money.'

He looked at me like he instantly understood. 'You need it for the next phase of treatment.'

'Yes, to get him on a trial drug that isn't yet widely available, we have to come up with the funds ourselves. Ordinarily I wouldn't ask, but . . . What can I say, it's a lot of money.'

'How much do you need?'

'Three hundred thousand. I can find some of that myself. A small portion of that.'

Terence thought this over. It was not clear whether the figure was more or less than he had expected.

With one finger he hit a high B on the piano and let the sound linger. I wished more than anything that he'd stop touching my leg.

'You know, you've always been a surprise,' Terence said. 'I had pictured Adrian with a different kind of girl. I don't know what he has done to deserve you. You're so honest and so loyal, you're ready to give yourself up when it matters most to the people around you. Maybe it's your background. When I worked in Hong Kong I met lots of women like you.'

He was playing at the keys randomly now, going up and down, producing something which resembled a pentatonic scale. But he didn't move the other hand, the one that was on my leg. I tried to get up, and he pressed on me firmly to indicate that I ought to stay still.

'Like the time you gave up that job at *Criterion*,' he continued. 'I admired your decision. I told Adrian that you would do the right thing, and you did.'

'Terence, I'm not here to talk about that.'

'No, but it's worth noting how beautifully you behaved on that occasion. You understood that your work was interfering with mine, that it was proving to be extremely inconvenient for many of my friends. You knew it had become an embarrassment to me, and you chose to side with me rather than your work.'

'You demanded that I give up that job. You told Adrian to demand it.'

'Is that how it happened?'

'Terence, you made it very uncomfortable for me to continue. You made things difficult between Adrian and I. I'm sure you remember.'

'Well, it all depends on the perspective, doesn't it. I'm not going to sit here and argue over semantics. The bottom line is that you stopped what you were doing to make things easier for me. That is a kind of devotion, fidelity. Which is why, as I said, people can become very fond of you.'

I had looked away while he talked. If I didn't, I might have picked something up and thrown it at him. And then I would have instantly regretted it.

'Back to the issue at hand, the money,' Terence said. 'Of course I would love to help him. But money can change things between people, render things awkward and uneasy. That is always my concern when it comes to money.'

'We would be very grateful, Terence. You mean the world to Adrian.'

'You don't need to keep selling it to me.'

'I'm sorry. It just makes me uncomfortable, having to ask you.'

'It's alright, Primrose. It's not naturally in us to grovel.'

'This is very far from where I ever thought I would be.'

'You merely want your husband to get better. You want to do the right thing to achieve that.'

Now he put his hand to my face, and it was only when he scraped his thumb across my cheek that I realised I was crying.

'Terence,' I said. 'I don't want to do this.'

But Terence didn't seem to hear. He put his mouth over mine and I let him do it.

'Come here,' he said, and he guided me onto his lap.

'Come here,' he said again. His voice had the crackle of someone in mild rapture.

I had to lift my skirt over my hips in order to straddle him. Again he put his mouth around mine, sank his teeth into me. I closed my eyes and tried very hard to think about the Beethoven, but I could no longer remember how the opening chords sounded or how the melody recapitulated itself. All I knew was that I hated everything around me, even the noise drifting up from the street below, even the air I was breathing.

I thought about pushing Terence away, about getting up and walking out of the door that was only a few steps away. But he was holding me down; he had locked himself firmly and irreversibly into me. Was there any point in untangling this transaction that had already begun?

'Terence,' I said.

'Be quiet,' he whispered.

He set about doing what he wanted, and I tried to calm myself down, to pretend I was a different person, unfeeling of his flesh inside me. And after a moment, a strange calm did wash over me. Each time he thrust himself against me, the need to struggle was diminished, and what seemed infinitely more important was a word from him that our deal was made.

'He's going to die,' I found myself saying. 'How else can I put it?'

Terence lifted his gaze – a dismissive smile and a hero's flare of the nostrils. Whatever words came out of his mouth next would be the solution of all solutions, the end of all discussions.

'I promise you that he won't. I'll take care of it.'

I was glad he said that, even happy. I nodded, and I made sure that I wiped away every last trace of tear on my face. I was holding on to him now, moving with his body to make it as nice as possible for him so that I could owe him nothing. This seemed to surprise him, this complicity which a moment ago had not been forthcoming. But he welcomed it as I made him swell inside me.

It did not, to my relief, last long. And once he had drawn the final, gratifying gasp, he wasted no time in moving me aside. He got up quickly and walked away from the piano.

The light coming from the window traced around him, made him look like an empty black space, a paper cut-out of a man. He didn't say another word to me that day.

A week later he sent Adrian an email to say he wanted nothing more than to help him get better. He said that he had heard about the issue with the money and he was happy to pay for the new treatment.

There was to be no argument about it, he said. And he would never want anything in return. This last point was stressed several times.

'Consider it a gift from one brother to another.'

21

Bebe comes down the stairs wearing a life jacket, singing that Rod Stewart song about sailing. She leans over the parapet, arms outstretched. The words are not precisely the right ones, but she warbles them like a bird, does not think twice.

Years ago, as a joke, Adrian and I would throw ourselves Rod Stewart parties in lieu of having a real social life. It was more for Bebe, who was going through one of those phases when bedtime must be preceded by an exhausting selection of incentives and inducements. Adrian would put all of our Rod Stewart CDs in the old music player and set the songs to a random shuffle. Bebe would join us, wrap her arms around one of our legs, and as we moved around the imaginary dancefloor, we took her with us. She must have been very little then. I never realised any of the songs had stuck.

'Careful, Bebe,' says Adrian, looking up the stairs towards her.

She pulls the inflation tag on the jacket. The thing sucks loudly, plumps up in a small cloud around her neck. Her head is as regal as the cherry on top of a cupcake; a winning smile crosses her face, lots of teeth showing.

'How appropriately dressed,' remarks Terence. 'But I'm pretty sure that life-saving devices are provided onboard.'

They have been waiting for her to get ready so they can head down to the marina. Terence has promised Bebe a sailing lesson. He has a friend whose yacht is free for the day. The weather, as it turns out, is perfect for it.

At the door, Adrian says, 'Are you sure, Primrose?'

He means that I should join them, but I know it would be madness to confine myself to a boat with Terence. I would go to Whistles.

I follow them to the front gate, watch as they walk to the end of the street and turn the corner towards the marina. I can hear the ringing of Adrian's phone. I can hear Bebe as she cries out to the swans, her voice short-lived in the morning breeze.

In the middle of the night, I woke in a fog of confusion. It felt, for a moment, as though I was in a hospital, having come to from anaesthesia. Then I felt Adrian's arm across my chest. It was so heavy, but when I moved it, I didn't feel any better. No matter which way I lay, I couldn't get rid of the weight inside me. I thought about Terence sleeping in the guest room downstairs, and how, after being here for four whole days, he'd be here for two more still.

He had barely spoken to me since he got here. He turned away from me whenever he said anything to anyone. Only once, as I passed him in the hallway, did he stop me and say, 'You must've been busy, all this cleaning you've been doing.'

It was possible that Adrian had discussed my preoccupations with him in private. Or perhaps he had figured it out on his own when he saw the way I was scrubbing at the floors. Whatever the case, he seemed to have been waiting for the opportunity to mention it. It made me think the whole purpose of his visit might have been to do just that.

In bed, I tried to reason with myself. Two more days, just two more. But even when he left, there would be no end to him. He would be back again one day, returning at endless intervals to present himself at the door. The future was filled with his visits.

I got out of bed and went to the window. Everything was dark except a room upstairs in Peter's house. I could see a figure moving about in it, flesh coloured and vaguely human; I knew it was him. I watched him pace about the room, I watched him leave and, after a while, I watched him return and move to the window. He looked out into the night, unseeing, then he switched off the light.

I went back to bed and stared at the darkness on the ceiling; I did that for hours. Eventually I thought of Harriet waiting for me at the first tee in the morning, as we'd planned. I thought of the drills, the invisible lines her hands would draw over the fairway, the expression she'd wear as she watched me send the ball into the distance. Thinking of that was like having the dawn come too soon, and without delay I rushed myself to sleep.

The water in the canal today is dark and unmoving. Even the ducks seem too afraid to test its temperature. They stay away, bake their wings on the island knitted from dead reeds.

It's one of those winter days that make everything appear very still. But the stillness is just a deception – every time I hit a ball, the whole landscape shifts imperceptibly against me, like someone has just picked it up while I wasn't looking, and moved it a few steps to the side. None of my shots go anywhere near where I intend. I don't know how many balls I've lost, but I'm down to my last two.

Harriet tugs me on the arm. 'Slow down, will you? What's the rush?'

She is wearing woollen gloves with the fingers cut off, and a beanie pulled so far down that it almost covers her eyes. Every time she looks at me, she's all mouth and nostrils.

'Relax your shoulders.'

She has welded her arm to mine so that we might move as one. 'Remember that the club goes in and around, in and around. Don't ever try to draw a straight swing. A straight swing does not lead to a straight shot.' She puts a ball down on the tee, steps away. 'Try again, will you?'

But she finds no satisfaction in the way I let my club come down.

'No, no, in and around.' She comes nearer again, stops me in my tracks. 'In and around, you see?'

'For God's sake, Harriet, stop saying that! Just let me hit the ball.'

'But you're going outside-in. You'll slice it too much.'

'What's the difference?'

'I would've thought the difference is obvious.' She gazes at me, bewildered by my mood.

Refusing to return the eye contact, I keep my head down and

smack the ball out low and fast, a half-circle into the open space. We are on the fourth hole, the one where you tee off on a little mound with the canal cutting in front of it. Without the necessary height, the ball has no chance of clearing the vegetation that guards the water. Like a misguided paper plane, it curves straight down into the thick of it all, lodges itself in the boggy bank. A pair of mallards come flying out of the grass, startled.

'You know,' says Harriet, 'ducks are not unlike people, they come in pairs. You take one out, the other can get quite upset about it.'

The mallards have made a short flight downstream and settled together on a log beside the water.

'Are you trying to make me feel guilty about endangering the wildlife?'

'It pays in more ways than one to invest the time in your technique.'

'You need to stop mistaking me for someone who cares about the technique. It's not why I'm here, Harriet.'

'I've often wondered that,' says Harriet, observing my difficulty in getting the club back into the bag. 'Why *are* you here, Primrose?'

'I don't know, but not for this. I don't care if the ball goes as straight or as far or as accurate as the next person's. I enjoy the fact that it's difficult and crushing. Frankly, I don't care if the ball ever goes into the hole.'

An awful noise from just outside the boundary. A truck has come to a screeching halt, pressing itself right up against the wire fence, so big that a tree must sacrifice two of its branches to make room for it.

It's just another one of the many trucks that have been arriving lately, to offload their mountains of building supplies, as if they were delivering reinforcements for war. Pile after pile of steel caging and precast chunks of concrete have been lined up along the perimeters, waiting for the final order to move in. A skip the size of a house is now taking up half the car park.

Harriet glances at the truck, at the driver who is trying simultaneously to alight and to do up the belt on his pants. He looks at us and, with pants firmly on, proceeds to inspect his cargo.

Harriet scratches her forehead. If she has any opinion at all about the truck, she is not about to share it. 'Let's go.'

She sends her buggy waddling across the bridge over the canal, and follows after it. She's handling the automation with a lot more grace than she used to. Walking together, they have the appearance of dancing a waltz, advancing in a zigzag motion, one led by the other.

We say nothing to each other for a long while. Harriet is playing like her usual consistent self. I bash about after her, making triple bogeys while trying to hold my head high.

On the seventh hole, we find Josh wandering beneath the grove of trees that guard the fairway. He's pointing his phone up, taking photos.

'Hi there,' he says, absently. 'Just pretend I'm not here.'

Harriet stops next to him, looks up at the branches that unfold against the sky like calligraphic strokes.

'Chinese elms,' she indicates.

'Yep,' confirms Josh.

'And what is it that you are doing?' Harriet enquires.

'I thought I'd take a few pictures, you know, before they're gone.'

'They are lovely trees,' I tell him.

Passing by, I've often stopped to admire the stark display of their bare bones in winter, the striking minimum of the trees' beauty. Each of them has chosen its own posture, none of them quite upright the way a tree ought to be. One of them is leaning at such an acute angle that you'd soon be able to scale its entire length without much danger of falling. Another fifty years, it will be lying blissfully among the grass, sleeping and living all at once. Maybe it still believes that this is its future; it can't possibly know that all the centuries it is capable of living will expire in a matter of weeks.

'Actually,' says Josh, taking a close shot of the bark, 'these are my great-granddad's trees.'

'Is that so?' says Harriet.

Josh nods. 'He was the one who planted them here one year, at the end of a bad drought, when it finally started to rain. For good luck, he must have thought. There's a story about it, actually, that the trees can be traced all the way back to one that grew in the summer palace, in old Peking.'

'That's quite a tale.'

There is a hint of embarrassment in the way Josh swallows a breath, in the way his smile turns to blush. He looks tired, like he's been skipping meals. He doesn't even seem to have any snacks on him. 'Who knows if it's true, right?'

Harriet shrugs, turns to leave. 'You're too young to be full of stories. Try to let go of some, would be my advice.'

*

At the car, afterwards, Harriet takes off her golf shoes, dusts down the soles with a brush she keeps for this purpose, and places them into a cloth bag. Changing into her boots, she says, 'We cannot let ourselves be carried away by this whole thing.'

'What whole thing?' I ask.

'The course is closing. That should be the end of it.'

'I noticed you were a little harsh with Josh back there.'

'Good. I wasn't trying not to be.'

'I think it's admirable that he holds so much pride in this place, and, in a way, his own family history.'

'Every single thing that happens to people is history. Would you like to hold on to it all?'

More trucks have arrived, and the air around us is filled with dust.

'I'm confused, Harriet. You've spent your whole life here too, perfecting your golf so that you can play it so beautifully as you do. I'm amazed you can let go of it so casually.'

Harriet looks at me with eyes that are almost colourless, the blue faded with the years. 'I'm simply pointing out that some things can be enjoyed and appreciated without having a higher value. Like golf, like this place, like most things in life.'

'I disagree,' I say to her. Suddenly I am thinking of the letter I discovered in my golf bag, that morning in the pool house: the little score card that sang like a wordless love song from the other side of the world. 'People find all sorts of things to be meaningful, to be of guidance to them in some way, so why not golf? And why not the land on which it is played, if they choose?'

'Is that why you are here, Primrose?' asks Harriet. 'To find something that is of guidance to you?'

'Something like that, I guess. If I have to encapsulate everything in one reason, that is probably it.'

Harriet gets up, boots now snuggly on her feet.

'Have you ever heard of a man named Ben Hogan?'

She knows I haven't.

'He was a golfer, one of the greatest, some people say. One day he was driving down the highway and a Greyhound bus going the wrong way smashed into him front on. Now he had a fractured pelvis, a broken foot, a blood clot in his leg and another in his lung. People thought he'd have to give up the golf. But eventually he got back on the course, played through all that pain in his leg and went on to win another six majors. Isn't that wonderful?'

'I don't know why you're telling me this. Comeback after setback, what's your point?'

'Well, naturally, younger golfers took to asking him for advice, some nugget of wisdom he must have gleaned from all those years spent on the course. After all the man was a legend of the game. And it did seem that golf was the one thing that saved his life, pulled him out of the hospital bed, kept him up when gravity wanted him down. So what did he have to say about it all? What was the one thing he had to offer to the golfers of the future? *Watch out for buses.*'

She takes a step forward, puts one hand on my shoulder. Her touch is almost weightless. Her face is very white and distorted by wrinkles, a pearl with an imperfect nacre.

'Watch out for buses.'

The more she says it, the more amusing she finds it. Her mouth crumples into a tilde.

'Primrose, what I am saying is that if you're looking for answers, you won't find them here.'

22

By the time I get home, the house is immersed in the blue shadow of a sinking sun. The day has gone by fleetingly, like a card being flashed in a memory game. The smell of burning logs is in the air as I get out of the car and walk up the footpath.

Adrian must have made a fire; smoke is coming out of the chimney in grey chiffon strokes. Finally, after all these years in the house, a fire. I can picture Bebe squatting in front of it, heaping twigs from the garden into the flames.

After I said goodbye to Harriet I sat in the car park, just watching people go in and out of Whistles. I watched as Josh talked to people about the way they swung their clubs, as more trucks came by to drop off supplies, as the clouds brought a brief shower and the wind blew it all away. I must have sat there for hours. I didn't want to go home knowing that Terence would still be there.

Now the house stares at me as if it knows I've been avoiding it. The lights are shining through the windows. The front door is ajar, and it opens as I near it. Adrian holds the handle, a concerned look on his face.

'Where have you been?' he says.

'I went for a walk.'

He looks down at the mud on my shoes.

'How was the sailing?' I ask.

'Bebe didn't like the bumpiness on the water. We were out there for about two seconds.'

'There goes her sailing career.'

Adrian tries a smile, but his face only manages to contort awkwardly. 'You left your phone at home. It's been ringing.'

'Well? Did you answer it?'

'It was the hospital,' he replies, and lets this hang unfinished. He hands me the phone, perhaps thinking that I need the proof to believe the claim. There are a bunch of missed calls from a number I don't recognise.

'What's happened?'

I have a sinking feeling that he will say it's my father. Who else could it be? My mother, perhaps – she has always had various ailments, been in and out of consultation rooms and put on new medications with minor side-effects. But all that medical attention over the years has left me with a sense that she has been thoroughly examined, well looked after. As for my father – I have no recollection of his ever taking so much as a vitamin tablet, which has only added to my suspicion that one day things will come to a head.

Now Adrian is saying, 'He's at Sacred Heart. Apparently he's been in some kind of altercation. I don't know the details. They said he didn't want to see anyone, but you're his emergency contact person, so . . .'

So it is him, but an altercation? The thought of my father in a fight is vaguely astonishing; he'd never let himself get involved in a violent situation. By altercation they must mean that he was attacked, though I can't think of a single reason anyone would want to hurt him. How could such a thing have happened to him? And by whom? Standing on the doorstep, I feel as though I might go mad pondering the whom.

Adrian touches me, and in a low voice, says, 'Primrose, you better go.'

This whole time I haven't realised that I've been wringing my hands in a knot. My fingers have gone purple, I can't feel them anymore. Maybe, I think, I'd be better off without them.

Terence walks into the corridor, glances in my direction. He hesitates for a moment, as if he wants to come nearer and participate in this emergency that has arisen. But he must sense from the way I'm looking back at him that I would scream if he did, that this time he is not allowed to intrude.

He steps away, turns towards the living room. His phone beeps and he takes it out of his pocket, checks. He's always doing that, as if something important is happening in his life every minute of the day. Adrian is still talking to me but all I can focus on is Terence, that thumb of his tapping in morse code on the blue-white screen of his phone, imposing his thoughts on the world. His entire being is the detestable opposite of everything I ever wanted to be near. And now, at last, I know for certain how much I hate him. I hate him as if he were the person who just put my father in the hospital.

'Primrose,' Adrian says. 'Don't worry, they said he was stable. Do you want me to come with you?'

'No, I'll be fine.'

'Are you sure? I think I better go with you.'

'You should stay with Bebe.'

'Terence can stay with her. You don't look so well, I think you need me with you.'

'No. I said no.'

I back away from the door, head down the footpath towards the car. But the footpath seems suddenly too narrow to walk on. My foot keeps getting stuck in the garden bed; the catnip hisses at my ankle. All the plants that in the summer had been an unsalvageable brown are thriving again in the winter, living large and vigorous in the cold. This house is full of things that grow out of discomfort.

Adrian is watching me.

'Stay there,' I warn him. If he follows me now I think I will scream at him too. 'I don't need you, I'm going on my own.'

The triage nurse frowns into the computer. She's sitting behind a partition smudged with fingerprints, which makes her face appear slightly blurred. The emergency room is filled with people either sitting or half slumped over the red plastic seats. Most of them seem to be suffering in private, exhibiting no outward signs of injury. Only a few appear obviously afflicted, either with a leg propped up or breathing in and out of a sick bag. One woman is saying something to another about eating day-old salmon.

'I don't seem to have him here,' the nurse says to me for the second time.

'Could you check again? I can't see how he could have gone missing.'

She rubs the bridge of her nose, adjusts her glasses. She's sighing in a way that suggests an inner conversation, one half of her telling the other to be more patient, forbearing. How long must she have been sitting here, fielding questions and concerns from agitated people?

Again she types into the computer, more keystrokes than the last time. 'Ah. Here we go. He's been transferred upstairs, that's why. He's had scans done. Go down the corridor, follow the yellow line on the ground to the lifts. Not the green line – that will take you to a different set of wards. The yellow line, up to Level Four.'

The yellow line takes me to a ward where patients are billeted in rooms of six, the same quiz show playing on the overhead TVs. A single nurse is running around fetching bedpans and water jugs, humming to herself. Helpfully, she gives me a run-down of my father's condition and directs me to his room at the end of the corridor.

It is the only quiet room in the ward, where the TVs are off and only one of the other beds is occupied. The mystery patient is hiding behind curtains that float above the floor like a magic trick ready to be revealed.

My father's bed is by the window, looking out over the tops of trees.

'I told them not to call anyone,' he complains upon discovering my reflection in the glass. 'I was clear that I didn't want anyone to come.'

'You look really awful, Dad.'

'I told them: leave me alone for a few hours and I will be ready to take myself home.'

'Fortunately, that's not the way hospitals are run.'

Someone has placed a plastic bag next to his bed, containing the clothes he was wearing when he got here. I would've recognised those clothes anywhere. The dark brown trousers still have the belt looped around the waist. The old white shirt, laundered so many times it has turned grey, is stained with blood. There is a large patch of it over the front, the shape of Russia.

'You should've stayed home,' he says. 'I can do this myself.'

The nurse explained that he would be woozy from the painkillers, but instead he is very alert, like his heart is racing after a lot of exercise.

'They had to call someone, Dad,' I say to him. 'They thought that you might've had brain damage.'

'As you can see, I am okay.'

'I can *see* that you're hurt!'

'I told them no one needs to know what has happened to me. Nothing happened.' Like a child, he is beating his fist on the bed as he talks, but only the fist on the good side, as the other arm has been wrapped up with a splint to keep it still. Someone has helped him raise the bed to a half-upright position and placed two pillows behind him. I suspect he must have asked for this, having refused to lie down and go to sleep.

According to the nurse, he was lucky not to have sustained any severe injury to the head, since all indications were that it made contact with the ground several times. The scans have come up clear. He has managed to escape with no serious injuries, though the less serious ones are numerous.

'What do you mean nothing happened?' I ask him. 'It seems

to me that a lot happened to you today, the concussion, the black eye, the broken tooth . . . should I go on?'

I must sound as if I am now the parent. 'Your arm is fractured in two places. Someone has fractured it.'

'It's not broken. It will be better in a few days.'

'Not according to the X-rays. You'll need surgery in the morning.'

'All the same, I want to go home.'

He is careful with his mouth as he talks, every word must be painful for him. His jaw has started to swell; it will soon merge with the purplish swelling of his eye. I can see, whenever his lips part, the pixel of darkness where half of his front tooth used to be.

I try to explain to him that going home right now is impossible, and, irrelevantly, he scolds, 'Stop speaking to me in English!'

The irony that he has said this in English dawns on him. He looks at the window, at the dark outside. The sounds of peak-hour traffic reach us from below; the air is tinted with the red glow of tail-lights. He blows some air out of his mouth, the way he used to when he smoked. 'Lucky your mother is out of town with her friends. She would give me no peace about this if she was here.'

He seems to want to go on about my mother's trip, to digress indefinitely from the issue at hand. 'Did she tell you where she has gone? A yoga retreat! Some place in the Blue Mountains, with a Sanskrit name, where they put wheatgrass and açaí in all the food. The yoga is going to her head, maybe from doing all those upside-down poses.'

'She's on her way back as we speak,' I tell him.

He tries to suppress a sigh and, in doing so, sends himself into a fit of coughs.

'Dad?'

'What?'

I can see the anguish when he moves his face.

'We need to get serious. At some point you will have to tell me what happened to you.'

'Don't you know already?'

'You were attacked, I don't know anything else.'

'Neither do I. Now let me be alone.'

My father did not cooperate with the police officers who visited him earlier. He refused to provide details about the events which led to his injuries, other than to confirm that they took place at the local park where he was playing the trumpet, as he normally did. And where was his trumpet? He was not able to say.

The nurse is the one who tells me all this, after I've been banished from the room by my father for asking too many questions. She talks to me in fragments as she darts back and forth from room to room, tending to IV drips and thermometers and wounds that require new bandaging.

In between all her talking, she offers me a plate of food which has been sitting unclaimed on the trolley – a piece of chicken breast with a green sauce, and a cup of jelly with bits of pear suspended in it. The sight of the food makes me squeamish, but I eat it as she showers me with a motherly expression.

'You know, my love, you don't look too good yourself,' she comments, as a mouthful of food works its way down my throat. 'You're not feeling sick, are you?'

The air in this place is so smothered by disinfectant that my lungs are refusing to accept it as the genuine thing. Plus the chicken, the sight of boiled meat on a plate, is all too familiar. During those months with Adrian in the hospital – every day it was the same chicken, no matter what meat they were serving.

'I'm sorry,' I say, stuffing my mouth with the jelly so it might dilute the taste of the poultry. 'I could be having some sort of reaction to the food.'

'Oops, shall we take that away from you, then? The food here is really not great, it takes getting used to.'

'The trouble is I'm too used to it, I think. I've spent a lot of time in here before.'

'Really?' she asks, as if surprised she does not already know that. 'Here? In this hospital?'

I nod, but stop short of telling her about all those times I walked the green line to Adrian's ward.

The nurse wanders off to take down blood pressures and heart rates. When she comes back, she says, 'Did you know there were witnesses? One of the officers who was here said that there were people around who saw what happened to your dad.'

She looks at her watch, writes something down on a clipboard, and slots it back into a holder on the wall.

'Apparently a bunch of boys had been taunting him – you know, about the usual stuff. They were trying to get a reaction out of him while he played his songs. He ignored them and kept playing. They went away, but then came back later, a bigger group of them. Then I guess they must've set on him.'

There is a plainness in her tone, no embellishments for emotional effect. It's probably something she sees a lot in this job, the shock value having worn off long ago. Which begs the question of why she cannot bring herself to explain 'the usual stuff'.

'I'm stumped as to why he's behaving this way,' I say to her. 'Why would he refuse to say anything to the police?'

The nurse shrugs. 'It happens sometimes. People can be in a hurry to move past things that are unpleasant to remember.'

'That's not like him at all. He's usually the one who seeks out unpleasantness and tries to correct it.'

Again the nurse shrugs. 'It happens, people change.'

There is a wailing opera in my head, a tenor in despair. It goes on, nightmarishly monotonous, neither building nor contracting. What is it getting at? Then the beeping starts, joining in with the low-battery singing, and finally, the female voices, merely speaking parts, not too many, just two. Their humanness is what finally wakes me to the hospital room, laid bare by the light from the open door.

'Mr Tagliaferri, please keep still,' one of two nurses is saying to the patient in the other bed. The curtain has at last opened around him, and I can see the parting of his feet, draped by the sheet.

'When did he take the medication?' the other nurse asks, checking the charts.

There must have been a shift change; the nurse who gave me the food is gone.

I am in the chair next to my father's bed. He is still asleep, with his hand on his stomach and his nose to the ceiling, a Snow White pose. I can't hear his breathing, but I can see the tug and pull of air in his chest, the float of the jutting bone in his throat. When was the last time I watched him sleep? I must've been a child, barefoot by his bed; how he hated being woken from a Sunday's sleep-in.

Mr Tagliaferri is murmuring something, his speech mashed into a paste by his mouth. One of the nurses tells him to stop pulling out his own cannula.

'It hurts,' he says, in sounds vaguely resembling the words.

'It will hurt more if I have to keep putting new ones in.'

The IV stand beeps, a pinprick of red light flashing over and over.

'Doctor,' the man says. 'I want doctor.'

He seems to want to rise from his bed; he has raised his knees. The nurse stops him, explains that the doctor will be here in the morning. While she reassures him, the other nurse leaves the room and returns with a tray of medicine. She picks up a syringe, puts it to his mouth.

'Mr Tagliaferri, please open up.'

He has started to cry. His voice is soaked, putrid. 'You're lying,' he spits. 'The real hospital is in San Marino.'

When I wake again, Mr Tagliaferri is gone. His bed is a mess, the sheets still puckered in his shape.

'They moved him to another room,' my father tells me, his face a blur in the measly light. Everything is as fuzzy as the snow on an old TV; it's the best my eyes can do at two o'clock in the morning.

'Oh. He seemed to be in a lot of pain,' I say.

'No, just crazy.'

My father's eyes are barely there beneath the swelling. If I were passing him on the street, I would not recognise him.

'Water,' he says, trying to prop himself up with his good arm.

'Here, water.'

With a straw he drinks from the cup, yesterday's water. His mouth can't close properly, which makes swallowing a struggle. The water spills from the corners of his mouth, drips all over his front.

'Leave it, it's fine,' he says.

He lies back down, touches his face, winces. He waits, as if he's counting in his head, before speaking again. 'It was difficult for you when Adrian was sick. I should have said that before.'

The words come out of his mouth mangled, bloody. Why is he bringing this up now? He must have thought about it, prepared himself, before saying it. He would never say a thing like that without thinking it through first, unless it's the pain-killers now doing the talking.

'At the time, I was unable to do anything to help you. I couldn't make things easier for you.'

'Dad, we don't need to talk about that now. In fact, it would be preferable if we didn't.'

'If not now, then when? Isn't that a song?' He tries to laugh but can't. He weaves his fingers together, puts them over his chest. 'No parent wants to see his child suffer. I think you suffered. Most likely you are still suffering.'

'Do you have a point? If not, you should sleep.'

'Okay, sleep.'

But he lies awake, practises his breathing like it's a new skill that must be learned from scratch. His nose is not working, and the air whistles through his lips, his broken tooth. I've always known he was growing old but only as a foregone conclusion, like something that did not require observable proof. Now he is the evidence of old, a crumpled reproduction of the man in my head.

'Consider things properly,' he murmurs. 'You can leave him if you want to. Divorce is not so terrible anymore, or so I hear.'

'What makes you think I want to do that?'

'I think you are not sure. You should always be sure.'

Neither of us is looking at the other, we must sound like two people talking over the phone.

'If something requires a conversation, even a confrontation, you should have it with Adrian. Sooner better than later.'

'I wouldn't know where to begin, Dad. I wouldn't know what to say.'

'That's an old problem for you. When you were little, when we first brought you here, you didn't talk for two years. I thought it was the language, but even after you learned, you never really talked again.'

My chest is burning. I want to cough, but all that comes out is a laugh so small it barely tips over the edge of my mouth.

'That must run in the family,' I say, feeling a rage come

over me. 'Dad, why didn't you talk to the police about what happened to you?'

'I'm not sure what happened to me,' he answers.

'It seems pretty clear, both the act and the motivation.'

'We can't assume we know what goes on in people's heads.'

'You mean, you don't know *why* they beat you? Isn't it obvious?'

'It's arguable. It's not clear.'

'Alright, Dad, okay. But you can't disagree that the act itself was committed. They beat you, it's a fact. Is it not right to speak up against aggression?'

'Leave it for someone else to do that. Not me.'

'Why not you? Isn't that why you go to the park, play your music all these years – to create some common ground between people so that they might behave civilly to one another? What happened to you is everything you wanted to prevent.'

He touches his face, forgetting that it is tender and fragile, damaged beneath the skin. He says, 'They were too young.'

'Who? Your attackers?'

'They were just boys.'

'Boys who tried to smash your skull against the ground, because of the colour of your skin, where you were born and who you were raised by. You know, the usual stuff.'

'You put them through the system, their whole life is ruined. What good would that do to anyone?'

'That's for the court to decide.'

'No, each person must decide, and that is what I decided. I want all this humiliating business behind me, as quickly as possible.'

'But Dad, things are changing. Can't you feel it? Aren't you aware how every little thing in the news these days is shifting the way people look at you?'

'I don't know what you mean.'

'You do. You understand enough about geopolitics in the year 2019 to know exactly how every single person like you, like me, is getting caught up in the world's affairs. And who knows what else will happen next year, and the year after that. If someone in your situation chooses not to speak up, then won't the target on your back just get bigger and bigger?'

My father shakes his head; his body stiffens. 'I'm afraid you are not making any sense to me.'

With his good hand, he pulls at the blanket, tries to twist it into a knot. He has become agitated, as if struck by a panic. 'Too hot,' he complains. 'Too, too hot.'

I try to feel his forehead, but he bats me away. I can see the bulging sinews of his throat, the storm of red and purple that has taken over his skin. The time for argument has passed. Now he must rest.

He holds up a fistful of blanket. 'Off. Take it all off.'

I help him pull the blanket away, and, relieved, he sinks back into the bed. The air gushes out of his pillow. He must have closed his eyes under the swollen flesh; suddenly a calm settles over him.

'Go to sleep, Dad.'

'Okay.'

He quietens, and, after a while, sleeps. His body becomes nothing but a space beneath the hospital gown. For the first time since I got here, I can see his legs, the raw, timid flesh on his knees where he was dragged and skinned over the asphalt.

The green man lights up; the pedestrian crossing *tak-tak-tak*s for no one. The street is deserted at this hour, and everything is bathed in the post-apocalyptic silver of the street lamps. A street sweeper rounds the gutters, whirrs in the cold, brittle air.

'Hi, are you awake?' I say into the phone, into the fog of my own breath.

'Where are you?' the voice says back, soaked in sleep. 'You sound like you're outside.'

'I'm at Sacred Heart.'

'What happened? Are you okay?'

'Yes, I'm fine. It's a long story. Can you get here? I don't feel like being alone right now. Sorry, I know what time it is.'

The words rattle in my throat, the world is disorienting after the last ten hours inside.

He doesn't say anything. For a moment I think he must be about to hang up, but then I hear his footsteps going down the stairs.

'Wait for me, I'm coming.'

23

Still hours till dawn, we burrow into the darkness of Whistles, through the hole in the fence left by Matthew. The loose wires nip at my clothes, scratch me across the top of the ear. The space is barely big enough for a child.

Peter asks, 'This Matthew, he does this every day?'

'With golf clubs and war medals and the whole world watching on.'

I think he smiles, but it's too dark to know.

'I haven't been here for twenty years,' he says. 'It's different from my memory of it, smaller. Maybe it's just that I've never seen it in the night-time.'

'That, and the fact it's not exactly Lost Cove.'

Peter thinks about this carefully, as if I've set some complicated puzzle for him to solve.

'No,' he says eventually. 'I know what you mean.'

Slowly we begin to clamber down the tumbling rough towards the fairway below. Our hands touch by accident. It's dark all around us, except for the faint light of the moon, the blade of a scythe. The air is sharp, the sky wide open.

A chill strikes me as I think about my father's damaged

body on the hospital bed, the excuses he was making for the people responsible. I had to get away from the hospital, even if just for a while.

I have a blanket wrapped around me, one which Peter found in the back of the car, the kind that people take with them on picnics. But even with it, I'm no closer to feeling warm again. The temperature seems to have dropped further; this is the hour in which frost will be made.

'Hey, slow down a bit,' he says, catching me by the tail of the blanket as I stumble over something in the grass. 'Primrose, you need to calm down.'

'I don't know why people always say that. Why do we *need* to calm down? Why is that a requirement?'

We've reached the bottom of the incline. From here, the grass is shorn to a smooth carpet that stretches all the way up to the green. My eyes are adjusting to the dark now; everything around me has regained a basic shape and texture.

'You're bleeding,' says Peter.

'It's the fence.'

'There's your first reason to calm down.'

He touches my ear with his thumb, wipes away the blood that has trailed down from the wound. I must not look human in this light; a ghostly rage has followed me from the hospital.

'Listen, it's terrible what happened to your dad. It's the stuff of nightmares. I'm sorry.'

'It was his own fault. He thought that if he insisted on everyone accepting each other, then it would simply happen. In the end he only made himself more visible to those looking for prey. It was a dumb idea from the beginning.'

'Do you really think that? That his ideology was flawed?'

'Yes. He's too logical. It doesn't work in a world gone mad.'

'What happened to him – this attack – it doesn't represent the world,' Peter says. 'It's an aberration.'

'It's cancer. It has more life than any other living organism – it multiplies continuously, exponentially. It can only be restrained by something that is even more toxic. And maybe that's the point of it – it lures people into self-destruction.'

My teeth are chattering. Any minute now, I might freeze like one of those women in my father's stories.

'Let's go back to the car,' says Peter, looking up at the stars. 'We shouldn't have come out here.'

'I don't want to go back. Can we please stay?'

'Primrose, even if you believe the world is going mad, the last thing you should do is go along with this madness.'

'What are you saying? That I should just go home and forget about it, let it lie? I've always done that. Now I think I have wasted my entire life being wrong.'

'It's right that you should have a reaction to these things, a response. You should speak up. But what I'm saying is that it's not useful to do that here, at Whistles, with me, in the middle of the night. No one can hear you.'

'But you can. Maybe you of all people should hear it.'

'I don't get what it is that you want to say to me.' He seems genuinely perplexed, as if he is hearing words meant for another person.

'That's the problem, Peter. You don't think you're part of the problem because people around you have always told you that you're not. You've never needed to consider who you are.'

He folds his arms, looks away at nothing in particular. 'I'm getting the distinct feeling I'm being attacked by you, again.'

'All I'm trying to say is that you are identified by your tasteful houses, your expensive art, by all the cool people who go to your luncheons and soirees. It only reinforces the idea in people's heads that the only acceptable Asians are the ones who are just like them.'

'Honestly, Primrose, is that why you woke me up in the middle of the night? To give me a lecture?'

'No, of course not.' I want to say more, but I find myself searching too long for the words.

Peter sighs into his fist, says, 'I know exactly who I am, Primrose. I've always known that, and I haven't needed anyone to prove or disprove it to me. What you are asking me to do is to be completely literal about myself, to say that I'm either white or I'm Asian, I'm either poor or I'm rich, I'm either liked or I'm detested. But as long as I can live with myself as a human being who is good and decent, why should I have the need to draw these circles around myself? The emancipation lies in *not* having to do that – in rejecting the need for a definition altogether. I won't stand here and be prosecuted by you for simply never feeling like I have to explain myself.'

'Really, now? *I won't stand here and be prosecuted by you?*' Irrationally, like a child, I want to throw the words back at him. 'Things are always so clear, so straightforward for you, aren't they, Peter? And you just ignorantly assume it is the same for everyone else too.'

'Wrong. I've never assumed anything about you, I don't

even understand you! I didn't when you were sixteen, and I definitely don't now. I have no idea what's going on inside your head because you never really want to tell me anything.'

'That's not true. It's not a question of wanting to. I'm just not wired like that, like the way you are, how easy it is for you to do and say what you mean.'

Exasperated, he replies, 'Primrose, I'm at a loss as to why you always insist that my life is so easy.'

'Because it is. Everything comes easily to you.'

'Not everything,' he says, hesitating. He steps closer, his shape larger than it was before. 'You weren't easy, Primrose. You turned out to be actually impossible.'

It doesn't seem dignified to laugh, so we wait. We wait until we can't anymore. It's pathetic and sad and funny all at once to recall the past and realise how small everything now looks from a distance.

The proportions have changed. New things are growing where old things have faded.

Peter reaches out, touches the cut on my ear where the cold has numbed away sensation. I take his hand, kiss it, place my face in it. The warmth of his skin resembles sun-baked earth, the shell of an egg kept safe in its nest. I remember having fallen asleep like this long ago, against the palm of his hand, his pillow, his body, with the curtains in his room opening and closing like a lung that would never run out of air.

There are movements from high up in the trees, a rapid fire of leaps across the branches. We walk again, across the fairway, across two more fairways, towards the canal and the little bridge at the fourth.

'You know what's crazy?' I say. 'That you still have the same phone number from high school.'

'And that you still remember it.'

The water in the canal is a dark syrup, viscous and without reflections. We cross the bridge and meander along with the water. The silhouette of the clubhouse watches us from afar, the old painting sleeping inside it.

Somewhere on the ninth hole, we sit down beside the fairway, among leaves and the roots of the trees. There is nowhere further to go. Everything is luminous now, the grass a moon-coloured river, the flag a zephyred sail above the green. This could be Whistles, and us, on any night in any year.

That summer, Peter was standing right about here with a five-iron in his hand, his gaze pinned to the green as he measured up for his second shot. From the tee, he had driven the ball well beyond his normal range, and once the ball had hit the ground, it had rolled along the dry earth for an extraordinary distance, longer than anyone would have expected. It astonished him, how far a ball could travel over baked ground, in drought-like conditions.

'I've only had one shot so far,' he explained to me, barely able to contain his excitement. 'If I get the ball in with the next one, it's an albatross! Can you believe it? That stuff almost never happens.'

He was screwing up his chin, looking at the ball he was about to strike for a second time. His face was full of concentration.

As for me, I had never heard of the albatross until then. 'Why do they call it that? Isn't it meant to be a bit of a curse?'

'No way,' Peter replied. 'It's a good fortune bird. It's only when you mess with them that your luck turns against you, like in that old poem.'

It was so hot that day, maybe too hot to be in the middle of a golf course. No one else was around. There was no water in the canal and the ducks were nowhere to be seen. The sun fried everything it touched, and the shadows beneath the trees were so black they looked like they were scorched into the earth.

Peter's hair was wet, plastered across his forehead; he tried to wipe it away with his arm.

'This is epic,' he said to me, though he was clearly also trying to pump himself up. 'In any given year, you'd see about thirty holes-in-one on the PGA Tour, but there's only been a dozen albatrosses over the last one hundred years. If I get one, that would be the real deal.'

'But it's still a long way away.' I laughed, looking over at the remainder of the hole, perhaps another 200 metres or so in length. 'You'll never make it.'

'Stranger things have happened. This iron is more than enough to make the distance.'

Peter looked up. A plane was flying above us, drawing white lines against the blue sky. It was working on an A. Suddenly he seemed deep in thought. Instead of readying himself for the shot, he relaxed his club; something else had to be resolved first.

'Listen, if I make it, it's got to be a sign of something, don't you think?'

'A sign? Like what?'

'I'm not sure . . . Like maybe I don't go to America.'

'What?'

'Yeah, I mean, not right now. I could stay here, wait for you to finish school. Maybe then we'll go together.'

He waited for me to say something, perhaps to tell him whether I thought he was joking. I didn't know what to say, what I wanted to say. It seemed that whatever came out of my mouth would be premature. In the end, I simply settled for telling him, 'Take the shot. Let's see what happens.'

He got himself into the right spot, feet apart, club pointing up at one o'clock. The club came down smoothly but buckled a little at the end. Did he mean to do that?

He struck the ball. It sounded menacingly satisfying, like a nutcracker at work. The ball sailed over the brown land, high towards the green. But it was not enough, or maybe it was too much. It sliced to the right, going wide into the rough.

Peter kicked the dirt off his shoe, let go of his club. When he moved into the shade I thought I could see the faintest trace of relief on his face.

'Next time,' he said.

He never finished the hole. It really was too hot, and he had a flight booked for New York the next morning.

Now he says to me, as if all of that were only yesterday, 'I felt pretty bad about that albatross. Do you remember?'

'I do. But the thing is, no one seems to think it can ever be done on this hole, so you shouldn't feel so bad.'

'I don't mean that, Primrose. When I really thought about it, years after that day, I couldn't be sure that I actually wanted to make that shot. And even if I did, I don't know if I would've stayed here like I said I would. It was inconsiderate of me to have made a joke of it, got your hopes up. You probably hated me after that.'

'Hate was not exactly how I felt. Did you hate me?'

'Yeah, a little, when you didn't come to visit like you'd promised. But not for very long. I mostly just thought that you must've had a good reason.'

He is leaning against a tree, his arms over his knees. What time must it be?

'Do you know what you want to do now?' he asks.

'I wish we could be that age again,' I say, 'only this time, be doing things differently, better.'

'We could still do that now, in the present. We can try to pick it all up from here.'

'But do you think it's too late? Now there are other people we've met along the way and become attached to. Everything is more difficult. If we couldn't make it in one shot, could we really make it in two?'

'Primrose,' says Peter, firmly, clearly. 'You have to tell me what you want.'

I am tired now, and no longer cold. He draws me nearer, his breath in my hair.

When we were younger, I used to think that we were perhaps a kind of science experiment in which two superficially similar yet fundamentally different people had failed to connect and react to each other, to congeal and combine into a recognisable form. Now I think it must have been simpler than that. We were just two kids in a room, with the door open, having no idea how and why to stay together.

The dawn is invading the dark now, bleeding into the

horizon with a yellow of richness and disquiet. The sound of traffic swells around us like waves brought in by the tide. There is cooing from the trees, birds sharing stories of strange voices heard in the night.

It will all happen quickly. In a minute, there will be enough light to lift Whistles out of the darkness into another day, a day on which it is destined to die a little more. Josh will arrive to unlock the gate, and people will come. Soon we'll have to leave – now I must say what I mean.

'This is what I know. I won't spend the rest of my life living adjacently to yours.'

We get up. I take Peter by the hand.

'We will have to figure it out.'

Acknowledgements

To my parents, George and Su, thank you for your adventurous spirit, for our journey of wonders, and for loving me more than I deserve.

To William, thank you for your belief, your bravery, and for putting that golf club in my hand. To Katie and Erik, you are my joy, my light, and I love you. To my grandparents, wherever you are, thank you for being the reason I write. To Bin and Desmond, I am grateful for your support and unwavering optimism. And to my extended family, thank you for the gift of being a part of something bigger.

My immense gratitude must go to the wonderful Cate Blake, for believing in this book and seeing ways to make it better. My warmest thanks also to Belinda Huang, Emma Schwarcz, Allison Colpoys, Clare Keighery, Adrik Kemp and everyone at Pan Macmillan, for your tireless work in bringing this book to readers.

To Clare Forster and Benjamin Paz at Curtis Brown, thank you for your invaluable support and guidance throughout this journey.

My heartfelt thanks to Neil Chenoweth, for being an

early supporter of this book, and to Richard Walsh, for your encouragement and extraordinary kindness. To the Premier of Victoria, the Wheeler Centre and to Ronnie Scott, R.W.R. McDonald, and Tresa LeClerc, thank you for all that you have done for the Victorian Premier's Literary Award for an Unpublished Manuscript. To Pauline Lynch, Ian Benjamin, Lee Kofman, Rhett Davis, and Tom Trumble, I am grateful for your friendship and generosity.

The Whistles golf course in this book was inspired by the old Elsternwick Golf Course in the Melbourne suburb of Brighton. I would like to acknowledge the Bunurong People of the Kulin Nation, on whose land the course stood for more than a century before its recent closure. I would also like to thank the many golfers I met there, whose names I never knew, but whose company I enjoyed from afar.

Finally, to the people of Ward 7B, you revealed to me the beauty of living. You are in my thoughts, always.